Quint McCauley

Brothers in Blood

Other Quint McCauley Mysteries by D. C. Brod

Brothers in Blood

D. C. Brod

Walker and Company
New York

First published in the United States of America in 1993
by Walker Publishing Company, Inc.

Published simultaneously in Canada by Thomas Allen & Son
Canada, Limited, Markham, Ontario

Library of Congress Cataloging-in-Publication Data
Brod, D. C.
Brothers in blood / D. C. Brod.
p.   cm.
ISBN 0-8027-3239-9
I. Title.
PS3552.R6148B76   1993
813'.54—dc20   93-3636
                          CIP

Printed in the United States of America

2 4 6 8 10 9 7 5 3 1

For Rachael Tecza,
a true believer

Acknowledgments

I'd like to thank Stan Bodner of Merriehill Farms in Marengo, Illinois, for confirming my suspicion that the Morgan is a very special breed. Thanks also go to Miriam Baily, Marilyn Nelson, and, as always, DFB.

Brothers in Blood

▽

1

Iᴛ's ᴛʜᴇ ʟᴀᴛᴇ-ᴡɪɴᴛᴇʀ blizzards that seem to hit Illinois the hardest. The temperatures are warmer, so the snow never lasts long, but that's not much of a consolation when there's a big one swirling around you as you're creeping down a narrow, unfamiliar country lane. The wipers were about as much use as my drunken companion, and I was depending on him to guide me to a place I wasn't sure he could find: his home. My feet were cold and wet, and so was my disposition. I just kept on, hoping I'd notice any curves in the road before I slid off into a ditch. The silence was dense and thick like the snow, and every now and then my passenger would slice through it with a snort and a groan. He'd told me his place was five miles down this road, then proceeded to lapse in and out of consciousness.

I hoped he knew what he was talking about. It had taken me almost ten minutes to gain one of those miles. Four more to go. After tonight, I wanted him to be like that tree the philosophers are always referring to. The next time he fell, he'd be way out of earshot, ergo he wouldn't exist. Meanwhile, I vowed that in the future I was going to make a point of remembering what day it was and celebrate by staying home.

Until I walked into the Tattersall Tavern and my senses were assaulted by shamrocks, green beer, corned beef, and cabbage, I hadn't realized it was St. Patrick's Day. That's a helluva thing for a guy who's part Irish to admit, but there you have it. Dates just don't seem important to me. Elaine tells me I'd forget Christmas if it weren't for the fact that every time you turn on TV, *It's a Wonderful Life* is on. To me, it was just Tuesday, March 17, and my chances of getting a quiet beer had been reduced to nil.

I was debating whether to hang around for one beer or go home before the snow got bad. At least I wouldn't have to worry about waking up with a green tongue. Maybe I'd spend some time with the electronic chess set Elaine had given me for Christmas. I had yet to beat it at its most elementary level, and it was fast becoming an obsession. As I pondered the similarities between the white queen and Moby Dick, a small man with thick-lensed wire-rims split off from the *Chronicle* crowd and joined me at the last vacant table. Jeff Barlowe dropped into the chair while balancing a three-quarters-full stein. "Quint, my man." He jerked his head back in the direction of the newspaper group. "What d'you think of the blond with the glasses?"

I glanced at the other table. "You mean the one your editor's hitting on right now?" Her head was cocked to one side, and she was laughing at something he was saying.

"Aw, shit, man," Jeff said after verifying my observation. "These newly divorced guys just don't let up, do they?" He shook his head and ran a hand through his mop of hair that curled over the collar of his fatigue jacket.

"Tell me about it," I muttered, then, noticing Jeff's hangdog expression, added, "Stay. Have another beer. That's how long it'll take her to see behind the beard and the Springsteen platitudes to the guy who refuses to sit in the bleachers at Wrigley Field." Jeff frowned as he watched them. "If she doesn't, who needs her?"

"Yeah." Jeff drew the word out, unconvinced. But he downed a substantial portion of his beer and gestured at the empty space in front of me. "Don't let me drink alone. Remember, I'm depressed." The jukebox was playing "In Heaven There Is No Beer," and a nearby table was loudly debating the theory. Why not?

After Ginny brought our Guinness, a brew that could not be turned green, I drew a swallow up from beneath the stiff foam and enjoyed the bitter, velvety sensation. Someone jarred my elbow as I lowered the glass to the table, and a dollop of stout splashed down the side of my glass and over my wrist.

"I'm sorry."

I looked up and saw a young woman standing with her hand over her mouth. She wore her dark hair short with heavy bangs, and her eyes were wide, reminding me of one of those big-eyed waif paintings you used to see all over the place.

"S'okay," I said and smiled.

She tentatively lowered her hand, which covered a shy smile, and shrugged another apology, then stepped back and slid into a chair that was waiting for her at the next table. Two men were waiting for her too—one older and the other closer to her age, mid-thirties maybe. The way the older guy was watching me, I was glad I wasn't the sort of jackass who made a scene over losing an inch of beer. He shoved his chair right up next to hers and sat so close it looked like they were working on the same crossword puzzle. There was something familiar about the guy, like maybe I'd seen him selling cars on one of the local stations. I figured the other man might have been his son. He appeared to have the same solid, stocky build and the same thick head of hair, although the older man's was considerably grayer. The younger man was watching the Bulls trounce the Pistons on the wide-screen TV. I guess if my dad were nuzzling up to a woman my own age, I'd be grateful for a basketball game to focus on. Even if I couldn't hear it. The woman was smiling and nodding at something—a puzzle clue, no doubt. Both of her hands rested on the table, one cupped over the other, as though she were sheltering a small bird.

I watched her for a moment, wondering what an attractive young woman saw when she looked at Quint McCauley. Probably a dark-featured, slightly weathered man on the other side of forty who's given to frequent contemplation of the world's complexities. Not that I do, I think it just seems that way. When my mind goes blank or is in low gear putting together a shopping list, I've been told I appear to be analyzing some quantum theory or constructing an esoteric poem.

"You two ready for another?" Ginny had moved to our table and scooped up Jeff's empty glass.

"Can we get more popcorn too?" Jeff asked, gesturing toward me. "If he's eating popcorn, he forgets about smoking."

While I didn't really forget, just found it easier to abstain, I didn't argue. It was getting so the only place you could smoke anymore without incurring the wrath of law-abiding citizens was in your own house. And there only if the windows were sealed shut. I said to Ginny, "If you have any normal kernels, that'd be real nice. I'm going to be picking green hulls out of my teeth for weeks."

"Easier to spot if they're green." She winked at me. "But suit yourself. I'll see what I can do."

Jeff had asked about Elaine, and I was telling him that she was taking riding lessons. All of that was fine, and I wished her well, but she'd also mounted a personal crusade to get me to go along with her.

He shrugged. "Why don't you just tell her you prefer your horses under the hood of a car?"

Instead of answering, I drank some more stout.

Jeff's eyes widened and in a tone that implied dawning comprehension said, "Ohhh, I think I get it." He nodded. "You're afraid Ed Carver's gonna start thinking that maybe Foxport PD needs a mounted patrol. And by gosh, the only time he can take lessons is when Elaine takes hers."

I looked away. "That's not it."

"Sure it's not." He snorted. "Hell, I don't blame you. If I thought the chief of police was in hot pursuit of my lady, I'd be watching my back end too." He began tapping the fingers of his right hand on the table, keeping time with "McNamara's Band."

"That's not all of it."

Jeff shrugged. "Well, you can relax as far as Carver goes. For a while, anyway. I just heard he's on vacation for a month." I raised my eyebrows. "I know. Stop the presses, right?"

"With Ellie?"

"Well, she's not around, but you never know, they might be taking separate vacations. I doubt they could put up with each other for a month." Now both of his hands were going. "I don't know what in the hell you're worried about anyway. You and Elaine are a given."

"Sure," I said and drained my glass.

"Which one of the horse palaces is giving Elaine lessons?"

When I told him, he stopped tapping and smiled. "Windemere Farms? No kidding. That guy at the next table, you know, the one whose lady you were admiring, he owns the place." As I turned to study him from another perspective, Jeff added, "Name's Brig Tanner. Maybe you've heard of him. He's running for mayor. He's a cinch to win the Republican primary"—he made a face—"which means you're looking at our next mayor." Then, as he followed my gaze, he added, "Uh-oh."

The three at the table had been joined by a fourth but apparently weren't aware of it yet. Standing behind Brig Tanner was a big man—easily six feet and stocky. He wore a down vest over a black-and-blue plaid wool shirt. Like Brig, he had thick white hair and a weathered look. Only it didn't work as well on him. On Brig it made him look distinguished, but this guy just looked like he'd aged hard. He didn't do anything, just stood there, looking down on Brig, swaying like the Hancock building on a windy day. In no apparent hurry, he drank about an inch off the top of his glass. A few of the surrounding tables, like ours, were watching, waiting, and the noise level dropped perceptibly. Then the younger man drew his attention from the game, his mouth open like he was ready to relate the score. But when he saw the man standing there, his eyes widened and his mouth froze.

Finally Brig raised his head and saw everyone staring at
him as though the big shillelagh was poised to bash his head
in. His shoulders sagged and his sigh was audible. It was like
he knew what he'd find when he looked up. But he did, and
there was no surprise on his face when he saw who was
standing behind him. He smiled the way you do when you'd
rather sneer and curse and pushed his chair back so he could
look at the man, but he didn't stand.

"Jubal. How's it going?" The words came out flat.

Jubal looked down at Brig and the woman, his jaw
clenched.

After a quick glimpse at the big man, she fixed her gaze
on the table, looking like a student who'd been caught
reading the answer off her shirt cuff.

As Jubal studied her, he finished off his drink, working
the gulp around his mouth like it was Listerine, then
swallowed and turned back to Brig.

"Talked to Hines this afternoon. He says you two made
a deal."

I had expected his words to be slurred, barely comprehen-
sible, but his enunciation was good and his deep voice
carried like a stage actor's.

Brig shrugged. "I offered him more, and I offered him
cash." He leaned toward the next table and grabbed an
empty chair, pulling it up. It made a ratchety noise as it
scraped the floor. My ears hurt. "C'mon, sit down."

Jubal barely glanced at the chair. "I told you to keep your
hands off that horse. Don't listen too good, do you?"

"All depends on who's talking." Brig tried to soften the
statement with a grin. "C'mon, Jubal. Have a seat." He
patted the chair slats. When he saw no movement on Jubal's
part, the smile dissolved and he added, "Besides, you're not
the only one who raises horses."

"Morgans?"

After a moment's hesitation, Brig said, "It's been a while
for you though, hasn't it?"

Jubal shifted, and the knuckles of his hand gripping the

beer went white. I thought the glass was going to shatter as he held it.

Brig frowned and shrugged, rubbing his chin. "A magnificent animal is just that, no matter what the breed."

Jubal glanced at the young woman but didn't say anything.

"Jubal," Brig continued, raising his hands, "Hines needed the money. Now. Not in a couple of months. Not whenever you and your cronies got it together. Plain and simple. If he hadn't sold to me, he had about three others lined up ready to put good money down. Now." He jabbed a finger on the table for emphasis.

Jubal pressed his lips together and narrowed his eyes. Then he relaxed his features and nodded as though suddenly it all made sense. "You think that's all it takes. Money. Well think again."

The younger man had been watching the scene unfold, his features tense. He stood slowly. "That's enough, Jubal. You're drunk. Go on home."

At that moment, Ginny, apparently oblivious to the situation, stepped between Brig and Jubal with a tray holding three green beers and two Guinness.

Jubal eyed the tray, and I could almost see the idea taking shape. "These are on Brig here," he said, and before anyone could stop him, he grabbed the tray from Ginny and dumped it all on Brig. Fortunately, he was too close to get much momentum going, so while taking five full mugs point-blank in the chest didn't do Brig any good, his leather jacket incurred most of the serious damage.

Except for the lyrics to "Danny Boy," the tavern had become still as death. The eyes in the room were divided between Brig, wordlessly wiping the beer from his chest, and Jubal, smiling and nodding like an artist who's just applied the finishing stroke to his canvas.

The young man was the first to move, grabbing Jubal's wrist. "You drunken old son of a bitch."

Jubal pulled his wrist free and turned on him, finger

stabbing his chest. "Careful boy, that's your grandma you're talking about."

The Tattersall Tavern didn't need bouncers. It's a quiet, well-mannered place, and on the rare occasion when someone gets out of order, there are usually enough regulars to bring him under control. The only cops Sammy gets in there are off duty, and that's the way he likes it.

When Jubal turned back to Brig, he saw that the occupants of several tables had risen and were waiting for his next move. The odds were at least twelve to one against him, but for a few seconds, as Jubal clenched and released his fists, I thought he was going to take them on. Every one of them. But then he scowled, waved off the whole lot, and turned toward the door. The wooden floor creaked beneath his boots. He had almost reached the door when Brig stood, but before he could speak, Jubal turned on him and, his voice low and measured, said, "You're gonna be sorry. Know that. You're not the only one who knows how to take." Then he left.

The room hung in suspended animation for several long seconds, and I half expected Brigham Tanner to snap out of it and wonder how in the hell he got his jacket all wet. But it didn't happen that way. The jukebox clicked, the Irish Rovers started singing about some hapless unicorn, and people began to move, sit down, drink. But, at least for now, some of the rowdiness had gone out of the crowd, and when Ginny asked us if we still wanted a drink, I said yes.

Brig Tanner looked as though he was ready to follow Jubal out there and kick some ass, but the other guy was talking him out of it, telling him it wasn't worth it, that Jubal didn't need any help in destroying himself. The woman was just sitting there, recovering, with her forehead braced in the palm of her hand. While Ginny went to get their drinks, Sammy was wiping up their table, apologizing. Not that it was his fault, but that's the kind of guy Sammy is. He takes it personally when any of his regulars have a bad time. It's like it reflects on his role as host. Now he was telling the three of them that the next round was on the house.

"As opposed to Brig," Jeff muttered.

As I replayed the scene in my head, my memory snagged on something. "What was that Jubal said about the kid's grandmother?"

Jeff smiled and folded his hands. "Yeah. Jubal said not to call him a son of a bitch because he'd be talking about his own grandmother." Just as the light bulb was clicking on, he added, "That was Jubal Tanner. He and Brig are brothers. The younger guy is Will Tanner. Brig's son. Jubal's nephew."

I was only half aware of the return to normalcy, and when Ginny brought our drinks, I took a couple swallows and watched as the crowd gradually filled in the silence and the space where Jubal Tanner had stood. After a few minutes I pulled my gaze from the door in time to catch Pippen put the Bulls up by seventeen.

I imposed the two-Guinness limit on myself, not so much because I thought three would send me over the edge, but because it was a good excuse to leave. The number of sing-along groups had doubled, and there didn't seem to be any effort to coordinate numbers. I glanced at my watch. Besides, if it was St. Patrick's Day, then *The Quiet Man* was probably on the tube. It wasn't ten-thirty yet. Maybe I'd be able to catch most of it. I zipped up my jacket and wished Jeff luck as he gravitated back to the *Chronicle* table.

I knew we were in for a bad one when I stepped out the door and planted my foot in four inches of snow. An hour and a half ago when I'd walked into the Tattersall, it had barely started. Now it was a full-fledged blizzard and showed no sign of letting up. I pulled up the collar of my corduroy jacket, relieved that I had only a few blocks to drive. A plow slowly working its way down Main Street sounded muffled, distant. I could tell from the ridge of snow against the curbs that the street had been plowed already, but a couple inches had accumulated since then. I figured those guys had their work cut out for them tonight. Hands sunk into my jacket pockets, I bent into the swirling flakes and plodded through the street. Boots would have been more practical than the low-cut, all-purpose athletic shoes I was wearing, but then I only had to walk across the street.

At the time, I'd considered myself lucky to get a space in the parking lot the Tattersall shared with Foxport Federal, but now I was glad I carried a snow shovel in the trunk. The space had been on the end, next to a City of Foxport dumpster, the front of which was shielded from the street by a redwood fence. It was a good thing I had a landmark to follow, because underneath several inches of snow, cars tend to look the same. I scraped the snow off the lock with my bare hand, started the car, and got the defroster running. While it warmed up, I knocked the snow off with a brush. It was heavy and fell to the ground in clumps—the kind of snow that's great for packing. I couldn't resist just one fat snowball, which I lobbed at the side of the dumpster. STEE-RIKE ONE! Its impact dislocated a chunk of snow, which dropped on a white bundle next to the dumpster. Strange. Foxport usually doesn't tolerate out-of-place garbage. I tried to ignore it and almost succeeded, but it was too large to write off as a bag of groceries or a laundry sack.

My knees cracked as I crouched next to the pile. By then I was close enough to realize it was a person, lying on his stomach with his cheek resting on his hand. Like he was taking a nap. I had to brush only a small amount off the face to determine that it belong to Jubal Tanner.

▽

2

AT FIRST I assumed he was dead; then I wondered if he wasn't just drunk. "Jubal!" I touched his face. It was still warm. I felt for a pulse and found one. "Jubal!" No response, so I brushed off some more snow and slapped his face a couple of times. "C'mon, Jubal." Still nothing. I slapped him harder and was rewarded with a low moan.

"Jubal, wake up." I slapped him again. His eyelids fluttered, his lashes thick with white flakes.

The glow from the streetlight made his skin gray. He looked like he'd been frozen and I guess by morning he would have been.

"C'mon, Jubal, get up."

I went to slap him again, but this time he grabbed for my wrist. His voice cracked as he said, "Quit hittin' me."

"Then get up." I took a fistful of his jacket and tried to haul him up. Talk about a deadweight. I looked around for someone to help, briefly considered going back to the Tattersall, but discarded the notion when I recalled how popular he was there.

"Jubal, I'm gonna hit you again if you don't help me out."

"Can't get . . . my head on straight." He looked at his snow-covered forearm like he couldn't figure out where in the hell it came from. "Dumb sonofabitch. What's he trying to do?"

"He's trying to keep your sorry ass from freezing to death. A little assistance would be appreciated."

"Huh? What?" He looked up at me, squinting. "Who the hell are you?"

"Quint McCauley. You don't know me from Adam. Now help me out."

He rolled over on his side, propping himself up with an elbow. Encouraged by the movement, I didn't push him. Moaning, he ran a hand through his hair, rubbed the back of his neck, and shook his head, as if that might help clear it. Then he glanced at his hand and wiped it on the snow, leaving a slash of red. At that point I figured he must have smacked his head on the dumpster when he fell.

"Let me help you up."

"Don't need no help." Bracing one hand against the dumpster, he rose to his knees first, then slowly worked his way up. Halfway there he stopped and doubled over, and I thought he was going to heave his guts in the snow. I stepped back. Nothing happened. After a few seconds, he groaned and continued his ascent. When he finally stood, a smile of triumph played on his mouth for a few seconds; then he lost his balance and slumped back against the dumpster. I caught him before he went all the way down, then wrapped his arm around my neck and my arm around his waist. Though he wasn't much taller than me, he must have outweighed me by about thirty pounds. We began to move toward the car. Slowly.

"Hey. This isn't my car. Where the hell'd I park the damned thing?"

"I'm taking you home."

He stopped. I stopped too. "The hell you are. Jubal Tanner doesn't need nobody taking him home."

"Shut up, Jubal, or I drop you here and let you walk home."

He wrenched himself away from me and fell against the car's door. Once he'd adjusted to the new support, he reached into his jeans pocket, groped around for a minute, then pulled out a ring of keys. He hadn't had any trouble standing up in the bar, so I wondered if he might have done some serious head damage when he fell by the dumpster.

Either way, I couldn't let him drive like this, and I briefly ran down my options as I studied the man leaning against my car. There was no way I could get him in my car unless he was willing. The only advantage I had was my sobriety. "Okay, why don't you relax a minute, I'll go start your car, get it brushed off." I held my hand out for his keys.

Tilting his head back, he studied me through narrowed eyes. "You know where your car is?"

"Course I do. Let's see." Chin raised, he surveyed the parking lot. "Over there somewhere." He nodded toward the back of the lot.

That eliminated about half the cars. "You're going to have to be a little more specific."

Scowling, he swung his arm toward the back of the lot. Apparently he didn't have a real firm grip on his keys, because they took off in that direction. So much for the psychological approach. Jubal looked at his empty hand. "Crap."

"C'mon, Jubal. You can get them tomorrow. Let me take you home."

He squinted at me, and after a few seconds his eyes widened and he said, "I know. I've got another set at home. You give me a lift, then we'll come back for my car."

"Great idea." I unlocked the door on the passenger side and helped Jubal onto the seat. He had trouble maneuvering his legs into the car, so I had to pick them up and swing them in after him. His boots smelled like they'd been through a lot. As I slammed the door shut, I hoped he wasn't the puking kind of drunk.

Had I known my mission would take me down five miles of unplowed road, I might have dropped him at the police station and let them deal with him. But he said he was "just outside of town," and I was already there by the time I realized that wasn't quite the case. Foxport is forty miles west of Chicago—the far edge of the city's suburbs. So far, we'd gone quite a ways over the edge. Jubal had given me instructions, then fallen into a silence, broken now and then by a snore or grunt. Now I was creeping along through a blizzard, unable to see more than ten feet in front of me. And given his condition, I wasn't overly optimistic that Jubal Tanner knew where he lived. If there really was a farm at the end of this road, how did I know it belonged to him? I decided I didn't care. I'd just prop him up against the door, ring the bell, and run.

"If I don't know you, how do you know me?"

Momentarily surprised by my passenger's consciousness, not to mention his acumen, I glanced at him. Maybe he'd slept it off. He was frowning, the creases in his face etched deep. "I was at the Tattersall."

"Oh," he grunted. "You a friend of Brig's?"

"Didn't know who he was either until tonight."

For a minute I thought he'd gone back to sleep. Then he said, his speech thick and clumsy, "Now you know who we both are. What d'ya think?"

"About what?"

"Who d'ya like best?"

"You've got all the charm, Jubal."

He chuckled. "I'm not so bad. Brig, he's a pain in the ass."

"What were you picking a fight about?"

"A horse. What else? He don't know horses. Just thinks he does." He chuckled again.

"You wanted the horse he bought?"

He sighed and shifted his bulk. "He's gonna be sorry. That I know."

"Oh yeah? How come?"

He didn't answer for a moment. Then he said, "Too much horse for him. Too much trouble."

"Is it worth you two clashing over? I mean, there are other horses."

"Not like Kessler. Nope. He's one of a kind. One of a kind."

"Jubal, you sure we're on the right road here?"

"Think so. Just taking a while 'cause you're driving so damned slow." His voice faded, and he finished the thought with a snort, then settled into deep, even snores.

According to my odometer, we'd come five miles down this road and had nothing to show for it. "Think so" wasn't good enough for me. This road had five minutes to come up with a house or I was turning back. Out of the corner of my eye, I saw lights to my left. When I looked, I saw that they belonged to two snowmobiles cutting through the field we were passing. As their buzzing faded in the distance, I was thinking how I wouldn't mind swapping my front-wheel-drive Accord for something a little more practical. Even a dogsled. I turned back to the road just in time to see the deer dart in front of the car. Fortunately for the doe, she was moving faster than I was. All I needed to do was adjust my steering to miss her. But I braked like I was trying to come to a dead stop on a clean, dry highway. The car began to slide sideways. I released the brake and downshifted, steering into the skid. It wasn't so much my after-the-fact maneuvering that stopped us as it was the roadside ditch. Not much of a ditch, but enough to send Jubal, who I hadn't belted in, onto the gearshift. He grunted like he'd just had the wind knocked out of him.

Still draped over the shift, he said, his voice muffled, "Shoulda hit the damned thing. We'd have eaten for a month."

We were wedged into the ditch at a forty-five-degree angle, and I didn't hold out much hope of pulling out of it. But I tried anyway. The wheels spun in the snow. Same in reverse. Useless. The mishap had apparently brought Jubal around again, because he was muttering something about the great venison stew someone named Claude made.

"How much farther, Jubal?"

With some difficulty, he pushed the door open and held it there as he stepped down into the snow. Hands tucked in the back pockets of his jeans, he squinted up into the sky. "Snowin' like a sonofabitch."

"Thank you, Willard Scott," I muttered. "How far, Jubal?" I repeated. He slogged his way onto the road, looked ahead, then back. "Just around that bend. I can walk it from here.

Thanks for the lift." He waved at me and began to shuffle down the road.

I know it does you no good to get mad at a drunk. It's sort of like yelling at a cat—being amoral, they're immune to your opinions. All I could do was hope that Jubal Tanner's hangover would be one to remember. In the car's headlights, I couldn't tell if there was a bend up ahead. I killed the lights and bailed out of my seat belt. The flashlight I kept in the glove box didn't work until I slapped it against my hand a couple of times. "Hold on there, Jubal." I climbed out on the passenger side. "My car's not going anywhere. Mind if I use your phone?"

He shrugged like it didn't matter to him and continued to scuff through the calf-deep snow. God, it was black out. And quiet. The flashlight had about the same effect as the car's headlights and was only good for about five feet. Jubal seemed to know where he was going without it, and we both plodded on for about fifty feet. I figured it was the fresh air that steadied him, because when we started out Jubal didn't look like he needed any help. But then he stumbled and dropped to his knees, one hand buried in the snow and the other rubbing the back of his neck. He let me help him up and then let me help him walk. Moving down the road as one, we continued the trek.

"You sure your place is just up ahead?"

"S'long as we're on the right road."

Great comfort, I thought as my ears went numb. I remembered how my mother always told me to wear a hat. How most of your body heat escaped through your head. A hat would have been nice. A hat and a dogsled. I started cutting deals with God.

We had slogged along for about fifteen minutes when I stopped. "Jubal—"

"Just a little farther."

"No offense, but I don't believe you. I think we're on the wrong road."

He pulled away from me. "Suit yourself. See ya around."

He took three steps and dropped like he'd been shot.

Shit. And I thought he was sobering up. In the flashlight's glare I examined the wound on the back of his head. It was wet and sticky but didn't seem to be bleeding anymore. I rolled him over and felt for a pulse. My hands were too numb to feel their own fingertips, let alone someone's pulse.

I hooked my arms under his armpits and managed to drag him to the side of the road. We were fifteen minutes from the car with both of us walking; there was no way I'd make it back there with him in tow. "I sure hope you knew where you were going, Jubal."

I kept going. I didn't know how long he'd last in the snow. Hell, I didn't even know if he was still alive. I thought about Elaine and tried to imagine what she'd be doing right now. Probably drinking a glass of cabernet and watching *The Quiet Man*, feet curled up under her on the couch, wearing her argyle socks and that bulky gray sweater. I held that image in my head like a treasured snapshot and trudged down the road, trying not to count the parts of my body I couldn't feel anymore.

▽

3

I HADN'T BEEN walking for more than five minutes when the road began to curve slightly. I didn't exactly get giddy with optimism, but I managed to pick up my pace a little. Somewhere not far away, a dog began to howl. Jubal's dog? My relief was short-lived when that howl was joined by another, then another. I'd read somewhere about the packs of wild dogs that preyed on livestock, but I couldn't remember whether there were any in the area. I wondered if they also preyed on stray humans and wished I'd paid closer attention.

I saw the beaten-up mailbox before I saw the lights. It defiantly held its own in a drift of snow. Sticking up through a six-inch snowcap was a red flag. On the sheltered side of the mailbox, TANNER was painted in awkward black letters. Eureka. The snow had long since buried whatever passed as a driveway to the house, but when I looked I saw lights flickering between the snowflakes, maybe a hundred feet away. That was also where the dog sounds were coming from. Wonderful.

As I closed the distance, I wondered what I'd do if no one was home. There was no plan B to fall back on. I could make out a house and a barn, illuminated by a gas lamp in the yard between the two buildings. Two dogs moved into the lamp's sphere of illumination. They weren't more than ten feet from me. One looked mostly like a shepherd, only stockier. The other was a black Lab. They were approaching me slowly; the shepherd seemed to be in charge, being several feet in front of the other. His head was down, and I could see big shoulders shifting beneath his fur. I kept moving toward the house, hoping I'd reach it before they stopped me. Then, from out of the shadows, a third dog appeared in the path between the house and me. I immediately reevaluated my leader theory. This guy had to be in charge. He was only a little bigger than the shepherd, but something about the shape of his head and the feral look in his eyes made me think there was some wolf in him. The door was only a few feet away—I was close enough to make out the patches of peeling paint—but it felt like miles. The dog wasn't moving, just watching me. Weren't you supposed to let a strange dog sniff your hand? Right. What if he didn't like the way it smelled? I kept my fists buried in my pockets and took a step forward. The dog growled low and deep, and the other two closed the distance between us.

Then the door opened, spilling light out onto the snow and revealing the silhouette of a woman holding a rifle. The lead dog allowed himself a quick glance over his shoulder before pinning me again with his stare.

"Who are you?" the woman demanded. "What do you want?"

"Is this where Jubal Tanner lives?"

After a moment's hesitation, she said, "Yes. I'm his wife. What do you want?"

"He needs help. He's up the road about a hundred feet. Out cold."

"Oh, my God." She turned, and I caught a glimpse of a slim neck and a sharp chin. "Melissa," she called back into the house, "get down here. It's your father." Then she stepped back from the door. "Come in for a minute. You look frozen." Her voice was soft but with subtle rhythms that made it carry the distance.

When I looked to the dog for permission, she said, "Bear, it's okay. Relax, boy."

Bear raised his head and backed off a couple feet. I think he was disappointed.

A rush of warmth greeted me as I stepped into the house

and the small entryway. I tried not to get too comfortable, which wasn't as tough as it might have been seeing as she made no move to close the door. Bear found a spot on the small concrete stoop and continued his vigil over me.

"How'd you get here?" The woman had propped the rifle up against the wall and was yanking a jacket out of the closet as she spoke. The gray of her hair was threaded with silver, and it fell in a thick braid to the middle of her back. She wore a heavy knit sweater and jeans.

"My car's back a ways on the road. I missed the deer but hit the ditch."

She regarded me, and the lines around her eyes deepened as though she were suppressing a smile. But all she said was "Here, put these on," and she thrust a pair of heavy work gloves at me.

It's difficult to get numb hands into a pair of gloves, but I managed. I flexed my fingers and willed the feeling back into them.

She was shrugging into the car coat as she fished through its pockets. "Melissa! Get down here."

I heard no movement in the house, and the woman twisted her mouth and shook her head. She was hurrying, wasting no movements, but there was something almost placid beneath her surface. It was as though this scene had been played out many times, and she knew all the marks. Pulling a set of keys out of her pocket, she said, "Let's go. We'll take my jeep."

Fortunately, the four-wheel drive vehicle had an easier time of it than my Accord, and it wasn't more than five minutes before we reached Jubal. In that time I learned that the woman, Jubal's wife, was the Claude he'd mentioned. "Short for Claudia," she'd explained and said nothing more until we found Jubal. There he was, by the side of the road, and for the second time that night, he'd been reduced to a snow-covered clump.

She knelt in the drift next to him and brushed the snow from his face and took it in her hands. In the jeep's headlights, Jubal looked like a corpse. "He's more than drunk, this time, isn't he?"

"He either hit his head or someone did it for him."

She glanced at me, eyes narrowed. Then, with long, slender fingers, she probed until she found the spot where the blood was caked. Frowning, she brushed snow off her husband's shoulders and said, "Let's get him in the jeep."

Between the two of us we managed to dump Jubal into the backseat. As I drove back to the house, Claude sat with him, cradling his head in her lap. I pulled right up to the door. As we unloaded Jubal and carried him into the house, Bear paced and whined like he was concerned about the big guy. The other two dogs sat and watched.

We deposited Jubal on an overstuffed brown plaid sofa. Bear tried to climb up with him, but Claude remanded him to the braided rug by the door. Once we got Jubal settled, Claude lifted his head and slipped a pillow embroidered with irises beneath it. When I looked up, a young woman was standing on the steps leading up the second floor. Her hair was wrapped in a faded blue towel, and she wore a red flannel robe and held a brush in her right hand.

"Where were you?" Claude's tone was sharp, accusing.

"I was in the bathroom. What's wrong? Is it Daddy?" Her eyes were wide, and she gripped the brush so tight her knuckles were white. Then she looked past the woman to the figure on the couch, and her mouth dropped open. Jubal's face looked like granite. "Oh, my God. Is he—?" She took a tentative step.

"He'll be fine. Get some blankets," Claude said, then added, "and a basin with warm water and a cloth." Melissa hesitated, apparently drawn toward the body on the couch. "He doesn't need you gawking at him. Do as I said." The brush clattered to the step, and she spun on the ball of her foot and ran up the stairs. "And some bandages," Claude called after her.

I helped Claude get Jubal out of his down vest, no easy matter.

As we worked, she asked me what happened. I told her, trying to skim over the part in the bar, but she wouldn't let me.

"Who was involved?"

"Well, his brother was there, his brother's girlfriend, his nephew."

"What was that fight about?" She tugged a boot off, revealing a heavy gray-wool sock. That came off too. Jubal was showing signs of life as we worked, emitting a low-pitched groan every now and then.

Before I could tell her, Melissa came down the stairs, two blankets tucked under her arm and carrying a metal basin of water.

Claude turned to me. "There's Scotch under the kitchen sink. Bring me the bottle and a glass."

The kitchen reminded me of my grandmother's with its peeling tile and ribbed porcelain drainer that emptied into a single oversized sink. True to Claude's word, there was a bottle under it. I found a glass in one of the white metal cabinets.

As I brought it into the living room, I noticed that Bear had managed to cut the distance between him and Jubal in half, apparently by crawling. Neither Claude nor her daughter seemed to notice. Melissa was adjusting the blankets covering her father, tucking them around his feet. "He'll be okay. Won't he, Mom?"

Claude shot her daughter a tired look and said, "He always is." Then she thanked me, took the glass, and poured about an inch of the Scotch. I don't know what the treatment is for being half frozen, with a probable concussion, but she seemed to know what she was doing. Propping his head up, she poured a bit of the Scotch between Jubal's lips. Nothing happened for a few seconds; then he coughed and sputtered and fell silent again. Melissa watched as her mother ministered to her father, hands sunk deep in her flannel pockets. When she saw me observing her, she returned the stare, and I went back to observing Jubal. At first I'd figured Melissa to be in her late teens, early twenties. But her face showed

traces of baby fat she hadn't quite shed yet. I reevaluated and
put her in high school.

Claude dipped the cloth in the pan of water, wrung it out,
then gently turned Jubal's face toward the back of the couch
and began to work at the dried blood at the base of his skull.
Melissa sat at her father's feet, rubbing them through the
blanket. She had pulled the towel from her head, and her
hair fell, dark and wet, past her shoulders. Hard to believe
that a couple of hours ago, this guy was thrown out of a bar
and sleeping it off under a pile of snow. Now he had three
individuals (I was counting the dog) hovering over him,
willing him conscious.

Feeling had returned to my hands, and now they were in
the hurting stage. But they were dry, which was more than
my feet could say. I dropped down into a brown vinyl chair
and worked at the ice-encrusted knot that was my shoelace.
It was going to take a while.

"These should help get your feet warm again."

When I looked up, Melissa was standing there with a pair
of socks. They were gray wool and had the nubby imperfec-
tions that made them look like they'd been hand knitted.
Probably the same kind Jubal wore, and I wondered if Claude
had made them. As I pulled them on, I realized they were
also warm.

I rejected Melissa's offer to take my jacket. At this point
it was busy helping to raise my body temperature. I figured
it wouldn't take much longer. The house was small and
warm, and a fire was dancing in a painted-brick fireplace at
the narrow end of the room. Above the mantel, against a
paneled wall was a large painting—maybe three by four feet.
Above the painting was one of those little lights you see
above oils in funeral homes. Only instead of Christ in some
impossibly green setting, a brown horse, sturdy and well-
muscled, stared down at me from the wall. The unsettling
thing was that the creature's wide, intelligent eyes seemed
to be watching me, and I was sure if I were to cross the room,
it would continue to stare. I looked away.

Jubal coughed and moaned, and I saw that Claude had just given him another dose. Bear had wormed his way right up to the couch and lay with his chin resting on a cushion. Jubal was trying to raise up, but with her free hand Claude pushed him back into the couch. She set the glass on the hardwood floor. "Jubal?" she murmured, stroking his cheek with the back of her hand. "Jubal."

"Ohh," he moaned in response and touched the back of his head, feeling the bandages. His eyes popped open, and he looked around the room as much as he could without turning. As he reached down to pet the dog, he asked, "How the hell did I get here?"

"Mr. McCauley brought you." Still holding the wet cloth, she gestured toward me. I waved. Jubal frowned and squinted at me; then his head dropped back to the couch. He moaned again, and Claude began to blot his forehead with the cloth. He brushed her hand away like it was a mosquito. "Don't get my head wet." He ran his tongue over dry, cracked lips. "Got any more of that medicine?"

"Melissa, get your father a glass of juice. I think we've got some grapefruit."

Jubal made an appropriately sour face. "Forget it, honey." He began to push himself up, and this time Claude and Melissa helped him gain a sitting position. Elbows on his knees, he cradled his face in his hands for a minute. Slowly he looked up at me. After he seemed to get me in focus, he said, "You ready to go back for my car?"

We were real democratic about it. It was three to one against Jubal. Afterward Claude told Melissa to get a pillow and another blanket for me, and Claude and I helped Jubal up the stairs to their bedroom. Bear was right behind us.

Jubal dropped on the bed's thick comforter with a groan, and we hoisted his feet up. He squinted and pointed his finger at me. "First thing tomorrow we gotta go back for my car." His voice was hoarse and thick.

"You bet." I hoped "first thing" didn't happen before the snowplows.

Claude gave him a wry smile and, with a light hand at my elbow, maneuvered me out of the room, pulling the door shut behind her. "I'm sorry I can't offer you anything other than the couch." I assured her the couch would be fine and I would be asleep before my body knew it wasn't a bed. Bear was lurking at the door, watching me.

"I assume the wet dog sleeps up here."

"He's not nearly as mean as he looks." I could hear the smile in her voice. "Kind of like Jubal," she added. Then she placed her hand on my arm. "Thank you for bringing him home."

I turned to go downstairs, but Claude stopped me. "You never did tell me what the fight was about."

"Well, from what I could tell it was about some horse that Jubal wanted but Brig bought first."

It was pretty dark in the hall, and I couldn't make out her face very well, but I could feel her tense up. "Brig bought Kessler?"

"I think that was his name."

All that filled the silence was the creaking of the springs as Jubal shifted in the bed. Claude's voice was barely a whisper when she said "Thank you, again" and stepped into the bedroom, closing the door behind her. Bear lay down in front of the door and waited for me to move past him before dropping his chin to his paws.

As I descended the stairs, all I could think about was how good that couch was going to feel and how nice it would be to blank this night out for a while. But when I got downstairs, I saw that Melissa had settled on the couch with a glass of Scotch. With her free hand, she poured another and offered it to me. "You look like you could use this." She looked like she wasn't nearly old enough to drink, but who was I to argue with the bartender? Besides, she was on my bed. I took the glass and found my place in the vinyl chair.

"Maybe that will warm you up enough to take your jacket off."

I smiled. Not yet. I waved my hand toward the stairs. "This sort of thing happen often?"

She sighed and took a drink, and I was almost sorry I asked. But then she said, "Not so you can set your watch by it, but enough." I nodded and drank some of my own. It felt good going down. Melissa continued. "When he's not being like this he's really, well, he's a lot different."

"I figured."

Melissa watched me as she patted the ends of her hair with the towel. It felt like she was waiting for me to say something, but I was either too dumb or too tired to figure it out. As she sat there, her robe open at the neck and the point of the wide V nestled between her breasts, I wondered if the girls had been that provocative when I was in high school. Maybe I'd just been too worried about my zits to notice. Nah, I may have been dumb, but I wasn't blind. I guess there's a big shift in attitude when a girl's role model is Madonna instead of Gidget. I took another drink. It wasn't very smooth, but it was Scotch. I was starting to warm up.

Melissa placed her drink on the arm of the couch and proceeded to run a comb through her hair, carefully working out the snarls as she went. She had her mother's long fingers and slender build and the same arch to her eyebrows. I didn't realize I'd been staring until she looked up and then smiled like she knew that's where I'd be.

"You live out here?" she asked.

I shook my head. "Back in town. Foxport."

"What do you do there?"

"Private investigator."

She stopped desnarling. "You're kidding. Really? Like Magnum?"

"Just like Magnum. Right down to the red Ferrari."

"Oh, well, that's not really his." She settled into the couch, dipping her left shoulder slightly. The robe's V neck was getting wider.

"Do you have any girlfriends?"

I nodded. "One."

"What's she like?"

"Smart. Funny." I hesitated because the next word that

came to mind was "complex" and I didn't want to explain.

Melissa filled in the gap. "I'm dating two guys at once." She flashed me a smile, quickly covering it with her hand. I wondered if she'd recently shed a set of braces. "They"—she glanced upward—"only know about one. Don't say anything."

Since I never planned to see any of them again, I didn't think it would take too much self-control on my part.

"I've been going out with Bobby forever. Almost . . . oh, let's see . . . two years." She stopped, gulped some Scotch, and continued, barely missing a beat. "He's really nice, but kind of, you know, immature."

I nodded.

She wrinkled her nose as she ran her comb down the length of her hair. As it dried, it was curling some.

When she didn't continue, I found myself saying, "Who's the other one?"

She smiled slowly, then whispered, "He's top secret. My folks would have a shit fit."

"Why?"

"He's older." She made it sound sinister. Then she added, "Twenty-seven," and I flashed ahead forty years to me in a nursing home—a candy striper who looks a lot like Melissa is feeding me a spoonful of pureed carrots. My small, knobby head is tilted back and my tongue wags in anticipation. I am cheeping.

I shook my head to clear it. "Your dad is an interesting man."

She settled back into the couch, smiling as though I hit on one of her favorite subjects. "Did you meet Jubal in a bar?"

"Not exactly."

When I finished telling her the story, she nodded. "Uncle Brig. It figures."

"There's some kind of bad blood there, I'd say."

"No kidding." She exchanged her comb for the Scotch and studied me over the glass's rim. "You must be pretty new to town."

"Been here over a year and a half."

"You're kidding!" Overwhelmed by my ignorance, she lowered her glass and gaped at me. "And you haven't heard? The Tanner feud is legend around here."

The next swallow of Scotch convinced me I was warm enough to take off my jacket. Easier said than done. I seemed to be working in slow motion.

"People are always asking me if it's true."

"If what's true?" I was out of one arm and working on the other.

"What started it," she said, like I'd just asked what's on after "Wheel of Fortune."

"Oh. Yeah." The Scotch might not have been smooth, but it had other things going for it. "The feud."

"Uh-huh. Lots of people ask me about it."

I nodded, finally catching on. "What's the feud about?"

She shrugged, and her robe slipped off one shoulder. She left it there. "No one really knows for sure. You know what I think? I think there's this, you know, crazy streak in the family and this thing between Jubal and Uncle Brig, well, it's just part of it." After pouring more Scotch into her glass, she leaned over to refill mine. I held it out and stared at the floor. When I looked up again, she was sitting back, smiling. Her robe had slipped a couple more inches, revealing the swell of her breast.

I took a swallow of Scotch and closed my eyes as it ate its way through my intestines. "Crazy you say?" I stifled another yawn.

She curled her legs under her, pushing the blankets back. "My uncle blew his brains out." Her bare knees poked out from her robe.

The combination of Scotch and a warm room made the prospect of sleep irresistible, but her statement, delivered with a practiced nonchalance, roused me a bit. "How come?"

She raised her eyebrows, and for an instant I saw the resemblance between her and her father. "No one knows. Well," she hurried to add, "I guess everyone knows why, but the rest of it's this really weird thing." The last three words were drawn out, and she locked onto my gaze, waiting.

"So, what happened?"

She changed positions so she was sitting with her legs crossed and her elbows on her knees. In the process she unconsciously pulled the robe up over her shoulder again. I felt a little sorry for her, she'd worked so hard at getting it down there.

"His name was Cody." Gazing up at the ceiling, she chewed on her lower lip for a moment. "Let's see, my father is sixty-three so that would make Uncle Brig sixty-one. There was one other brother, Cody. If he were still alive, he'd be fifty something. But he died young. Before I was born." She leaned back into the couch and drank some more Scotch. If the stuff was making me numb, I wondered how well she could be functioning.

"What happened?" I figured I'd have to work for this.

"Well, a lot of people don't really know the story. Most, in fact. They figure that Jubal and Uncle Brig just don't get along, you know. I mean this happened back when Foxport was a lot smaller. Well, Cody was supposed to get married to this woman who worked as a secretary to one of the local lawyers. You know, real young and pretty, they say. Three days before the wedding, her mother found her in a tub full of blood, her wrists slashed. She cut them this way." Using the comb, Melissa drew a vertical line down her wrist. "That's the way that someone who really means business does it. Not the other way." I nodded. "Can you imagine? I guess it was really gross. They buried her on the day she was supposed to become Cody's wife. That night—the night they buried her—Cody went out to the cemetery, stood there on her brand-new grave, you know the funeral flowers were practically fresh"—she paused and drew in a breath—"and he blew his brains out."

After taking a few moments to digest all of it, I asked, "Why?"

She gave me the same look my fourth-grade teacher used

on me when I disappointed her. "Cause she was dead."

"No. I know that. Why was she dead? Why did his fiancée kill herself?"

Staring into my eyes, she drew the pause out. "No one knows. Of course, there were all kinds of rumors. Everything from Cody having another woman on the side to Cody having, you know, a male lover." She nodded to herself. "Yep. I think the family's cursed *and* crazy."

I nodded. "Sounds like it."

"Well," she said and frowned as if testing a brand-new notion. "Maybe it's the madness. Maybe there's madness in the family. You know, like some gene or something gone crazy."

"Melissa!" It was Claude, calling her daughter from upstairs.

"Yeah, Mom."

"Come upstairs to bed so Quint can get some sleep."

She scrunched up her nose and stuck out her tongue. "Right away, Mom." Leaning forward she poked her thumb in the direction of the stairs. "Guess it's a good thing I've got her genes on my side." She mouthed the word "boring."

"I said now!"

Melissa rolled her eyes. "I'm coming."

She took our glasses into the kitchen, taking the time to rinse and put them away. As she passed me on her way upstairs, she touched my shoulder. When I looked up at her, I saw that her eyes shimmered with tears. "Thanks for bringing my dad home."

$\triangledown$

4

IT WAS THREE days later, and I was making good on a deal I'd made with God and wondering if maybe I hadn't gotten the short end of the stick. All he had to do was make a farmhouse appear, a miracle that seemed pretty minor when compared to parting the Red Sea. Now I was about to spend an hour bouncing around in a ridiculously small saddle on top of this surly, oversized animal. Hardly a good trade-off.

From the way the old sorrel was eyeing me, he might have been in total agreement. But Elaine wasn't. She stood, long-legged in faded jeans, holding one end of a pair of reins, the other end of which was attached to the large, slightly swaybacked animal. Elaine had that look she gets when she's just about tired of this game. The horse was making crunching noises as he chewed some hay and regarded me with what I considered menacing indifference.

She offered me the reins. "C'mon, Quint. Scott's a sweetheart."

"That's another thing. Whoever heard of a horse named Scott? You name a son Scott, maybe a Highland terrier, but not a horse."

"What difference does his name make anyway? It's not like it's Killer or Screwball or anything like that."

I was about to tell her how very important his name was to me, then thought of a more promising tack. "He's too old."

"Aw, come on." Elaine stroked the white splotch on Scott's forehead. I'd been told it was called a star, even though it in no way resembled one. "He's gentle. You said you wanted a gentle one."

"I didn't say 'gentle.' I think 'laid-back' was the term I used. This guy is so laid-back he's barely breathing." Tight little lines appeared around Elaine's mouth, which meant she was suppressing either a laugh or the urge to tell me off. "Elaine, that horse is only ten years younger than I am. What if I climb on him, he takes two steps and drops dead?"

"Quint." She was showing signs of exasperation now, which meant it was a matter of moments before I caved in. I wished I hadn't promised her I'd try this. What the hell was I trying to prove? Let Ed Carver lead the posse. Be my guest. I had a bad feeling about it. Real bad. Elaine looked so natural with her boots and jeans, shoulder-length auburn hair pulled back with a clip. Even the little velvet hard hat with its leather chin strap looked great on her. But I'd sooner have Scott grind his hoof into my ear than wear one. The thing was, I wasn't so much afraid of falling off the beast as I was of making an idiot of myself. There's no way you can control an animal that outweighs you by a thousand pounds unless it's in the mood. Only now did I realize that from the time I'd made that promise up until I stood nose to muzzle with this Scott horse, I believed that somehow Providence would intercede on my behalf and spare me.

Scott continued to chew, though it sounded like he was just grinding his teeth together, and it occurred to me that no deus ex machina was going to swoop down and yank me out of this one. I noticed the shading of gray on his muzzle. Maybe if it had to happen, this guy would be my best bet. Elaine extended her arm, pulling his head toward me. He moved one step closer. It seemed to take him a while and involved four separate and distinct hoof clops. "Pet him." This wasn't a request. "Let him know you're his friend."

The six inches he'd moved had brought him that much closer to several bales of hay stacked against a stall. With speed I hadn't thought him capable of, he lunged at the hay, excising a chunk of it with his large, yellow teeth.

"No," I said. "I don't want to lead him on."

Just as I was coming to grips with the inevitable, I heard someone behind me. "There you are, Elaine." When I turned, I saw a small blond woman approaching us. Her jeans were even paler than Elaine's, and her boots had the scrunched and scuffed look you only get from lots of honest wearing. She smiled at both of us, and as she came to stop, she looked up at me and said, "You must be Quint." She offered her hand and we shook. "I'm Cindy Tanner." She was at least a foot shorter than me, and her bones were fine and felt fragile in my hand. Continuing to smile, she flipped a strand of hair off her face with a shake of her head. She wore her shoulder-length hair straight and with bangs, sort of like Mary Travers, and I warmed to her immediately. But then she said to me, "Ready for your first lesson?" and the chill came fast.

"I don't know. Scott here doesn't look like he's up for it."

"Aw, what's the matter, fella?" She patted Scott's nose, then took the reins from Elaine and handed them to me. "You two are going to get along just fine. I can tell when Scottie takes to someone." Scottie? The situation had degenerated. Now I was about to ride a horse named Scottie. He jerked his head up and gave it a good shake, accompanying the movement with a nice healthy snort, which coated me in a thin layer of horse phlegm. I smiled and swallowed as I wiped a denim sleeve across my face. I knew when I'd been beaten.

"Okay," I said, "let's get this over with."

"That's the spirit." Elaine patted my shoulder and moved ahead with her horse, a robust-looking gray animal with a dark mane. When I really thought about it, that bothered me too. Both of us would be in the same riding ring. Elaine would be on this handsome creature, and I'd be plodding along behind on good old Scott—excuse me, Scottie—who looked like he should be wearing a hat with earholes and daisies while he pulled a carriage down Michigan Avenue. I imagined Elaine posting her way around the ring looking smart and natural astride this horse whose name was something like Aramis. Then I saw myself, legs flailing as I tried to stay on top of Scott. I don't care to think of myself as someone hung up on macho images, but that one made me wince.

Elaine and Cindy were sharing a laugh as we walked past the rows of stalls. A few of the residents craned their necks over their stalls to get a glimpse of us, but most of them were more interested in eating or chewing on wood slats. We stepped out of the barn and into the twenty feet of yard that separated the stable from the riding arena. Even though it had been only a few days since the storm, the temperature was in the forties, and though we'd gotten eight inches of snow, a lot of it had already melted. The closer we got to the arena, the slower Scott was going. Or maybe it was me. Then just as we were stepping into the sawdust-and-dirt ring, he stumbled against my leg, coming down hard on my boot. He righted himself before inflicting any permanent damage to my foot, but when he took his next step, he was definitely limping. "Cindy," I said, trying not to sound too hopeful. "Scott just went lame."

She reminded me of a den mother who just learned one of her troop members scraped his knee—concern diluted with annoyance. Elaine just looked downright suspicious.

Cindy bent from her waist and hoisted Scott's hoof up between her legs. As she straddled the big animal's leg, she gently probed the underside of his hoof. Her hands looked like an infant's as she cradled it. "Well, I'll be damned, Scott. How did you manage to step on something in—what?— thirty feet?" Scott blew air out of his nostrils and shook his big head. Cindy probed a little more. "Yep, you've got a bruise there all right." Straightening, she released his hoof. He shifted on his three good legs and brought the bad one down so only the tip of the hoof touched the ground. Nice touch, Scott.

"Gee, I'm sorry about this, Quint," Cindy said. "You want to saddle up one of the others? Deacon's pretty good-natured." A smile tugged at one corner of her mouth as she waited for my excuse.

I didn't want to disappoint. "Oh, gee, I don't think so. I had my heart set on this fellow. Why don't you and Elaine go ahead, and I'll take a rain check for next week?" Maybe I'd have managed to break my leg by next week.

Standing with a hand on her hip, suppressing a smile, Elaine said, "You know, if I didn't know better, I'd swear you stuck a rock in the poor animal's foot yourself."

"Hoof, Elaine. It's called a hoof."

Cindy patted Scott's chest. "I don't know. I think both of them had this planned."

Neither Scott nor I admitted complicity.

Still smiling, Cindy said, "Why don't you just take him back to his stall and get him unsaddled. Then I'll have someone come down and take a look at him."

"Unsaddle him?" Elaine had saddled him as I looked on, promising to do it myself next week.

"You remember, Quint. Just do what I did before, only backwards."

"Thank you, Elaine." I glanced at Scott, who didn't look like he cared one way or another. "He doesn't seem to mind the saddle."

"I can't believe I'm hearing this from a guy who can't wear a necktie for more than an hour and a half without complaining of suffocation."

They were both laughing now, and I decided it was best to cut my losses while shreds of my dignity still clung to me.

Scott didn't need any help in finding his stall, and unsaddling him proved to be relatively simple. In fact, he was real cooperative about the whole thing. Both our moods improved, and Scott even started to nuzzle me. At first I thought it was his way of showing affection, then I realized he was going through my pockets.

I raised my arms. "Just leave me enough for a phone call."

Someone giggled. I looked up and saw a young woman standing in the corridor. She wore riding pants, high black boots, and a lightweight sweater and held a riding crop. It was a moment before I realized she was the woman Brig Tanner had been with the other night at the Tattersall.

"I'm being mugged by this horse."

"Scott just thinks you've got a goodie for him."

"Oh, I see. Sort of like tipping for service?" Convinced that I wasn't carrying, Scott was gnawing at some straw again. "Gee, had I known. What does he like to eat?"

"Oh, he's got a sweet tooth. Apples mostly. Though he wouldn't turn down a carrot."

"No, I don't suppose he would." I picked up the bridle and shook it clean of hay. "You wouldn't happen to know where his stuff goes, would you?"

"The tack room. I'll show you where it is."

I patted Scott's rump, hefted the saddle, and wished him a good day.

"My name's Gayle Millard." She hesitated. "I think, we've, uh, run into each other before, haven't we?"

"I guess you could say that," I said and told her my name.

"Sorry about spilling that beer on you."

"No harm done." We walked a few feet in silence. In light of the evening's other events, I barely recalled the incident. "Those two really put on quite a show, don't they?"

When she didn't respond, I said, "I'm not keeping you from riding am I?" I tried to sound concerned.

"Oh, no, I've already been out."

"Horses don't mind being ridden this early?" It was barely nine o'clock.

"Now's the best time." Gayle wasn't much taller than Cindy, but she didn't have as slight a frame. As she walked a few steps ahead of me, I couldn't help but notice the sway to her hips and the way she carried herself, back straight and chin up as though she was sniffing something. Once she turned her head and smiled at me, like she knew I was watching. She slowed to keep pace with me.

"What about you? You must have finished early. Were you out on the trail?"

"Nope. Didn't make it. Poor Scott, he seems to have bruised his hoof."

She smiled again, her dark eyes bright. "This is just a guess, but I'd say you're pretty relieved."

"Good guess."

"Why are you here then? Horseback riding is supposed to be voluntary, you know."

"A friend talked me into it."

As she walked, she tapped the riding crop against her boot and nodded to herself. "I'd say it's probably a female friend."

"You're right. She's taking her turn in the ring now."

"The one with Cindy?"

It wasn't that the saddle was heavy, but it was hard to keep all the straps and whatnot from dragging on the floor. I stopped to get a better grip on them. Gayle watched me, her arms crossed. Did horse people think that the rest of us folks were hopelessly inept? It could certainly seem that way. I hadn't felt this out of place since I took a class in ballroom dancing.

"She's the one with Cindy now?" Gayle pressed.

"Yeah, that's Elaine."

She nodded, as though confirming a thought. "She's pretty new at riding, isn't she?"

"Oh, she's been at it a few weeks. How about you?"

"How long have I been riding? Since I was little. I honestly don't remember a time when I couldn't ride."

"You must be pretty good then."

"It's like walking."

We'd reached the tack room, and Gayle took the bridle while I hoisted the saddle onto a wood support protruding from a wall. The smell of leather and sweat was heavy in this room and not at all unpleasant.

"So you've got some time to kill. Waiting until your friend's done."

"Just about twenty minutes. No big deal."

"How about some coffee?"

I frowned and shrugged. "Sure."

She led me to an office in the corner of the barn. It reminded me of the office in my dad's auto-body shop—small and dusty with institutional furniture. Only instead of smelling like grease and paint, it smelled like leather and oil, and instead of a comely, incredibly endowed young woman smiling down at me from March's '57 T-bird, a fully clothed man with a pinched expression was putting a high-stepping horse through its paces. Gayle poured a cup for me and one for herself using white mugs with a silhouette of a horse's head above the words "Windemere Farms Riding Club." She sat at one of the two desks, which was empty except for a computer and a pencil holder shaped like a horse's head. The floor felt gritty beneath my boots. I moved over to a small, smudged window, sipping the coffee, which was just this side of warm. It was a gray morning, and the sky looked like it was deciding whether to rain on us or not. A slightly built boy was leading a dirty white horse from the arena. As they passed by us, the horse seemed to be looking in the window, watching me.

I turned to Gayle. "That horse that Brig and Jubal were arguing about. Was its name Kessler?"

She gave me an odd look, then said, "Yes. How did you know?"

"Must have come up that night."

She was sitting with her boots propped up on the old wooden desk, blowing on the mug of coffee. "Brig's picking him up this morning. Should be back any time now."

"Must be some horse to be worth all that fuss."

"Oh, he is. He is. Just wait'll you see him. Kessler's bloodline is going to be apparent in Windemere horses for generations." After taking a sip of the coffee, she added, "Morgans are very prepotent."

I wasn't sure, but I figured that meant he had strong genes. A Kennedy among horses. But I didn't want to get into a discussion of a horse's breeding habits, so I looked for another subject. One of the office's paneled walls was covered with ribbons, and some were strung on a wire that spanned the wall. Horseman's trophies and silver mugs occupied several shelves with a few marksman and a couple bowling trophies thrown in for variety. There were photos too. Mostly the subject was horses, each looking expensive and posed, but several were of Brig and Cindy, with Cindy wearing English riding gear and Brig in some form of civilian dress.

I turned to Gayle. "Does Brig ride?"

She shook her head. "Not since he hurt his back a few years ago."

I nodded and touched one of the elaborate red, white, and blue ribbons. The surface was soft and shiny, and white letters read "Best in Show."

"Pretty impressive, aren't they?"

"Any of these prizes yours?"

"No. Those are Cindy's. Mine wouldn't be up there." The edge in her tone prompted me to glance at her, but her expression remained open, friendly. "I keep them at my apartment."

I gestured toward the desk. "Whose office is this?"

"Cindy and Brig run the farm."

"She's his daughter?"

Gayle nodded.

"What about his son, Will? Does he work here?"

"No, he's not in the horse business. He's an accountant. Works in town."

What was it about the Tanners? I wanted nothing to do with them, but here I was firing questions at Gayle. How did she fit in with the family? There was something that didn't quite mesh here. When I'd seen her the other night, she'd seemed timid—afraid I'd cuff her for bumping my elbow. I admit I was surprised by her familiarity and her casual manner.

"And what do you do when you're not avoiding a riding lesson?"

I shrugged. "I own part of an import shop, do a little consulting on the side."

She raised her eyebrows. "What kind of consulting?"

I was wondering what family dinners around here were like when I heard gravel crunching beneath the wheels of a large vehicle. A pickup truck was pulling a horse van past the stables and into the gravel area. Brig Tanner was driving.

"Don't look now, but I think your horse is here."

She squealed, jumped from the chair, and grabbed my arm as she passed me. "C'mon, you've got to see him." I put the half-full mug on one of the desks, shook the excess coffee off my hand, and followed her out of the office. I admit I was curious about this animal Jubal Tanner was ready to do battle over. Kessler had a ways to go to live up to his reputation. I didn't envy him.

5

B<small>Y THE TIME</small> we got out there, Brig was lowering the back flap of the horse trailer, which served as a ramp. He was several inches shorter than his brother but had the same stocky build and the same rigid way of carrying himself. A small crowd had assembled, consisting of two teenage girls wearing riding pants, one mother wearing jeans and a short jacket, and a man with dark, curly hair that was short in front and brushed his shoulders in the back. He wore a gray sweatshirt with the sleeves cut off and stood back from the crowd, slouching with his arms crossed over his chest. Then Brig spotted him.

"Don't just stand there, Jim. Give me a hand here." Jim looked to either side as though Brig might have been referring to someone behind him and, finding himself alone, approached the trailer as though it were carrying a load of scorpions.

I turned to ask Gayle if this was to be her horse, but she had moved several feet away and stood, hands clasped at her chest, bouncing on the balls of her feet. She looked like she was about to witness a vision. And knew it. Brig took a moment to give Gayle a hug, one hand working its way up the back of her sweater. Gayle giggled, pulling away. Brig released her body but took hold of her gaze with his. After a few seconds, he said, "Wait'll you see him."

Gayle grabbed his hand. "I can't wait."

Brig pulled himself away, looked around, and found Jim standing by the trailer, apparently waiting for orders. "He put up a real fuss on the way over. When Hines said he didn't travel well, he wasn't fooling." Brig took hold of the trailer's side and pulled himself up next to the horse, then turned as though expecting to see Jim behind him. But Jim was still a safe distance from the trailer and the horse's back legs. Brig scowled. "What the hell you doing down there, huh? You gonna talk him outta here?"

Gayle covered her mouth as she giggled, reminding me of a little girl. Jim glanced at her before following Brig up onto the back of the vehicle.

"I see you got front-row seats."

I turned and there was Elaine.

"It's the only show in town." I saw that she was without her horse. "Where's Abacus?"

She smiled. "In his stall."

"Did you get him out of his work clothes?"

"No, someone's riding him next hour."

I nodded. "Convenient."

She gestured toward the trailer with her chin. "Is this the wonder horse you told me about?"

"That's the word." I glanced around and saw Cindy had also come out and was standing back from the crowd. Her arms were crossed, her hip cocked, and her jaw set. If she and Gayle were to stand together they'd make an interesting study in contrasts.

There was some thumping around in the trailer; I heard a high-pitched whinny, more like a scream, and a bang against the trailer's side. Brig yelled, "For God's sake, get hold of his tail and pull." Jim started down the ramp, tail in hand, evaded a flailing hoof, then lost his balance and tumbled off the ramp. But the crowd barely noticed because the horse's rear leg was now visible. Its tail swished in the air, and Gayle brought her fist to her mouth, jumping up and down a couple of times.

"Jeez," Elaine murmured behind me. "You'd think the Beatles were climbing out of there."

After a glimpse of the animal's hindquarters, I could only

say so far so good. The horse stopped and began stamping its left rear hoof on the ramp, and the dull clang sliced through the still morning air. Brig's yell was muffled by the trailer, but I heard a slap against hide, and the horse jumped, then backed out the rest of the way, practically pulling Brig along with him. Jim stood and brushed off the seat of his pants, watching his boss handle the horse. Kessler was dancing in place, his eyes rimmed in white as he took in his new surroundings. Brig held the horse's reins at arm's length and watched as the dance slowed to a shuffle. Kessler continued to toss his head in a way that seemed familiar. Cindy used the same gesture to shake a lock of hair off her face.

Gayle breathed her admiration. "Oh, Brig. He's wonderful. He's heavenly." Brig offered her the reins, and she hesitated only a moment before accepting them. "Oh, big fella." She ran her hand along his back, down his shoulder. "You're a beauty all right." Then she stood facing him, and as he jerked his head up, she touched his muzzle with her left hand and blew gently into his nostrils.

I turned to Elaine and shook my head in disbelief. "Where am I?"

Barely suppressing a smile, Elaine whispered, "That's how a horse picks up your scent."

"Promise me you'll never do that."

Smirking, Elaine shrugged. "I don't know, it's a pretty powerful urge." Then she added, "Isn't he beautiful?"

After all the buildup this animal had gotten, I figured there was no way he could live up to the hype. But he did. There is a quality to all things that are exceptional—whether it's a painting, a sunset, whatever—something intangible that can't easily be described but elicits a strong emotional response. This guy had that quality. As he danced in place, the raw power and energy barely contained beneath his skin, I was reminded of something elemental and unspoiled. Then it occurred to me that if he stood still long enough to pose for a painting, he'd look a lot like the horse in the painting Jubal Tanner had hanging over his fireplace.

Brig Tanner stood back and admired his purchase, then turned to the crowd to get our reaction. When he saw me, he stopped, seemed like he was trying to figure out why I looked familiar, then nodded and looked away.

Jim, having brushed off his jeans and his dignity and keeping his distance from the horse, approached Brig. "If that's all you got for me, Mr. Tanner, I'll be going now."

Brig dismissed him with a nod.

"Quint, I want you to see something." Elaine took my elbow with her hand.

"What?"

"A horse."

"Another horse? Haven't I seen enough horses today?" I was trying to take in the chemistry between horses and the people who dote on them and didn't quite have a handle on it yet.

"The one Brig's selling. You've got to see him."

"Are you thinking about buying?" I hoped the distress wasn't as apparent as it felt.

"No. I don't know." Her shoulders sagged. "I just want you to see him."

"I thought Arabesque was your main horse. How's he going to feel about this?"

"Aramis," she said, stressing the name, "isn't for sale."

I let Elaine pull me away but not before I noticed Cindy twist her mouth in a disgusted gesture, turn on her heel, and walk away from Kessler and his entourage.

The horse's name was Sanchez. Compared with the Morgan he seemed like a ballet dancer, and it wasn't hard to see how Elaine had become smitten so quickly. He was spotted gray—"dappled"—Elaine said.

"Look at his eyes. They're so intelligent."

"Yeah, I've noticed that about horses. They've all got intelligent eyes. Even Scott. I just can't help but think that behind those eyes is one big, fat question mark." Elaine held her hand out to him and he nuzzled her palm. "See, he doesn't even believe his nose. He's gotta lip your hand just to make sure there's no cookie crumbs."

"Quint, for ten seconds can you stop being a cynic? Cindy tells me Sanchez is bright and a good beginner's horse."

I gave her a skeptical look but kept my mouth shut.

"I know. I know. I sound like I've already swallowed the bait, don't I?" She sighed. "Well, it doesn't matter anyway."

"How much?"

"They want a thousand, but she said she'd give him to me for eight hundred." She repeated the sigh. "Hell, it might as well be a hundred thousand."

We spent some time watching Sanchez eat, listening to him crunch. His ears were going the whole time, following noises and sensing movement. Actually, we stood there watching him long after the scene had lost its charm for me. Elaine was trying to figure a way to buy and keep the horse and still have enough money left over to subsist. Finally she shook her head. "I think the only way I could manage is if he moved in with me."

I nodded. "Imagine the size of that litter box."

When we left the barn, the crowd admiring Kessler had dissipated, and only Gayle and Brig were still with the horse. Gayle apparently couldn't get enough of him.

"Gayle." We looked toward the house. A short, plump woman with white hair stood on the ranch house's wraparound porch, drying her hands with a towel. She was wearing a blue apron with "Hildy" stitched in large white letters across the front. "Gayle! Telephone. Want me to take a message?"

Gayle hesitated a fraction of a second. "No, I'll get it." She kissed Brig on the mouth. "Be right back," she said and handed him the reins. "Don't let that horse move."

She breezed past us on her way up to the house.

"You certainly made her day, didn't you?" I commented to Brig.

"He's one of a kind. Won't be long before there's a line of Morgans out of Windemere that's gonna be known throughout the country."

"Prepotent, aren't they?" I commented.

He smiled and nodded. "Prolific too. You know what a shot of this guy's semen goes for?"

I told him I had no idea.

"Two thousand bucks."

I was impressed. I watched Kessler's muscles move beneath his hide. He did seem to have an extraordinary fluidity to his moves. "Just wait'll the mares hear about you." Kessler responded with a snort, and Brig smiled like he was accepting the compliment himself.

A screen door banged, and Gayle came trotting from the house. "Brig, hon, let me use your car, I've got to run out for a couple of hours. You know that saddle I was telling you about? The guy's ready to sell." She seemed more annoyed or distracted than pleased about the prospect.

"Can't it wait?"

"I better not. He might change his mind." She ran her hand down the horse's neck and patted his chest. "I just don't want to let him out of my sight."

"He'll be here when you get back," Brig said.

Gayle flashed him a smile and returned her attentions to Kessler.

Brig studied her for a moment, eyes narrowed. Then he glanced at his watch. "It's Saturday morning. You know I've got to go to the bank." Gayle was pulling a blade of straw out of Kessler's mane and didn't seem to hear him. He continued, "Well, that's okay. I'll get the trailer unhitched and take the truck." He pulled his keys out of his front pocket and a pile of bills out of his back. Peeling one off, he gave it to her along with the keys. "Drove out to Rockford yesterday. Might need some gas."

She gave him a kiss, then took the horse's head in her hands. He jerked his head slightly and backed up a half foot. "And don't you go anywhere." She planted a kiss on his white muzzle.

I watched as she climbed into a Lincoln Town Car parked next to the house, thinking that it seemed too big a car for her. It was black with dark-tinted windows—and looked like something Darth Vader might have driven. She backed out of the narrow gravel drive, waved, then the window slid up and she disappeared.

Brig turned to Elaine. "I hear Cindy was going to show you Sanchez. Fine horse. Think you're interested?" Thumbs hooked in his pockets, he might have been inquiring about the weather.

"I know I'm interested. It's just that right now it's not financially possible."

He jerked his thumb toward me. "Get your friend here to help you out." Then he winked and added, "That's what they're for, you know."

Elaine nudged a piece of gravel with the toe of her boot, then ground it into the dirt. She managed a smile and shook her head. "Doesn't work that way with us." Then she looked up at me. "You ready to go?"

We left Brig still admiring Kessler, shaking his head at his own good fortune. I wondered if it felt all the sweeter because he'd one-upped his brother.

"Brig's really wrapped around that one's little finger," Elaine commented.

"Gayle's or Kessler's?"

"Gayle's." She smiled. "Horses don't have fingers."

She glanced over her shoulder at Brig and his horse. "I can't believe Cindy's such a neat person with such a jerk for a father."

"He's not so bad," I said as we approached my car. "Maybe a little presumptuous, but don't write him off yet."

"You know he's running for mayor?"

"Of course I know. Do you think I don't keep politically current?"

Elaine smiled, then tossed her hat in the backseat and climbed in on the passenger side. "You know, maybe I should just forget about this horse thing. Maybe I'm out of my league."

I wasn't used to the new Elaine. Before she left Chicago for Santa Fe, she wouldn't have thought twice about being in anyone's league. If there wasn't a place for her, she'd make it. But while in Santa Fe, she'd been burned by a good friend who used Elaine's and her own money to help her boyfriend make drug investments. Not only had Elaine lost all her money and the catering business the two of them had started, but she'd also lost a lot of her pluck. I wasn't used to bolstering her confidence. I wanted the old Elaine back and wasn't sure how to help her get there.

I glanced at her and saw her watching the buildings slide by as we pulled out of the long drive. "Don't be silly. Who says you have to own your own horse to ride one?" When that didn't draw a response, I chuckled. "Gee, I'll bet you could get a good deal on Scott."

After a few seconds she smiled and said, "You know, I'll bet you two would be good together."

"Don't start." I turned the radio to Wynonna and Naomi Judd singing "Mama, He's Crazy." I cranked it up a little and pitched my voice a fraction above the volume. "How'd the lesson go?"

"Fine. You're changing the subject."

We were a long way from town yet, not even a mile down the road that zigzagged its way to Windemere, so I figured I couldn't stall with a response for that long. Might as well level with her. Sort of. "You know, maybe I wouldn't mind it so much if I were riding western. I mean, you want to eventually do the horse-show bit and everything. All I want to do is ride and go on picnics. I picture the two of us standing on a cliff—well, the horse would be standing; I'd be on his back. We'd be looking down at this huge herd, and the sun would be going down behind me."

"Oh," she said as though she were taking me seriously. "Why didn't you say so?"

"What? That I see myself in a Remington painting?"

"Not that. The western part. Why didn't you say you'd rather ride western?"

"What difference does it make? He's an English horse, isn't he?"

Now she laughed. "Yeah, but he can be ridden western too."

I should have known. "He can? Hmm. Good old Scottie's a switch-hitter?"

"Sure is."

Having called my bluff, she was watching me now, waiting. I gripped the steering wheel tighter. She deserved more than my disparaging observations about horses and their activities. Yet, it seemed infinitely more difficult to tell her the real motivation behind my agreeing to go riding, and it had nothing to do with promises made to God. Simply put, I was afraid if we didn't do this together, the other things would slip away as well.

Elaine gasped. "Oh, my God."

I saw it a fraction of a second after she spoke. We weren't more than a quarter mile from Dunkirk Road, and I had downshifted to make a sharp curve in the road. On the right was a slight ravine. Nose down in the ravine, its rear end sticking up like a top-heavy black bear, was a Lincoln Town Car with the license plate BTANNER.

6

"OH, MY GOD," Elaine repeated. She glanced over her shoulder at the road. "God, she must have been going fast."

I had to agree. In order to wipe out on a gentle curve like that, she had to be doing better than sixty. The car had gone off the right side of the road and taken a couple saplings with it. But the tree that stopped it had the advantage in size and permanence.

As I opened the door, I turned to Elaine. "Why don't you stay in the car?" The second I'd spoken, I knew I was exhibiting one of those latent macho tendencies that seem to strike me every now and then. I'd seen Elaine in bad situations, and she frequently behaved better than I did. She was out the door before the entire sentence was out of my mouth.

The ground was slick, still wet from the snow, but aside from the piles that had been plowed along the shoulder, now more gray than white, most signs of the blizzard were gone. I sidestepped my way down into the ravine, which was only about six feet deep and a fairly gentle incline. When I was close enough to see the shattered windshield, I stopped abruptly. Elaine slid into me, her feet went out from under her, and she landed with a slight "Oof." I reached down to help her up, wondering if she'd reconsider staying in the car. There was blood on the window, and if that was what had stopped Gayle's forward momentum, I wasn't sure I wanted to see what it had done to her. If she hadn't been wearing a seat belt, a six-foot drop, even at a gradual incline, could be

real nasty. Especially if there was a tree in the way. But Elaine
was up and moving, so I pushed away some of the dark,
shattered glass. Gayle was sprawled across the passenger
seat, lying on her side, facing the dashboard with her
knuckles of her left hand resting on the floor. Her jaw was
slack and her eyes wide and dull with surprise. A trickle of
blood flowed from her mouth onto the tan leather. There was
blood everywhere—splattered across the dashboard, her
head, her face. But it was that tiny stream from her mouth
that burned into my consciousness.

"Is she . . . ?" Elaine stuck her chin over my shoulder.
"Oh, my God," she pulled away from me.

In the few seconds we stood there, time seemed to hold
still, but the clock started ticking again when she breathed.
It was a shredded, gurgling sound like someone sucking the
bottom of a glass dry.

"Oh, Jesus, Quint. She's still alive." Elaine's hand covered
her mouth, and she'd lost some of her color. Then she
dropped her hand, gave her head a little shake, and said, "I'll
go get an ambulance." She hesitated, seemed about to add
something, then turned and took off up the ravine.

The passenger door was jammed against a tree, so I
climbed in on the driver's side and over Gayle. She'd taken
a bad cut to her forehead, but that didn't explain all the
blood. Where in the hell was it all coming from? And what
had taken the windshield out? None of the tree's limbs
seemed large enough to do the job. I gently pushed her
shoulder so she rolled onto her back, and I had my answer.
Her heart was pumping blood out of a hole in her chest. That
hole hadn't resulted from the car's nosedive. She'd taken a
gun blast to the chest. I needed to elevate her chest, and I
figured the best way to do that was to slide under her and
lift her so her head and shoulders were on my lap.

I pushed her hair, matted and sticky, back from her
forehead. Her face was white against red, and I thought I
detected a movement in her eyelids. "We're getting help,
Gayle. Just hold on." At the same time I felt foolish, but

what do you say to someone who's dying and probably can't hear you anyway?

I heard the car come to a thudding stall as Elaine popped the clutch. There was a second of silence, then she got it started. Gravel crunched beneath the wheels, sprayed as the wheels spun, then caught. I listened to the car until it was out of earshot, then there was silence, broken by Gayle's next breath. She sounded like she was drowning, and I guess she was.

I remembered I carried a towel in the trunk of my car and wished I'd asked Elaine to bring it to me before she left. But, you make do with what you've got, so I squirmed out of my khaki jacket and tried to stanch the flow of blood with it. But her heart just kept pumping out blood, and the jacket was crimson in a matter of seconds. You have no idea how much blood there is in a person until you see someone lose it like this.

She breathed eight more times before she died. I'm not sure how I knew the eighth breath was her last, but there was a subtle shudder, and it was like something passed from her. I took the wrist of her right hand. It rested on a sparkling gold belt buckle with a black horse's head. There was no movement beneath the skin. Not even a flutter. I held her for another minute, then eased myself out from under her. The glass grated as I climbed out of the car, and I felt a piece stick in the palm of my hand. I brushed it off on my jeans, noting that they were blood-soaked.

I scanned the woods, looking for something out of place, or a likely vantage point for a sniper. He must have been on the ridge and shot down into the car. There wasn't much green on the trees, but they were dense and revealed nothing. I kicked a clump of mud off the heel of my boot, wondering what I'd expected. Like the guy was going to stick around.

It wouldn't take more than ten minutes for someone to get here. I hoped it would be the police first, but my money was on Brig Tanner. I moved up toward the roadside, then turned to view the car from that angle.

There wasn't any sun, and the rear windshield seemed black as ink. Guess that was one purpose for those windows. Anonymity? Then why in the hell does he have license plates that scream his name? I glanced back at the road toward Windemere. Maybe Gayle Millard hadn't been the target after all. Maybe when it's Brig Tanner's car, you assume Brig Tanner's behind the wheel. Hell of an assumption to make when the stakes are on the high side. What a shock to walk up to the car and see that you'd put a bullet in the chest of a young dark-haired woman instead of a white-haired old man. If you'd even bother to check.

I heard the vehicle coming before I saw it and knew that if whoever was driving wasn't careful, he'd wind up in the ditch too.

The wheels had barely stopped spinning when Brig Tanner jumped out of his truck.

"Get outta my way," he warned as he plowed into me.

I knew better than to try to stop the guy; I just wanted to prepare him. I grabbed his arm. "It's real bad."

His jaw tightened and his mouth pulsed like he was holding back a sob. Then he noticed the dark stain on my jeans and shirt. "She was alive when I got here," I said. "Barely. She was having so much trouble breathing, I thought, well . . ." I trailed off. "She's . . ."

"Don't you say it," he warned, his voice soft and even. "Just get outta my way," he repeated, and I released his arm.

I glanced up at the embankment. Elaine was pulling my car off the road. I listened for the sound of sirens but only heard the heavy stillness of the woods, then the moan. Brig Tanner's hands clutched the car's door, shattered glass and all. He looked up into the bare trees and the moan crescendoed into a wail. Then the cry stopped, as sudden as a needle lifted off a record. He turned to me, as though he was hoping I'd say he was seeing things. His eyes were moist, and as I watched, a tear slipped out of his right eye and traveled down one of the deep creases in his face. I wanted to look away but couldn't. He blinked rapidly, then grasped

the car's door handle, squeezing it for a couple seconds
before yanking it open. He just looked at her, shaking his
head. "Oh, honey," he said, then climbed in the car. I almost
yelled at him. It was a murder scene, but, hell, I'd been
crawling around in there. Besides, how was I supposed to
stop him?

Seconds later he came flying out of the car, fists clenched,
his face red. "She's been shot! This wasn't any accident.
Somebody shot her."

"I know, Brig. The police are coming." Actually I didn't
know whether we'd wind up with the police or the sheriff.
Either way, where the hell were they?

He slammed his fist into the car's roof and looked up into
the sky. "That son of a bitch is dead." He raised one fist
toward the woods and shook it at the trees. "You hear me?"
he yelled. "You are dead."

"Quint."

Elaine was on the shoulder, looking down into the ravine.
"Did I hear you say she was shot?"

I nodded, and she glanced over her shoulder at the road.
"I think the police are here."

As she spoke I heard the sirens coming closer.

The ambulance arrived moments ahead of the police. Two
paramedics—a middle-aged woman with short, spiky hair
and a short, solid man in his early twenties—had almost
reached the Town Car when the squad car pulled up—
Foxport PD.

I was wondering who was being Ed Carver while he was
out of town, figuring it would be one of his two lieutenants
and mentally placing my bet on John Sturgis, who had
seniority over the other. I was wrong.

I recognized Gene Moore the minute he stepped out of the
squad car. Even though the sun was hard-pressed to work
its way through the cloud cover, he wore his trademark
aviator sunglasses. I think they're the kind you can buy only
in eyewear boutiques. As I watched the man with the

brush-cut hair approaching, thumbs hooked in his belt, I
noticed that he'd filled out some through the neck, shoulders, and upper arms. He must be squeezing trips to the
health club into his hectic schedule. Despite the cool
weather, he wore no jacket.

"Where's Carver?" Brig demanded. He'd left his vigil by the
car and was moving slowly up the ravine, studying the new cop
like he was some new, and possibly beneficial, bacteria. He
came to a stop and stood there with his hands on his hips, and
I saw that he'd cut them up some on the glass.

A muscle flexed in the police officer's jaw. Then he said,
"He's on a month's leave, Mr. Tanner. I'm Lieutenant
Moore."

From the way Brig nodded, I couldn't tell whether he knew
that already or was acknowledging Moore's right to be there.

As he descended into the ravine, past Brig and me, Moore
said, "Anyone see this happen?"

I stepped in front of him, blocking his descent. He reached
out to move me from his path, and I said, "She's been shot.
We didn't realize it at first. You'd better secure this area and
get a team down here."

He stared at me for a few seconds. At least that's what I
assumed he was doing behind the mirrors. Finally he said,
"Who are you?"

Before I could tell him, Brig jumped in. "I know what
happened here. I know exactly what happened." He pushed
ahead of Moore and stepped up to the wrecked car. Moore
followed. "That worthless piece of shit I've got for a brother
thought he was taking me out. Instead he got"—he glanced
into the shattered window and his voice softened—"he got
my lady."

"Her name's Gayle Millard," I mentioned, but no one
acknowledged me. I persisted. "You didn't see Jubal leaving
the scene, did you?"

"I don't have to see what I know up here." He tapped his
forehead.

Moore was eyeing the car as though it had taken on a new dimension. Swallowing, he looked directly at Tanner. "She's been shot?"

Brig stopped and stared at Moore for a few seconds, then gestured toward the car. "See for yourself," he said and waited.

Moore took a deep breath, like he was about to jump off the high dive, then stuck the upper half of his torso into the car. Another cop joined us. I recognized him as the sneering, overweight Henninger who had once referred to my dog as a wimp.

When Moore straightened, he exhaled deeply and wiped his forehead with the back of his arm. He turned to Henninger and said, "Call Wiley and Burgess. Looks like we got a homicide here."

Looks like we've got a regular Sherlock Holmes here, I mused to myself.

Moore looked directly at Brig and said, "Why you saying Jubal did this?" He put his hand on Brig's shoulder, steering him away from the car.

"Who else? It's pretty obvious, isn't it? How was anyone supposed to know Gayle was in the car? What with the windows and all you can barely see in. I always go to the bank Saturday morning, same time. Everyone knows that. Gayle wouldn'ta been in there except her car's in the shop." He pounded his chest with a fist. "I was supposed to be in this damned car."

Moore circled the wreck, taking in the dark windows, as though confirming that they were, indeed, all dark. As he walked, he withdrew a half stick of Doublemint gum from his breast pocket, unwrapped it, and popped it into his mouth. He stuffed the paper wad into his pocket. When Moore got back to his starting point, he said to Brig, "Well, we're sure going to bring him in for a talk, Mr. Tanner."

I had remained relatively silent, curious to see how long it would take Moore to rip his attention from Brig Tanner. Elaine, however, had other ideas.

"Aren't you interested in talking to us?" She had come up behind me and now stepped forward, fingers tucked into her jeans pocket.

Moore gave Brig a consolatory pat on the back before turning to Elaine. "Who are you?"

Elaine's mouth formed a hard line, and I heard her take in a deep breath. "I called this in. My name's Elaine Kluszewski." She spelled it, then nodded toward me. "And this is Quint McCauley. We were first on the scene." Moore nodded and waited. "We didn't see any sign of Jubal Tanner or anyone else for that matter."

Moore glanced at Brig before giving her a thin smile. "You don't think he'd stick around, do you?" He looked up at me. "You see anything?" I could almost feel the heat rising off Elaine.

"No, I didn't. But the thing is, it's a little early to be convicting anyone, isn't it? I mean, why don't we just stop at Ace Hardware and pick up a rope on the way over to Jubal's?"

Behind me, Henninger snorted. "We'd be doing the town a favor."

"McCauley," Brig said, his attention on Moore. "Why don't we let the police handle this?"

"Good idea, Brig. Why don't we?" I stressed the question, but again no one seemed to notice. A classic case of selective perception.

Brig gave us a sad smile and brushed a gravel-sized piece of glass off his jacket. "I'm grateful to you folks for calling this in. I really am. I hate to think how long she might have been out here." He looked away, blinking.

"She was coming from your place?" Moore asked Brig, who responded with a nod. "When did she leave?"

"Oh, let's see." He squinted up at the sky. "Must have been around ten. A little before. She got a call from somebody wanting to sell a saddle."

"Who?" Both Elaine and I piped in.

Brig regarded us for a moment before answering Moore.

"I don't know who she'd been talking to, but that ought to be easy enough to find out."

Moore nodded and shifted his feet. Then he pulled a small spiral notebook out of his breast pocket and began to scribble in it with a stubby pencil.

"We left a few minutes later," I added, in case he was interested.

"You know," Brig added, "I could have sworn I heard a gunshot. Didn't think much of it. Not around these parts. People around here like their target practice."

I glanced at the car and wondered if maybe they didn't like it too much.

Brig turned to me. "You hear anything?"

"I didn't. Did you?" I asked Elaine.

Elaine shook her head and added, "But we had the radio on."

"I think the shot must have come from that ridge." I pointed up toward it.

Moore turned toward me, his jaw working the gum with sharp, staccato punches. "Why don't you let the police handle this? Wiley and Burgess'll be here in a second. You can give them your statement. Meanwhile, why don't you wait up by the road?"

I don't have to be told twice. Or maybe I do. I put my hand on Elaine's shoulder. "C'mon, let's go." She hesitated, then backed away from the car. As we climbed out of the ravine, I remember thinking that Gayle Millard's murder could easily spin off into one huge Tanner grudge match. And though I barely knew the woman, I suspected she deserved better.

▽

7

ONE WEEK PASSED. The weather had turned warm, and green things were sprouting. I admired their spirit and hoped they didn't get zapped by another late snow.

Louise took advantage of the spring signs, which brought out the customers, marked a few items down, and called it a sale. Louise Orwell is both my landlady and business partner. I live on the second floor of her house, which sits about forty feet up from the Fox River. About a year ago she convinced me to invest my earnings in half of the Jaded Fox, an import jewelry shop. I use a room in back of the shop with its own entrance as my office. Louise is a spirited British woman whose age is difficult to decipher for two reasons. One, though her hair is a brilliant white, her face seems relatively young. There are lines, but they are fine and you don't notice some of them until she laughs. I suspect that's due, in part, to her careful maintenance. I've never seen her step outside in the sun without a hat. The other reason her age is tough to pin down is she lies about it. Depending on the situation, she might be anywhere from fifty-five to seventy. That's one of the things I like about Louise. She's flexible.

Louise had taken to Elaine right away, and when Elaine showed interest in the shop, she was more than happy to show her the ropes. Now Elaine runs the place when Louise isn't there. And though Elaine says she's still looking for "something permanent," I suspect that Louise would like nothing better than to turn the shop over to her someday.

It was just 10:00 A.M., and I wasn't quite ready to dig into my work yet and decided the distraction of the *Foxport Chronicle* was a good excuse not to rush into anything. Gayle Millard's murder was unresolved. Brig Tanner was still hollering that someone had better arrest Jubal, and Gene Moore wasn't saying much. Probably figuring that there was nothing like a little incentive, Brig was offering a $10,000 reward for information leading to the arrest of Gayle's killer. Everyone was wondering where Ed Carver had gone, but no one was talking. I'd learned from Elaine that he and his estranged wife, Ellie, were trying to make a go of their marriage again. I admit I was surprised by Carver's shift in priorities. I was also relieved and wished him the best of luck and tried not to wonder why he would confide all this in Elaine.

The success of Brig's mayoral bid would be decided in the primary, which was three weeks away. Our current mayor, Charlie Olson, wasn't running for reelection, so the contest had become a free-for-all. There were a number of candidates who just wanted a little name recognition, either for themselves or their businesses. Brig Tanner was one of the serious contenders and, at this point, was favored to win. He had just held some kind of fund-raiser, assuring his supporters that they were doing the right thing in voting for him and in paying two hundred a plate for the dinner and the privilege. I love this country.

When I finished the paper, I picked up the file for my only open case, hoping that the good weather would also bring out desperate citizens in search of answers. About all that was left to do on the case was inform my clients of my findings. I sensed they weren't going to be pleased. I was investigating the background of a young man engaged to marry the daughter of one of Foxport's reigning families. My sleuthing was to be done, of course, without the knowledge of either the daughter or potential son-in-law. So far, all my investigation had turned up was that the kid had two unpaid parking tickets, was one of probably eight or nine registered Democrats in Abel County, and belonged to the ACLU. I didn't know whether he carried his card or kept it tucked away in the sleeve of an old Bob Dylan album. Either way, I suspected the bride's parents wouldn't be pleased, probably preferring an ax murderer over a liberal as a son-in-law.

I'd brought Peanuts to the office. He likes to come with me, and on days when I'm not doing much running around, I sometimes indulge him. He spends the time curled up either in the L.L. Bean dog bed Elaine got him or in the Jaded Fox, charming customers. He's about 90 percent border collie and 10 percent something else. Con artist, I think. I'm sure that Louise has made more than one sale based largely on Peanuts' "starved dog" look. When people are talking about him, he sort of turns his head away like he doesn't know he's the topic of conversation. Then when someone stoops to pet him, he accepts the gesture graciously, sometimes with a small lick on the wrist. He's got it down to an art. He was full-grown when I got him at the shelter, so I can't lay any claims to molding his personality.

My office and the Jaded Fox are on Foxport's exclusive retail drag, and I have the distinction of being the only private detective in the high-rent district. I've found that the real estate people are right. Location *is* everything. I'm sure I've obtained some clients simply because I'm right on the way to The White Oak, a posh eatery. You know, "Let's stop and retain a PI before we do lunch." I also have learned to charge higher rates than I might elsewhere, though I've been known to negotiate. I usually don't have any trouble getting it either. There's an attitude that permeates this area that says you get what you pay for. Who was I to argue?

The Jaded Fox is on the corner, and you can enter my office either from the shop or from a direct entrance on Raymond Street. There's a tiny outer office, where I pretend to have a secretary who happens to take long breaks, and my office, which really isn't much bigger.

I'd just gotten off the phone with Elaine, who was telling me how, if she only ate one meal a day ("You know, a decent one. Macaroni and cheese or something like that") and got one more part-time job (as if two and half weren't enough), she'd be able to afford the horse.

"Yes," I'd said, "but when would you have time to ride it?" I found myself playing devil's advocate a lot lately and didn't much care for the role.

When I hung up, I saw Jubal Tanner standing in the doorway to the outer office. I hadn't heard him come in. He wore faded jeans and a white chamois shirt and was fidgeting with a battered black cowboy hat he held in both hands. He looked more like he was walking into the Longbranch Saloon than a PI's office.

"Jubal. How you feeling?"

He shrugged. "Been better." There seemed to be something hesitant about his gestures, but maybe that was because I'd never seen him sober.

I tried to remember what Melissa said her father was—sixty-three or something like that. I decided he looked every day of it, and then some. His skin was leathery and weathered, but he had a full head of thick, white hair. I wondered how I'd missed noticing his eyes—a startling shade of blue—then remembered that at our previous meeting they'd been either at half-mast or closed.

Peanuts' bed was in the corner, and he was watching Jubal, tail wagging cautiously. That's my dog. He always assumes the best out of someone.

"What can I do for you?" I gestured toward a chair, but he made no move from the outer office.

"You reasonable?"

"You're talking money now, aren't you?"

He scowled and slapped the hat against his thigh. "Hell, yes. Don't think I care about your attitude, do you?"

"Well, I charge three hundred dollars per day plus expenses. You'll have to decide the rest for yourself."

He whistled softly. "How long's it take you?"

"Hard to tell. It depends a lot on what you ask me to do." When he didn't move from his spot, I added, "But I don't charge anything to talk, so why don't you take a load off."

After glancing behind him, he slowly made his way into my office and sank into the chair, which creaked beneath his bulk. Then he saw Peanuts. His eyes widened, and he lifted one corner of his mouth. It seemed more an apology than a smile. "Isn't he one of them sheepdogs?" He reached down and extended his arm so Peanuts could sniff his hand. Once Jubal passed muster, he roughed the fur on the top of the dog's head and scratched him behind the ears. Peanuts closed his eyes and enjoyed. At this point, Jubal probably could have pulled a gun and shot me between the eyes, and Peanuts wouldn't have bared his teeth. Jubal gave him one final pat and turned to me. "Depends on what?"

I had to think a second to pick up the string. "Well, if you want me to find your girlfriend from fifth grade who left a paper trail a mile wide, then it's not going to take long." Jubal was watching me, eyes narrowed. "On the other hand, if she's become a part of the witness protection program, then it's going to take a while." He frowned and nodded, as though weighing my words. "What do you want me to do?"

"Find out who killed my brother's girlfriend."

"That'd take a while. In fact, I might not even be able to do it."

He frowned, and his eyebrows met in a bushy V. "How come?"

"I can't interfere with an ongoing police investigation. I could lose my license."

"You'd let that bother you?"

I shrugged.

"Hmph." I sensed that I'd slipped a notch in his estimation.

Jubal shifted in the chair, crossed his ankle over his knee, and hung his hat on his boot. "Well, what am I supposed to do? Sit on my ass and let them railroad me for that woman's murder. Hell, I didn't do it."

"What are you talking about?"

"Where've you been? They're trying to prove I killed her, thinking it was Brig in the car. Hell," he snorted, "if it'd been me, I'd a' been sure."

"You got a lawyer yet?"

"Hell, no. They're more expensive than you are. Besides, I haven't been arrested yet. They can't prove a damned thing."

"Then what are you worried about?"

He scowled, irritated with my denseness. When he spoke it was like he was explaining a fundamental principle to a not-so-bright child. "Cause as soon as they figure out *how* to railroad me, they *will*. Hell, that bastard brother of mine is offering a reward. A goddamned reward. Did you hear that?"

I nodded. "You have an alibi, don't you?"

"Yeah, but that's not gonna stop 'em. They're looking to get me on conspiracy to commit murder or something like that." He snorted his contempt. "Like I'd hire someone to do my dirty work."

"Well, if you didn't do it, then how can they connect you to her murder?"

"Now you sound like Claude. Like I tell her, if they try hard enough, they'll figure something out. Besides . . ." His voice trailed off.

"What?"

"Even if they can't prove anything and if they can't figure out who did it, my ass is grass anyway."

"How do you figure that?"

"That damned brother of mine. I know him. He'll kill me. He'll do it so he won't get caught, and because he's Brig Tanner and not his good-for-nothing brother, he'll get away with it." He paused and nodded. "That's what'd really kill me. He'd get away with it."

"Your brother is running for mayor. It's not too likely that he'd jeopardize a good shot at the office by being suspected of orchestrating his brother's murder." Jubal's expression didn't change, so I asked, "What makes you think he's coming after you?"

He took a deep breath and looked down at Peanuts. "I know him. If the cops don't get me, he will." He ran a gnarled hand through his hair and added, "And he's the type to hire someone to do it."

I hesitated, which was probably a mistake. By the time I managed a regretful shake of the head, he knew I was weakening.

"There's another thing," he said, his tone softer. He pulled his gaze away from Peanuts and directed it at me. "I almost had enough investors together to buy Kessler when my brother bought him out from under me. They're making like it's some revenge thing now."

"Investors? How many does it take?"

"Four. No, five. Me, three guys I've done business with before, and then a friend of Claude's came through at the last minute. Good old Margaret." He sighed and shook his head. "Almost had him. Almost."

"What does a horse like that cost?"

"One-twenty-five." Before I could react to the price tag, he continued. "And that's 'cause Kessler's pretty old—seventeen. Ten years ago you could easily get two-fifty. Thing is, at his age nobody knows how many years he's got left."

"Seventeen isn't that old, is it?" I wasn't sure what that came to in horse years, but using Scott as a measuring stick, it didn't seem old.

"I'm not talking about years of living. I'm talking about years of being a stud."

"Ah." I nodded my comprehension. "How many babies can a horse produce in a year?"

"Fifty's a pretty good number."

"Must keep the horse on the road a lot."

Jubal regarded me for a moment, and it was as if he were trying to figure out whether I was pulling his leg or really was that dense. I was. Finally, he said, "He doesn't have to leave his stall. They just ship the semen."

So much for romance, although I had to admit it made sense. I did a quick mental calculation. At two thousand a baby, Brig Tanner would earn the money back in just over a year. "You plan on buying another horse then?"

"If I can keep the investors interested. But that's the thing. I get my name fouled up in this mess, they'll drop me like a hot potato."

I nodded. "You looking for another Morgan?"

"Far as I'm concerned that's all there is." It was a statement of fact.

"What's so special about the Morgan?"

He rubbed his jaw for a minute as he studied me. Then he leaned forward and patted the edge of my desk. "Here's a cliff. Say you're on a horse heading toward that cliff. Say you're on an Arab. Well, it's been spooked by some partridge a quarter mile back and doesn't even see the cliff. You and the Arab go over." He slid his hand off the desk. "Say you're on a quarter horse—it sees the cliff, and just keeps right on going. You're on a walker. It goes over just to stop the pain." He leaned back in the chair and continued in a lower, more respectful tone. "You're on a Morgan—it stops at the edge of the cliff, asks if you want to keep going, and if you say yes"—he arched his hand down into a dive—"he goes over. No questions asked." Then he folded his hands on his lap and waited.

I had a few questions about the scenario, but none of them were relevant. Jubal was convinced the Morgan was the greatest thing since baseball. No one else here had to be. "You used to raise Morgans?"

He sighed and turned his gaze down to the floor. "Some of the best in the country came out of my farm."

"What happened?"

At first I didn't think he was going to answer me, but then he seemed to draw himself out of a reverie. "About ten years ago I lost my stallion. Wayward's Robert. Bobby." I swear he was blinking back tears as he told me how the horse succumbed to some strange virus.

"He wasn't your only horse, was he?"

"Might as well have been." He seemed to be studying a framed print of Belmont Harbor that hung, slightly askew, on the wall. "I've gotta get back to them, though. I need 'em." He spoke quietly. "Morgans are the only thing I'm good at. Nothing else feels right." Turning to me, he asked, "You know what I'm saying?"

I nodded but didn't respond. What was there to say? I knew exactly how he felt. You don't realize how bad a place fits until you find one that does.

He shook his head and kneaded the skin on his forehead for a few seconds, perhaps interpreting my hesitation as indecision. The fact was, there was something about this guy that was starting to grow on me. I tried to fight it. "That night in the parking lot—who hit you?"

He appeared genuinely confused. "Hit me?"

"Yeah, you didn't just pass out. Someone helped you along."

Rubbing the back of his neck, he shook his head. "I honest to God don't remember anyone hitting me. I just figured I slipped and smacked my noggin on that dumpster. Why? You think someone's trying to kill me off too?"

"No. Maybe you're right," I said, though I didn't see what he was doing by the dumpster when his car was on the other side of the lot. I did concede that the blow might have affected his recollection of the night.

Jubal continued as if I'd never brought up the subject. "I know what the problem is. It's the money, isn't it? You figure there's no way I can afford three hundred a day. Well, you're right. But I tell you what I'll do. I think I can cut you a deal you'll like real well."

"Jubal," I leaned on the desk, preparing to make the final rejection.

He continued before I had a chance. "I tell you what I'll do for you. I'll give you three hundred total and throw in a horse. A real nice one. I mean it. She's an . . ." He hesitated. "A pretty little gray thing. Hate to lose her. Worth at least twelve hundred."

I stared at him, my mouth frozen in the open position.

He genuinely expected me to deal in horse currency. When I finally got my mouth moving again, I said, "Jubal, what would I want with a horse?"

He shrugged and grunted. "Learn to ride. Give her to someone who does. Makes a great gift." He smiled and raised his eyebrows. "A lady's horse."

I watched him. There seemed no doubt in his mind that I would accept this animal as legal tender.

"Jubal, have you ever threatened to kill your brother?"

He leaned back in the chair and crossed his arms over his chest. "Well, I don't know. I get pretty mad sometimes."

"Jubal, answer me."

"Aw, hell. Maybe once or twice. If I've been drinking."

"Everyone saw you and him arguing the other night. You were hot about that horse. Threatening him."

He frowned. "I know. But I didn't want to kill him." He took a moment, forming his next words. "I kill my brother, my life's perfect. Who needs it?"

I almost believed him, but the little corner of my brain that lets me know when I'm about to do something bone-headed was flashing the yellow lights. "Jubal, I want a horse just about as bad as I want a hemorrhoid. In fact, I could see how the two would go together."

"But they're trying to railroad me!" He slammed his boot on the floor again. This time Peanuts jumped out of his bed, claws clicking against the wood floor. Jubal's face reddened and his eyes bulged. "That Moore guy's either incompetent or crooked, and believe me my brother knows how to use both. Moore's had me in twice for questioning and they keep asking me the same damned things. Over and over. So what am I supposed to do? Sit around and wait until they get tired of trying to figure out how I did it and just throw me in jail?" He jabbed his chest with a fist. "I'm Jubal Tanner, for God's sake. I'm not Brigham Tanner, with all kinds of folks standing in line to wipe my ass. I'm the black sheep. I'm the throwaway. They'll toss me in jail and forget about me. I know it."

"Jubal . . ."

"I know they will."

I shook my head, dazed. He was so emphatic. I didn't know whether to believe him or write him off as paranoid.

Jubal settled back into the chair and studied me for a minute. "Listen," he finally said, "you're probably not a bad guy. Even though you got no time for horses. I'm telling you, I need help. Who am I supposed to go to? I don't trust lawyers. You walk in their office and they turn the goddamned meter on. I don't know any other detective types. You got any pull with the cops?"

I had to bite the inside of my cheek to keep from laughing out loud. "Probably not."

Jubal considered that a moment, then shrugged it off. "That's okay. Guess I don't either."

He was talking like there was no doubt I'd take his case. How did he know that? I was ready to say "Okay, I'll see what I can do," and I didn't know why. I studied him. I guess I felt the pull of this guy. Here he was—a walking, breathing, living anachronism. He belonged in another century. Back when he could bellow, beat his chest, and fling his arms out without breaking anyone's nose. Sometimes I think we're too civilized. Then I look around and shake my head. Nah, we just think we are. Still, I can't help but believe we'd be a whole lot healthier if we could bellow every now and then.

I took a deep breath and released it. "Okay, here's what I'll do. I'll go talk to Moore. See if I can find out what he's got on you, see if he's trying to railroad you. If I tell you he's not, that he's just conducting an investigation, will you believe me?"

He frowned and shrugged. I waited. Finally he nodded and said, "Yeah, I guess," without much enthusiasm.

"And if that's the case, you'll either stop being paranoid or get a lawyer."

"What if he is trying to railroad me?"

"Then I look into it. After I check the horse out."

He nodded.

"And . . ." I paused. "I get the horse plus food and board for a year."

He sat up. "The hell you say. You're already getting a deal on the horse. You know how much one of those things eats in a year?"

"I have no idea." He opened his mouth to interrupt me, but I kept going. "And I don't care. But that's got to be part of the deal."

He rubbed his hand along the rim of his hat as he thought. Then he arched an eyebrow. "Six months."

I waited a beat. "Nine months."

He shook his head and sighed. "Okay, but you damned well better produce." Then he muttered, "Goddamned highway robbery," but a smile tugged at the corner of his mouth.

After he left, I spent a moment pondering why I do these things. Was it the three hundred dollars? Nice, but no. The horse for Elaine? Real nice, but no. Preservation? Yep, that was it. I guess I'm a sucker for endangered species.

∇

8

GENE MOORE HAD something of a reputation in Foxport. He'd been with the department since he got out of the marines about fifteen years ago. He was the PD's explosives and firearms expert and had organized and trained their version of a SWAT team. He was also one cold-blooded piece of work.

I'd seen him in action about a year ago but figured he wouldn't remember me. It was an incident that I'd been witness to, but only as a bystander. As I recalled it now, I had to concede that maybe Jubal did have something to worry about.

Timothy Williamson had been one of Foxport's most influential lawyers and, some believed, was on his way to Congress as the district's representative. He and Moore had become pretty good friends; Moore and his wife were frequent guests of the Williamsons at the country club. They were sort of an odd-looking pair—Williamson with his slicked-back hair and silk suits and Moore with his brush cut and polyester blends—but it was probably a mutually beneficial relationship. Williamson was the kind of man who liked being able to flash a law officer around. And Moore, well, he probably figured he'd latched on to a winner.

Then Williamson's only child died suddenly of a cerebral hemorrhage. She was ten. It was a fast train downhill for Williamson after that. He started drinking heavily, and public displays became common. I was up at the Tattersall one day when he started getting abusive with one of

Sammy's waitresses. Sammy called the cops. When Moore showed up, Williamson was urinating into a basket of popcorn. Moore just stood there and looked at him like he was a million-dollar thoroughbred whose leg just snapped. I half expected Moore to take his gun out and shoot the man. Instead, he called for a backup and let a couple of patrolmen take Williamson in. Not long after that, Williamson disappeared. No one knew what happened to him, but most assumed it wasn't anything good. And Moore, well, apparently he'd managed to cut his losses.

I was genuinely surprised that Carver would leave Moore in charge, but then I'd never been much at second-guessing the man. I looked forward to forming my own opinion of the acting police chief.

When I got to the police station, Moore was spread out in Carver's office like he'd always been there. It occurred to me that, aside from the incident at the Tattersall where we didn't get very close, this was the first time I'd seen him without his sunglasses. His eyes were a watery blue and puffy, like he'd just woken up. I guess I'd wear them too.

He sat back in Carver's chair, relaxed, elbows perched on its arms, and eyed me with a mixture of suspicion and contempt as I voiced Jubal's concerns. Then he sighed and shook his head like I was too dense to breathe. "McCauley, I'm not trying to railroad anyone. I don't know what kind of department you think I'm running here, but that's not the way I do it. I'm not out to get anyone."

I regarded him for a moment, noting his choice of singular pronouns. "Yeah, well, Jubal Tanner's just kind of paranoid, I guess."

"Maybe he should be."

"Why? I mean, everyone knows there's bad blood between him and Brig, but it's been like that for years. The other night at the Tattersall wasn't the first time they've had a public falling out." I could tell from the slacking of his jaw that Moore knew nothing about the incident at the Tattersall. I could also tell from the way he snapped it back into

place that he wasn't going to stoop to ask me about it. I
continued. "I mean, Jubal may not be a stellar citizen, but
he's a long way from being a murderer."

"Jubal Tanner is a crime waiting to happen, and everyone
in this town, except maybe you and that ditsy wife of his,
knows it."

"Yeah, well, as convenient as it might be to pin every
unsolved crime on the guy, it just won't work. He's got an
alibi, you know."

Moore snorted. "Yeah, he was doing the grocery shopping.
The wife says she was sitting in the car. If you want to believe
her. We haven't got anyone at the store who can positively
say when he was there. Even if they could, Jubal probably
has enough resources to hire him someone to do the dirty
work."

I shook my head. "That's where you're wrong. If Jubal ever
figured it was time to kill his brother, he'd want to do it
himself. There's no way anyone would rob him of that
pleasure."

He took a few seconds to straighten his tie against his
khaki shirt. "McCauley, I've got men working on this.
Maybe there's nothing conclusive yet, but before long I know
there will be."

Just then one of his "men" stuck her head in his office. I
didn't know her name but recognized her as one of Carver's
officers. She was a little on the heavy side, with blond hair
and, as I recalled, a nice smile. There was no sign of it now.
"Lieutenant, Mr. Tanner's on line one for you."

He sat up and folded his hands in front of him on the desk
blotter. "Ah, Helen, would you tell him I'll get right back to
him. No more than three minutes."

She hesitated long enough to fire a few daggers at him out
of her honey-colored eyes. Apparently Moore had his sensi-
tivity shield up, because he didn't seem fazed.

"No question about which Mr. Tanner that was, I see."

He shrugged. "Jubal Tanner hasn't exactly made himself
available to us."

"Who could blame him?"

He narrowed his eyes, creating an extra set of bags. "I don't think I care what your opinion is. If Jubal's got a lawyer, I'll talk to him, but all you are is a cheap PI. I don't have to deal with you."

I resisted the urge to point out that I was anything but cheap. "Come on, think about it. Jubal Tanner's not the only possibility. I can't believe Brig hasn't got any other enemies. He's running for office. You ever think this might be politically motivated? Maybe someone doesn't want to see him get into office. You check that out?" Except for a twitch in his right eye, his expression remained bland, unreadable. "If you manufacture enough evidence to get Jubal tossed in jail and someone pops Brig at his victory celebration, that's gonna leave you looking pretty inept, isn't it? Or what about Gayle? Do you know who made that phone call? I know this would be a major blow to Brig Tanner's ego, but maybe he wasn't the target."

"You sound like a guy being paid to twist the facts." He sighed and leaned back into the chair, smirking. "Carver warned me about you." He patted one of the drawers. "In fact, I think I've got a three-page memo in here on people who are likely to make my life miserable. Your dog even rates a line. You're near the top of the list."

"Maybe that explains why I'm so lonely." As I stood to leave, Moore's expression didn't change, but his eyes fogged over.

I almost ran into Officer Helen on my way and, as we sidestepped each other, was rewarded with a glimpse of that smile I remembered. As I threaded my way through the desks in the crowded squad room, I could feel Moore's gaze on me. At the door, I turned to wave. He didn't look away. He didn't wave either.

I should have been used to feeling uncomfortable in that office. My first encounter with Ed Carver had hardly been auspicious. Later meetings in that very office had been strained, to say the least. But at least Carver had a reason to feel some resentment toward me. Maybe that resentment wasn't justified, but I'm not sure I'd have risen above it myself. It had been almost two years since I'd picked up Ellie, his wife, in a local bar, assuming she was like me—lonely and unattached. To Ed Carver, it was just like yesterday.

I was hungry and figured maybe Elaine would be up for something besides macaroni and cheese for lunch. As I pulled into an angle space next to the Jaded Fox, I was reasonably convinced that Jubal Tanner was not going to be given a fair shot in Foxport. Still, did I want to get involved in the middle of an investigation that could, if I were to get careless, get my license yanked? Sometimes I get so cautious I scare myself.

Elaine and Louise were discussing the pros and cons of horse ownership. Louise sat on a stool behind the shop's glass counter, resting her pointed chin on a fist. "You know, I think it would be wonderful to go riding on a nice fall day, when the air is crisp as the leaves. On the other hand, I can't imagine it would be quite as lovely in August when it's insufferably hot."

"Louise," I said, "you think eighty is insufferably hot. It's those British genes you've got."

"That may be, but I can't imagine the horse would be any more comfortable. What with that fur and all."

Elaine smiled as she placed a pair of freshwater-pearl earrings in the loop of a necklace on a glass shelf. "You know it's not just having a horse. It's more than that. I need something to concentrate on right now. Something to work at being good at." She straightened and looked at us. "You know what I mean."

Louise frowned. "Well, of course I know what you mean, but you're very good at what you do here. You learn so fast. It's one thing to sell a piece of jewelry like that," she said, gesturing toward the pearls with a pink, glittery nail, "but you've gone out of your way to learn how they are created. People love to hear that. Husbands give their wives the gift of knowledge along with a lovely necklace."

Elaine made a face and shrugged.

"Now, don't go underrating yourself," Louise warned. "Young people today, I don't know why they can't just say 'Yes, I did well, didn't I?' without getting all modest." She looked to me for confirmation, then shook her head. Lately she'd been spending a lot of time bolstering Elaine's ego. I thought some of it had taken, but there was still a ways to go yet.

"How about some lunch?" I asked when it seemed an ideal time to change the subject.

"You be okay alone here for a while?"

Louise studied her watch. "Let's see. We've had an average of two customers an hour today. I should manage." Then, "Oh, I have an appointment with my manicurist at two." She held her hands out at arm's length. "What do you think? Is it going to be a good week for candy-apple red?"

The Tattersall was a different place when it wasn't crammed with people whose idea of a good time was to get drunk enough to put the moves on someone else.

We sat at our usual table—right by the fireplace. I was too warm for a fire, but habits die hard.

"When do you think Sammy will give me my own mug?" she asked as I took my first sip of Guinness. Sammy favored his regulars with their own mug, initials inscribed. It wasn't something you could ask for; he just gave it to you after you'd been coming there awhile. Of course, he had to like you.

She frowned as though this had occurred to her. "Do you think he doesn't like me?"

I shook my head as I finished chewing a bite of the smoked turkey sandwich, absently brushing the QCM etching on my mug with my thumb. "Of course, Sammy likes you. He wouldn't flirt with you if he didn't like you." Elaine conceded my point with a sheepish smile. "The thing is," I continued, "you don't drink beer very often. What he does with these is he hangs them up on hooks behind the bar. How's he gonna hang up a Seven-Up or a wineglass?"

Elaine was silent for a minute, then said, "How do you think I'd look with a beer belly?" Before I had time to answer, she continued, this time on the offensive. "And why is it that you can guzzle that stuff all day and you never show it? It's not fair."

I shrugged. She was right. "I know it's not, but in fairness to me, I do not guzzle this all day long."

"Yeah, but I look at a mug of stout or even ale and a pound appears on my thighs." She paused long enough to drink from her glass of Diet 7UP and made a face. "How do you do it?"

I shook my head. "It's the McCauley men. All four of my brothers are the same way. Dad's got a gut though, so there's some evidence that this catches up with us."

"Hmph. You know I have to plan for one of those a day in advance?" She nodded toward my Guinness. "I cut back on everything else for a day or two, you know, seriously diet so I can splurge on just one of those."

"I had no idea. I think you deserve a mug."

"Damned right I do."

Elaine was seriously into her tuna salad sandwich when I began to tell her about my meeting with Jubal. "You know, I almost hate to admit it, but I kind of like the guy."

"Do you believe him?" She picked up a piece of tuna that had fallen into the paper-lined basket and popped it into her mouth.

"Yeah, I do. I really do. But I guess that's not the point."

"What is the point?"

"Two things. One, Carver's replacement is less happy with me than Carver is. And without a good reason. Plus he seems to have Brig Tanner on his side, at least as long as the investigation continues to focus on his brother. Or maybe Brig has Moore in his pocket. The other reason is, what Jubal really needs right now is a lawyer, not a private detective."

"Well, he's already told you a lawyer's out of the question. He doesn't have a lot of money, does he?"

"Doesn't seem to, though he must have had some money to invest in the horse. And then I guess he comes from some money."

Elaine nodded. "He does. At least that's what Cindy says. Apparently their parents left both Brig and Jubal quite a bit of money and some land. Brig made some good investments. I guess Jubal didn't."

"Yeah, I guess not. Do you know if Brig has a job outside of the house, so to speak? Aside from running for office, that is."

"He owns a chain of hardware stores. Though I guess you could call him semiretired. He's been real active in the community for a number of years before he decided to throw his hat in the ring. City council and all."

"How do you know all this?"

"Cindy and I talked some at my last lesson. You know, the one you missed because you had to do 'surveillance.'" She enclosed the word with finger quotes.

"I did." Now it was my turn to get defensive. "Some guy was—"

She stopped me with a raised hand. "I know, I know." Pausing to brush crumbs off the tips of her fingers, she studied me. "Quint, I know you don't want to do this riding thing, and that's fine. But why are you pretending to want it?"

She'd posed the question when my mouth was full and before I could swallow added, "Is our relationship in that bad a shape?"

A simple "no" seemed inadequate and perhaps not accurate either.

Nodding, she sighed. "It is, isn't it?"

Now I had to say something. "How do you mean?" This was unfair of me, but I felt I'd been bushwhacked and needed time to collect words and phrases that made sense of what I was thinking.

Cocking her head, she seemed to be deciding how much of that response was reflex and how much was thought out. "When's the last time we made love?"

"I don't know. Maybe a week ago."

"Eight days. The day after the blizzard. You know, you

came straight to my place from the Tanners and we spent the afternoon in bed."

I smiled at the memory. "Yeah. That was great."

She hesitated for a moment, then, to my relief, nodded. "Yeah. It was. But that was really an exception. I mean, lately we're usually just not as connected as we used to be. Sexually, I mean." She took another bite out of her sandwich. Dammit. She always did stuff like that, stopped talking when I thought I was about to be served the punch line.

"I don't know what you mean."

"Think about it, Quint. Okay, last week was the exception. But, really you were so thrilled to be alive, not to be a human ice chunk, that it was more the"—she fluttered her hand in the air—"the joie de vivre that was energizing you. I'm not saying you didn't want to be with me or that I might have been an inflatable doll. I'm not saying that. It's just that . . ." She paused. "Have you noticed lately how we spend a lot of time talking?"

"Talking? Haven't we always? I like talking to you." I paused a beat and added, "In fact, I can't think of anyone I'd rather talk to."

"Well, me too. I'm not talking about our friendship. That's as healthy as a"—she smiled—"well, as one of those big, four-legged things." Trading the smile for something more serious, she continued. "I'm talking about our relationship as, you know, lovers. As two people romantically involved." She paused and added, "I'm not sure it's there anymore."

I knew what she was saying, because I'd had the same feeling only hadn't acknowledged it head-on. And I'd never dreamed of putting words to it. One of the qualities I admired most about Elaine was her courage. My gut reaction was to deny. "Well, I don't know about you, but there's nothing I'd like better than to rekindle things back at my place this afternoon." The second it was out of my mouth, I knew it was a mistake. I wasn't even sure I meant it.

She twisted her mouth in the way she does when she's

disappointed with me. "That's not what I'm saying. You know it's not." She was watching me now.

I wasn't sure how to respond. Sure, I'd felt some of what she'd been talking about, maybe even wondered what it'd be like to let go, but always retreating from the subject when I got that far. When I opened my mouth to say something, I still wasn't sure what was going to come out.

I guess I'll never know, because I was saved by the sound of a familiar voice. "I've been looking for you," Jeff Barlowe was saying as he descended on our table. "Hi, Elaine." He patted her shoulder and pulled up a chair. At the same time he waved at the waitress for a beer. Then he took a second look at the two of us. "Hey, did I interrupt something here?"

"No, that's okay. It can wait."

Elaine shot me a look, then nodded.

"Thought you both might be interested in this." He took his initialed mug from the waitress. "Put it on his tab."

Mary Ellen looked to me for approval. I shrugged and nodded. "This better be good."

"It's worth at least one of these." He held up the mug. "But then you can always wait for the paper to come out tomorrow."

"We're waiting for you."

He consulted his watch. "About an hour ago Charlie Olson announced that Ed Carver is out and Gene Moore is in."

"What?" Both Elaine and I said that.

"You heard me. At an emergency city council meeting at ten o'clock last night, they voted Carver out as the chief of police and voted Moore in." He glanced at the ceiling. "God help us."

Elaine looked like she'd been gut-punched. I took another drink of stout.

"How can they do that?"

Jeff shrugged. "Well, apparently they can. And did. All it takes is a unanimous vote on the council's part. I don't think it hurts any that Charlie's on his way out and you-know-who is favored to be our next mayor."

It figured. "What were the reasons?"

"Well, they're saying that Carver's lost touch, both literally and figuratively. His men can't work with him anymore, and he went off for a month's vacation without telling anyone where he was going."

"He told—" Elaine cut herself off and tried to take it back by swallowing several gulps of soda.

Jeff jumped on it. "He told you?"

"I didn't say that." She answered Jeff and concentrated on tucking a piece of tuna back into her sandwich.

"No, but you almost did."

"What I was going to say was 'He told no one?' " She faltered. "It was supposed to be a question."

Jeff and I exchanged a look. I changed the subject. "Would it be farfetched to assume that Brig Tanner had something to do with this?"

Jeff drew his attention from Elaine reluctantly. "He called the meeting and made the motion. Surprise, huh? It's amazing how much power you wield when you're favored to win a primary."

"Jesus," Elaine said under her breath.

"So, Carver's going to come back from vacation and find himself out of a job."

Jeff took one of the potato chips from my basket. "Looks that way."

Elaine pushed her basket, full of chips, toward him. "Here, eat mine. I'm dieting."

He smiled his appreciation and pulled the basket closer. "You going to eat this other half of your sandwich?"

She shook her head. "Take it."

"Thanks."

I tried to make eye contact with Elaine, but she looked away. "What's the *Chronicle* going to say about all this?"

"Just what went on at the meeting and what we can pick up from sources. Of course, there's always the editorial page." He spoke while chewing, then swallowed. "Clever timing on the council's part. By holding the meeting that late, they made sure they wouldn't make the paper until tomorrow." He swallowed the last of his beer. "Well, don't mean to be rude here, but I gotta get back. Just figured you'd want to know."

"Why would you think I'd care?"

"Well, knowing your devotion to Carver for one. Also, I heard Jubal came to see you."

"Where'd you hear that?"

Wiping his hands together, he pushed back the chair as he stood. "I saw him walk into the Jaded Fox. Figured he wasn't buying jewelry. You working for him?"

I shook my head. "Not so you can quote me."

"I'll call you tonight," Jeff said, then eyed Elaine. "You sure you don't know where Carver is?"

She drained the glass of 7UP. "No, Jeff. I don't."

He gave the table a farewell tap. "Well, see you guys later."

Both Elaine and I watched him leave. When the door closed behind him, I turned to her. "You do know where he is, don't you?"

She sighed and looked at me but didn't answer. Not out loud anyway.

More than anything I wanted to know how she knew. Why would Carver talk to her about plans he wouldn't share with anyone else? But I knew that wasn't going to buy me anything at this point. "If you know where he is, probably the best thing you can do for him right now is call him."

She sighed and nodded. "I know. I know where to call, but I can't be sure he'll get my message right away." She watched me for a minute, then said, "It's not the way it looks. Ed and I are friends, you know that. He was trying to work things out with Ellie and was looking for a place he could take her that would be good for that sort of thing, and I made a suggestion. So, that's how I know where he is." She seemed to be waiting for my response, which I hadn't figured out yet. This was either really good news or really bad news. I wasn't sure. Finally she added, "He didn't tell me to call if anything happened though."

I was the last person on the face of the earth who'd want to interrupt an Ellie-Ed reconciliation. But even if they came home feeling like newlyweds, this bit of news would hit him like a cold shower. So, it was with some reluctance that I said, "Well, he probably didn't think this would happen." Elaine rubbed her forehead. "Don't you think he'd want to know?"

After a minute, she nodded. "I'll call him if you'll do something for me."

"What's that?"

"Take this case for Jubal. I don't even know the guy and I'm feeling sorry for him." She shrugged. "I guess I hate to see someone like Brig Tanner acting like a bully and getting away with it. It burns me. Besides," she added with a smile, "you need a change of pace. You're getting too set in your ways."

She was right. I was getting too staid for my own good. And there were ways to do this without getting in the way of the police department. I just hadn't bothered to think them out. "There's another thing," I said. "Jubal doesn't have much in the way of money. So, as partial payment for my services, he's offered to give me a horse and put it up at his place—you know, room and board—for nine months."

She laughed. "That's perfect. No wonder you didn't want the case. You don't want to ride a horse, much less own one."

"I'll take the case, but I'm taking the horse too. He's yours."

Before giving herself the chance to even consider it, she shook her head. "I can't. It's too much."

"I want to. Think of it as an early birthday present."

"Quint, on your last birthday I gave you a shirt and a book."

"Yeah, but I'm tough to buy for." This called for a strategy change, and I went with it before thinking about the consequences or flaws. "Okay, it's not a present. It's your fee."

She looked at me, interest tinged with suspicion creeping into her eyes.

"You're gonna work for this horse." I'd only half formed my idea, but I went with it as best I could. "You keep telling me how I need to computerize the business. I know you're right, but the main reason I've been stalling is because I don't know a RAM from a byte. You, on the other hand, used to work with the miserable things."

"What would I be doing?"

"Pick out a computer, software, whatever. Get it set up, run it."

"Do I get to teach you how to use it?"

"If it comes to that."

She tilted back her glass and let a half-melted cube slide into her mouth. Then, arching her right eyebrow in a suspicious manner, she said, "What kind of horse?"

"I don't know," I said, feeling stupid for not having asked.

She crumpled up the napkin and dropped it into the basket. "Is this a guilt thing on your part? I mean are we really back to the original subject?" She seemed more amused than angry.

I shrugged, not willing to admit one way or the other. "Think about it. If you don't want the horse, I guess I can sell it. Still, I want you to take a look at it. You know, make sure I'm not getting a lemon."

"I'm not sure I'd know. We'll have to find someone who knows horses better."

"Whatever." I dropped some bills on the table and we left. Neither of us dredged up our lack of connection, but I could feel it—vague but insistent like a question waiting to be asked. It wouldn't go away.

9

ON THE WAY back to the Jaded Fox, out of the clear blue Elaine said, "What about Cindy?"

"What about Cindy?"

"Well, maybe she'd take a look at the horse."

"Are you forgetting whose daughter she is?"

"Well, even if she won't, maybe she can suggest someone." She turned to me, and I could hear the smile in her voice, "Unless, of course, you feel qualified to check her out yourself."

"Yeah, I guess I qualify as an expert. Calling on my vast storehouse of horse knowledge, I'd say that Scott's hipbones stick up in a way that I wouldn't call attractive, and his back is probably a couple inches lower than it ought to be. So, if she looks anything like Scott, we should work out an easy payment schedule for Jubal. One that doesn't involve horses."

Back in my office, Elaine made two phone calls. The first was to Cindy, who, after the initial shock of Elaine considering one of Jubal's horses, agreed to take a ride out to Jubal's place with us later in the afternoon. I waited in the outer office while Elaine made the second call. She didn't ask me to, I just wasn't sure I wanted to hear the sound of her voice when she talked to Ed Carver.

I lit a cigarette and dragged a Chicago Cubs ashtray across the desk top. When I was a kid, I remember making an ashtray for my folks in second or third grade. We started with a plain old glass ashtray, and then the teacher took a picture of each one of us. We mounted that photo on a piece of green felt and glued it to the bottom of the ashtray. So every time Dad snuffed a cigarette, he usually got me right on the nose. Funny the things that were okay thirty-some years ago. Dad still had the ashtray even though he'd given up the habit years ago. I think he empties his pockets into it every night. I knocked an ash off my cigarette, and it landed in the middle of the Cubs emblem. After the last season, they deserved it.

Further reflection on the significance of personalized ashtrays seemed pointless at best, but easy to justify. I am great at pondering trivialities when there's serious thinking to be done. Elaine was on the other side of the door right now, talking to a man who was not only interested in her but who, if he reacted to this call as I suspected he would, would soon be divorced.

For the second time in our relationship, we'd hit a "now what?" point. The first time I'd chalked it off to the lull after the storm. We'd come together at a point of turmoil in both our lives, and after the initial passions, there was a letdown. She admitted trying to force the issue by telling me she was moving to Santa Fe. I hadn't stopped her, convincing myself that she needed the time to herself. But now she'd been back for six months and we were hitting that same point. I valued our friendship. I depended on it. But even when I couldn't see us married, it hurt to imagine her married to someone else. Sometimes I'm a selfish SOB.

Of course, just because she was talking to Ed Carver didn't mean she'd be married to him inside of six months. But who was I to stop that? I could see me at the wedding where I'd been invited over Carver's protests. The minister has just posed the objection question and is asking us to speak now or forever hold our peace. I'd get up slowly and say something like "I'd really prefer that Elaine devote the rest of her life to being my friend. She can't do that if she's married, especially to Ed Carver." I flashed ahead five years. They've got three kids and Elaine's pregnant with a fourth. Over Ed's protests, the oldest son is named Quint. Ed has finally become a family man. Takes his kids to the park every day, pushes the little girl on the swing. Hell, he's got the time, he's night watchman at one of Brig Tanner's hardware stores.

"I can't get hold of him now."

I spun the chair slowly. Elaine was leaning against the doorframe her arms folded over her chest. "He's at one of these back-to-nature things. No one can get in touch with him until he gets back to the lodge."

I nodded. Picture that. "How long before they send out the search party?"

Smiling, Elaine said, "He's due back either tomorrow or the next day."

"Did you leave a message for him to call you?"

Her eyes widened. "Oh, sure. The guy's there to try to save his marriage and he gets a call from another woman. Wouldn't that make his day?"

"Well, the nature of the message isn't going to make his day either. Are you going to keep calling? Try to catch him between nature walks?"

"No. I left a message for him to call you."

I nodded. "I can see it now. He's going to drop whatever he's doing and dial his favorite person."

She giggled. "He may be angry, but you've got to admit he won't ignore it." She watched me as I studied her through a stream of smoke. "Besides, what would Ellie think if she knew I'd called him."

"I don't know. What would she think?"

Gazing off into space, she spoke more to herself than to me, ignoring my question. "He's going to take this hard. No matter what the circumstances are. And he's going to come back. No matter what it does to his marriage." Then she scanned the tiny office and the wobbly desk that held only the ashtray and seemed to be straining at that. "Is this where you want the computer set up?"

"I'd rather have it in my office."

"I'll probably be in your way for a while."

"I'll compensate."

She pulled one of the chairs out of my office. "Is this going to work?"

"The desk?"

She positioned herself in the chair so we sat knee-to-knee. "You know what I mean. Us working together."

I'd wondered about the wisdom of my suggestion, but I knew she wouldn't let me give her the horse. "Why not? Besides, once you've trained me your job is over. Though I guess that could take a while." After a moment's thought, I added, "If it's not working out, you just leave the manuals with me. I'll be fine."

Nodding, she leaned back in her chair and studied me. Her eyes are a no-nonsense shade of brown—medium tone without flecks of gold or any other mineral—but they are her most expressive feature, and right now they were telling me not to treat this lightly. I cleared my throat. "Look, let's put this 'connecting' stuff aside for a minute. I know you've been frustrated lately. And I know why. Nothing's working for you; you're trying to find a place to fit. So, yeah, in a way I offered you this because I figured it would be good for you. But the bottom line here is I wouldn't have asked you to help me out if I didn't think you were the best person for it." I jabbed my cigarette into the ashtray, using the movement to avert my eyes. She reads me too well. But at that point there was no way I could come right out and say: It feels like we're breaking up here, and I don't know how or even if we should stop it. Right now I'm feeling guilty, stupid, and ungrateful, and I'll do just about anything to get rid of that. Knowing that you have this horse is gonna make me feel better. You won't let me give it to you so I've gotta figure out something else.

I glanced at her to see if she was still with me. She was smiling a little, nodding. Finally she said, "Okay, we'll give it a try."

It was after four when we got to Jubal's place. The day was clear and mild, and frankly, I wasn't sure I'd recognize it without the blizzard. Bear led the pack this time. They didn't start to bark until I got out of the car.

I was curious to see how Cindy and Jubal would react to each other, seeing as this was enemy territory. Jubal came out of the house to greet us and hush the dogs up. In his right hand he carried a large red apple. He was just a yard from the car when Cindy climbed out. She walked right up to him, raised up on her toes, and kissed his cheek. "Hi, Uncle Jubal." She gave his forearm a squeeze.

Jubal smiled when he saw my mouth sagging.

His arm around Cindy, he chuckled. "Don't tell her daddy. He'll never let her out of the house again."

Cindy didn't seem to be squirming, so I figured it had to be something deeper than family that brought them together. Maybe it was something that had four legs, a tail, and the ability to crush the bejesus out of you.

I introduced him to Elaine and explained that she would be the primary rider. Jubal gave her the once-over, and I had the feeling he was appraising her not so much as a woman but as a woman who rides horses. Either way, she seemed to get his approval.

He took us behind the house to the barn and paddock. I'd never seen this part of Jubal's farm. It was a large area, but like the house, it had run down some. Most of the barn's red paint had long since given way to weathered, rotting wood. The inside was a different story. The place was as neat as I imagined the inside of a barn could be. A wide dirt aisle separated two long rows of stalls. Most of them appeared empty, reminding me of vacant storefronts in a town hit hard by the recession. The few that were occupied had fresh straw on the floor, and the horses didn't seem to be complaining about the lousy paint job.

A gray head bobbed over the side of one stall and greeted us with a whinny. Jubal took a bite out of his apple, then offered it to the horse, who, of course, accepted, taking a much larger bite. "Yeah, I hate to lose B.J. here, but she's too small for me to ride and Claude and Missy aren't much into horses. I was planning to sell her, so I guess she's as good as money, isn't she McCauley?" He took another bite out of the apple and gave the rest to the horse. I thought I was going to lose my lunch.

Jubal turned to Elaine and Cindy. "Why don't you two take a look at B.J., and me and Quint'll go inside for a beer. You got any questions, just holler."

As we walked back to the house, Jubal said, "Elaine's gonna love that horse." He paused and nodded to himself. "She's a good one," he said, not bothering to add whether he was talking about Elaine or the horse.

I had real mixed feelings about the Tanner's house. On the one hand I saw it as the proverbial port in a storm, but on the other I don't recall ever being so relieved to get out of a place. Claude was sitting in the small living room; an embroidery hoop stretching a nubby cream-colored fabric rested on her lap. When we walked in, she smiled and rose, setting the project on the arm of the old vinyl chair.

"It's nice to see you again, Quint." She kneaded the knuckles of her right hand with the fingers of her left.

Jubal motioned me onto the couch. "Why don't you get us a couple of beers, hon?"

When she left the room, Jubal lowered himself into her chair. It sighed as he settled in, and Jubal pushed Claude's needlepoint back on the arm. It was too early in the work to tell what it was supposed to be, but the primary color seemed to be red. Roses, maybe.

Jubal winked at me. "She's gonna love that horse. You're gonna score lots of points."

I acknowledged his insight with a nod. "So, tell me," I said, "how do you and Cindy manage to maintain a relationship?"

He dismissed it with a wave of his hand. "Ah, she's the best of the bunch. She's the only one who really knows horses. She's her mother's daughter, I guess. Barbara, now she was all right."

"Is she dead?"

"Yeah, she died 'bout fifteen years ago. Went out riding

one day and the horse came home without her. They found her a couple hours later, her neck broken." He shook his head. "Took a bad fall. It happens."

I thought of Elaine's long, slender neck and swallowed.

"So," Jubal said, "you think they're trying to send me up the river?"

"Not necessarily. But I think there's so much pressure to settle this thing that certain formalities might be overlooked." I crossed my leg over my knee. Diplomacy wasn't my strong suit. "In fact, I think certain formalities already have been overlooked." I told him about Ed Carver's permanent replacement.

Jubal listened, then whistled softly under his breath. "Damn."

"What does that mean?" Claude had returned and was handing Jubal a mug of beer. She set mine next to me on the end table.

"It means we've got an asshole running the police department," Jubal explained.

She looked to me for confirmation, and I nodded. "And I think we can assume that Brig Tanner's opinion is going to weigh pretty heavy with this administration."

She smiled nervously, fluttering her fingers against her mouth. "I don't understand." Her hair was a long, single braid that fell over her right shoulder, and the gray was a stark contrast against the deep blue of her sweater. "Jubal went grocery shopping for me that morning. Lots of people saw him, so they know that Jubal couldn't have killed her. Why are they so certain that Brig was supposed to die and that there's a conspiracy of some kind and Jubal's behind it?" She sat on the end of the couch nearest Jubal's chair. "It's ridiculous."

"Well, they've got a good reason to believe that Brig was the intended victim. If it really was Gayle, then whoever called her had to be involved. Otherwise, how would anyone know she'd be driving Brig's car at ten o'clock on a Saturday morning when he's usually driving to the bank? If the phone call was a setup, then chances are there were at least two people involved. One to make the call and the other had to be in place with a rifle. Otherwise whoever made the call would have to move pretty damned fast to get in place."

Jubal thought for a moment, then frowned. "There's always those car phones."

"Maybe."

"Okay, what if Brig was the target, then why's it got to be a conspiracy?"

"A conspiracy's less likely with him, but still possible. If someone was hired, I've got the feeling he's not a pro, which means maybe he came cheap."

"Why's that?"

"Well, he shot a car without being sure who was in it. Professionals don't get paid if they kill the wrong person."

Claude had retrieved her needlepoint and was jabbing a needle into the taut fabric. "It's all so hard to believe," she murmured, shaking her head.

Jubal sucked on his beer for a minute, then wiped his mouth with his shirtsleeve. "Still," he said, "that don't make it a conspiracy."

"No, it doesn't. It could have been someone with a grudge."

I turned to Claude. "Does Jubal always shop with you?"

She started as though caught in the act of daydreaming. "I'm sorry."

I repeated the question.

Chuckling, she said, "Only when we need salt for the water softener."

Jubal smiled at her like she'd just paid him a compliment. "Claude did her back in a couple summers ago."

A door slammed, and moments later Cindy and Elaine joined us in the living room. I could tell from the color in Elaine's cheeks and the brightness of her eyes that the horse checked out okay.

Cindy brushed her aunt's cheek with a kiss and sat between her and me on the couch. "She's a beauty, Uncle Jubal. You're gonna hate to lose her, aren't you?"

"It's like losing a kid."

If that was supposed to make me regret this transaction, it didn't work.

"What're you making there?" Cindy looked down at the needlepoint.

"Roses," Claude replied. "For a pillow cover."

Cindy pulled her gaze away from the red blotches. "How's Melissa?"

"She's fine. Should be home any time now."

Cindy nodded without much enthusiasm and turned to her uncle. "You have any luck scouting out another Morgan?"

"Not yet. I'm gonna hit the shows this spring. See what I can drum up." He hesitated. "How's Kessler?"

After studying him quietly for a moment, Cindy said, "He's beautiful. But you knew that." She hesitated, then added, "You should have him."

"Ouch. Damn." Claude jerked her hand up and squeezed the tip of her middle finger. A drop of blood appeared. She licked it off, then shook her hand, as if drying it. "You'd think after fifty years of doing this that I'd have figured out how to miss my finger."

Jubal regarded her absently before saying to Cindy, "Your old man treating Kessler okay?"

"Oh yeah. He dotes on him. Last thing he does every night is go out to the stable to visit him." Her voice drifted off, and she avoided Jubal's gaze.

"Will those investors still be interested later this spring?" I asked Jubal.

With a half shrug, he said, "Who knows. Depends on how the wind's blowing." He turned to Claude. "You think Margaret will still want to go in on it? She's not exactly a horse type." He turned to me and clarified. "Claude's friend's a nice lady, but doesn't know a Clydesdale from a Paso Fino."

"Jubal," Claude gently chided him, "she trusts your judgment. She knows your opinion is highly regarded."

Jubal frowned as though the jury were still out on that one.

Since there were no other chairs in the room, Elaine had dropped down on the Indian rug. Now she put her hand on my knee. "She's wonderful, Quint. Why don't you come out and take a look at her? She's an Arabian."

"An Arabian?" I turned to Jubal, who was hiding his smile behind the beer. "Aren't those the ones who panic at the sight of a rabbit and go charging off cliffs?"

He waved off my question. "Illinois is as flat as a pancake."

"Don't worry, Quint. B.J.'s got a fine disposition. Uncle Jubal thinks if a horse isn't a Morgan, it's not good enough to be called a horse."

"What's wrong with Arabians?" Elaine was appealing to any of us for an answer.

"They're wound as tight as a Chihuahua on speed," I said. "That's what's wrong with them."

"No." Elaine looked at me, wounded. Jubal was laughing, enjoying himself knowing I didn't have a choice here. "Come out and see her for yourself."

"No, that's okay. I already got a glimpse of her. I think I'll see lots more of her later."

"She's fine," Cindy said, laughing.

I squeezed Elaine's hand. "We should get going."

Claude sat forward. "Why don't you stay for a while, Cindy? Melissa should be home from school within the hour."

Glancing at her watch, Cindy said, "Thanks, but I've got a lesson in an hour."

"She'll be sorry she missed you."

Jubal walked us out to the car and pulled me aside as Elaine and Cindy got in. "Claude, she's not taking this too good. I used to think she could handle anything, but I guess everyone's got a limit." Hands on his hips, he looked up from the ground, then out toward the west and the stripes of pink and purple in the sunset. "She's scared to death I'm going to jail. Tries not to act like it, but she is." He finally looked at me. "You gotta get me out of this."

"I'll do my best, Jubal."

He nodded, resigned.

As we pulled away from the house, Bear sat down next to him and the two of them watched us leave.

On the way back to Windemere, I asked Cindy how she'd managed to stay close to Jubal and his family.

"Well, my dad doesn't know, of course. And it's not like we're real close either. It's just that I don't have any reason to hate them, so I don't." She paused. "This isn't a family feud or anything like that, you know. The only quarrel is between my dad and Uncle Jubal."

"Is Melissa their daughter?" Elaine asked. She was riding in the backseat.

Cindy snorted and turned so she could talk to both Elaine and me. "Yeah, she's a strange one."

"How's that?"

"Well, she's kind of dreamy, I guess. Head in the clouds. Sometimes I wonder if she's all there."

"Sounds like a fairly typical teenager," I commented.

She smiled. "Yeah, maybe. The last time I saw her was, oh, a couple months ago." Brushing some dust off her jeans, she seemed to be debating whether to continue. "I was at a party one of the instructors over at Dunkirk Stables was giving, and Melissa was there. Now I know she's only sixteen, but she looks older. And, well, you know how she dresses kind of . . . oh, I guess eccentric's a good word." She glanced at me for confirmation.

Actually, I'd only seen her in a robe, but I didn't feel like explaining myself, so I just nodded.

"She was telling me about this great guy she'd come with, and who does it turn out to be but Jim Dworski?" She made a face. "Hardly my idea of a great guy. By about midnight, they were both pretty drunk and all over each other. I didn't want her driving with him, so I told her I'd take her home. She didn't want to come with me, but one word from Dworski changed her mind. Guess he didn't want to get on my bad side. So, Rich and I drove her home, poured her out of the car. Aunt Claude was fit to be tied."

She must be an old hand at it. "What's Claude like?"

"She's great. Adores Uncle Jubal." She paused. "Missy and Claude, well, they don't get along real well, but I guess that's not unusual for a teenager and her mother." She finished there, but I wondered if growing up without a mother had something to do with Cindy's closeness to Jubal's family.

No one spoke for a minute, then Elaine said, "What does the way Melissa dresses have to do with anything?"

"Oh," Cindy said like she'd forgotten herself. "Well, at the party she had on one of those cat suits." She turned toward Elaine. "You know, sort of a body stocking."

"Oh yeah," came the voice from the backseat. "I bet every woman at the party wanted to string her up."

"Just about. I mean, guys were hitting on her right and left."

I nodded soberly. "Body stockings have that effect on us."

"But she didn't have eyes for anyone but Dworski." She shook her head. "I don't get it. I mean, you've seen him. He's really no prize."

I figured Dworski must have been the older man Melissa had referred to that night of the blizzard. "Yeah, well, sometimes just the idea that Mom and Dad would have a shit fit is enough to make a guy interesting."

Cindy paused and pushed a lock of blond hair behind her ear. "I suppose."

"Is Melissa close to your dad or your brother?"

"I don't know if 'close' is the word. I mean, we get along, but don't really see much of each other. Though Melissa does some work for Will after school a couple days a week. And on Saturday morning. You know, at his accounting firm. I think she's got a couple part-time jobs. I've gotta hand it to her, she's working hard to earn some money for college. She's told me more than once that she wants to have a psychiatric practice in Chicago."

"She wants to be a shrink?"

Smiling at the disbelief in my voice, Cindy said, "I know. But she's really serious about it. She does volunteer work at Abel County Hospital and loves it." Sighing, she added, "I'm just not cut out for that kind of thing. It's not for everyone, you know." She nodded to herself, as though acknowledging her fault and forgiving herself for it at the same time. She was silent for a minute, gaze fixed straight ahead. Then she turned to me. "My dad doesn't know you're working for Uncle Jubal, does he?"

"Not that I know of. And I'd like to keep it that way."

She emitted a dry chuckle. "I won't say anything, but you can bet he'll find out. There's not much going on around here worth knowing that he doesn't know about."

I turned onto Dunkirk. "What did you think of Gayle?"

"I'm sorry she's dead, but I'm glad she's out of our lives. I think it's pretty obvious what she was after."

"Money?"

"And whatever goes along with it."

"Do you think she and your dad would have gotten married?"

She shifted in her seat, crossing her ankle over her knee. "I guess we'll never know," she said, raking a lock of hair off her face.

We rode in silence for a few seconds. It was the point in the day when it's hardest to see shapes, and things take on a purple cast. "Brig and Jubal. How long have they been at each other's throats?"

She paused before she said, "As long as I can remember. My dad's always been more successful in almost everything. I guess after a while Jubal got pretty resentful."

"You said 'almost everything.' What's the exception?"

"Horses." I could hear the smile in her voice. "Uncle Jubal knows horses like my dad never will. He may be a lousy gambler, but he's a respected horseman."

"Lousy gambler?"

"Yeah," I could feel her looking at me. "Didn't he tell you about Bobby?"

"His former horse?"

She nodded.

"Yeah. He said he died of some weird virus."

Cindy chuckled. "You've just gotten a taste of Uncle Jubal's tale-spinning talents. He didn't lose Bobby to a virus, he lost him to an inside straight."

"Damn." I pounded the steering wheel. "I bought the whole damned line. Horse dying with its head in his lap and all."

"Well, I can understand his lying. That was really the beginning of the end for him. That same night he lost four of his brood mares trying to win him back. After that it was downhill." She paused. "Then he went away for a while, and when he came home, he brought Claude with him. She's so good for him. I think he'd have killed himself by now if it weren't for her and then Melissa."

"I suppose your dad likes him better when he's down."

After a minute she sighed. "Why do you think he bought Kessler? My father raises horses as an expensive hobby. He didn't need that horse. He just didn't want Jubal to have him."

"If horses are just a hobby to him, why does he tuck Kessler in every night?"

"That's easy," she said after a moment. "Kessler reminds him of Gayle."

$\triangledown$

10

IT WAS ALMOST dark when we pulled into Windemere Farms' long gravel driveway. Elaine and Cindy were discussing the virtues of B.J., and I was doing some calculating. When Gayle had gotten the phone call, there were about eight of us there, including Elaine and me. Would it have been possible for any one of us to get in a position with a rifle so he or she would be sitting in wait when Gayle went driving by in the Town Car? Jim Dworski, Tanner's hired hand and Melissa's paramour, left early. He could easily have been there. I made a mental note to check out where he was going and when he got there. Although the drive was less than five minutes, someone on foot taking the winding road never would have made it. But what if that person had gone the cross-country route? On foot or by horse? I wondered if I could rule out anyone who had been standing there gaping at Kessler. Maybe not.

"Cindy, are there any riding trails between here and Tyler Road?"

"Sure. There are trails all through this area. You can also cut through the woods to Dunkirk." She studied me for a moment. "Why?"

"I was just trying to figure how Gayle's killer could have gotten in position without a car."

Nodding, she turned away. "I guess they could have ridden. Or walked from Dunkirk. If they knew the area."

I pulled the car up to the Tanner house. Lights burned in

several of the windows, and I could see Brig Tanner talking on a portable phone, squinting out at us. "How long would it take to get from here to that spot on foot?"

She paused, watching me, and her jaw muscles flexed a couple times. Finally she said, "You could do it in ten minutes if you had to. It's practically a direct diagonal."

Elaine leaned forward, resting her arms on the back of my seat. "What are you thinking?"

I put the car in neutral and yanked up the emergency brake. "I'm not sure."

Cindy turned to face Elaine. "He's wondering if I could have run down there with a rifle in time to kill her." Back to me. "Isn't that right?"

When I didn't answer, Elaine gave me an accusing look but kept silent.

Cindy pulled the arms of her jacket down so only her fingers peeked out from the cuffs. "Well, it's no big secret. I didn't care much for Gayle. Like I said, I think she was an opportunist who was more interested in my father's money than anything else. She was one of the those people who was real nice to you if she wanted something or until she found someone who was more useful to her. Then she barely acknowledged your existence."

"What would you have done if she'd married your father?"

Without hesitation, she said, "I would have left Windemere. I'm good at what I do, I wouldn't have any trouble getting another job." She watched me for a moment, then added, "But, despite what you hear, not all Tanners are into frontier justice."

"But some are?"

"That's not what I meant," she snapped.

"Was Gayle a good rider?"

I could feel her eyes on me. After a moment, she said, "Yes. Very good."

"Better than you?"

A hesitation. "Maybe."

"Did she ride any of your horses in shows?"

"She hadn't." Cindy drew in a breath and added, "But the show season doesn't start for another month."

"Would she have ridden?"

Now she looked at me, eyes brimming with anger. "Dad never mentioned it to me, but it would have made sense. A farm's reputation is built on how well it does in the ring. So, yes, it's possible that we might have shared that job."

"How would you have felt?"

"It would have hurt. I told you I didn't care for her, and showing is something I've always done. But I want what's best for Windemere too. I could live with it." She paused a beat, then added, "I sure wouldn't kill someone over it."

I digested that for a minute and rubbed my face with my hands. I liked Cindy, had trouble picturing her killing like that. Besides, how would she know it was Gayle in the car and not her father? God, it was getting confusing. At least I could rule Brig out. There was no way he could have beaten our car down there, then run back in time to be making Kessler comfortable when Elaine came back for the police. Unless he had someone do it for him. Who else had been there?

"I'm not accusing anyone, Cindy. How did your brother feel about Gayle?"

She paused. "Will doesn't have much to do with any of us."

"How come?"

A small shrug. "He doesn't like horses."

It could be that simple. "What about Dworski?"

"He left early, didn't he?" Elaine said.

"Yeah, I think he did. But"—she turned so she could address Elaine—"he was just hanging around to help Dad unload Kessler. He usually comes in the early morning to clean stalls and help with the feeding, is gone by nine or ten to another job, then comes back in the late afternoon."

"Then he doesn't live here."

"Oh, no. He's got several jobs and his own place." She looked toward the barn where I could see a light. The horses were up late reading, no doubt. "But he might still be here, finishing up." Her voice drifted off, as though caught at the end of a thought.

"What is it? Something about Jim?"

"No, I don't think so." She turned back to me. "It's probably nothing, but I just remembered a couple weeks ago . . ."

I waited.

"Yeah, it was maybe a week before Gayle was killed. Some tack had turned up missing—a saddle and a couple bridles, I think. Dad confronted Jim and finally came right out and accused him of stealing. He denied it, of course, and since Dad couldn't prove anything, he just told Jim he was being watched."

"Was Gayle there?"

"Um, yeah, I think she was." Cindy closed her eyes for a minute, as though conjuring up the image. "Yes, she was. She was sort of standing behind Dad. Didn't say anything though."

"Anything else turn up missing?"

"No. Not that I've noticed anyway."

I tried to imagine how offended Jim Dworski would be if he were accused of a theft he didn't commit. Staring at the barn's lights wasn't going to tell me anything. Maybe it was time to ask him.

I left Elaine to smooth Cindy's feathers and walked across the yard. Strains of the Stones' "Under My Thumb" met me at the barn's open door. As I followed the sound, a black-and-white cat came out of a shadow and brushed up against my leg, arching its back. The music grew louder as I walked down the corridor toward the offices. Jim Dworski was sitting in the office Gayle had shown me the week before, tilted back in the chair, his feet up on the metal desk, eyes closed, accompanying the Stones with an air guitar. His smile had a beatific quality to it, as though he was at one with the world or had gotten hold of some excellent pot. I didn't mean to sneak up on him, but it was hard not to with the music blasting. It came from a boom box on a filing cabinet. I reached out and switched it off. Jim's chair slammed to the floor, and he almost slipped out onto a rough landing on his butt.

"Who the hell are you?" He wiped his hands on his jeans, as though rubbing out any traces of the guitar.

I told him.

"Yeah?" He squinted at me even though the only light in the room came from a desk lamp. "What do you want?"

I stepped into the office and leaned up against the other desk, folding my arms over my chest. "Just wanted to ask you a couple questions."

"What if I don't want to answer them?"

I shrugged. "I can't make you talk. You don't want to, I'll leave. I just figured you work here, you see a lot of what's going on. A lot more than, say, a Brig Tanner, who's kind of in the middle of it all, if you know what I mean." I didn't even know what I meant, but Jim sat there, chewing on the inside of his mouth, studying me. Black high-top sneakers protruded from a pair of faded black jeans, and he topped it all off with a Van Halen T-shirt. Black, of course. His build was small and wiry, and his arms were corded with muscle.

"You ain't a cop, are you?"

"Nope. Private."

"Who you workin' for?"

I glanced out the door, then back to Jim. From the way Brig Tanner was treating him the other day, and from the story Cindy told me, I figured it was a safe bet that Tanner wasn't one of Jim's favorite people. I jerked my head in the direction of the house. "His brother."

Jim smiled for the first time. Actually, it was more of a smirk, but probably as close as he got. He propped his feet back up on the desk and folded his hands on his stomach. I noticed there was manure on the bottom of one of his shoes. "What d'you want to know?"

"You worked for him long?"

"Six, eight months."

"What's he like to work for?"

"What d'you think?"

I considered for a minute. "I think maybe he doesn't exactly appreciate people who work for him."

"You'd be right there." He clasped his hands behind his neck. His underarm skin was fishbelly white against the black T-shirt. "Most people don't."

"This isn't your only job?"

"Hell, no. I got an auto-repair business on the side. This"—he waved his hand toward the door and the rest of the stable—"this shit is just till I get that going."

"You do work on foreign cars?"

"Sure do." He sat up and dug in his back pocket. "What've you got?"

"Accord."

"Good car." He handed me a white card with his name and address below AUTO REPAIRS in large letters and REASONABLE in smaller type. "You having trouble with it?"

"Not right now, but that's bound to change." I pocketed the card. I'd take my car to Jim Dworski when I was ready to take myself to some guy with a card that read "Appendectomies . . . Reasonable." But maybe I could buy myself a little cooperation.

"Do you work for any other farms?" I asked him.

"Yeah. A few other places."

"You specialize in horses?"

"Guess so."

"You like them?"   •

He screwed up his nose like he was smelling something bad and shook his head. "I tell ya, people around here are horse nuts. So I learn to take care of horses. Don't like 'em." He jerked his thumb toward the rear of the barn. "Especially that new one. We go back a ways. I do work for Hines too. He's the guy who sold Tanner the horse. And I'll tell you, far as I'm concerned, it's a pain in the ass. God, you'd think it shits caviar the way people go on about it. To me, the only horse worth spit is the one who comes in first when I got my money on him."

"You knew Gayle."

He frowned and shrugged. "Just seen her around. She never talked to us hired folks except if she was bitching about the way you do something. Like the stall ain't clean enough. You know, like I'm standing there, waiting for the horse to crap so I can catch it before it hits the floor."

"How long has she been coming around?"

"Three, four months maybe." He raked his hand through his hair. "At first she just came for the riding. You know, renting a horse. She wasn't bad then. But then old man Tanner takes a liking to her. Horses ain't the only thing she's riding anymore." He smirked again. "All of a sudden she hasn't got the time for anyone whose name ain't Tanner."

"Did she get along with Cindy?"

"Cindy didn't have much time for her. 'Specially after she and her old man became an item. Musta burned her but good." Then, as if to emphasize the point, he lit an unfiltered cigarette with a wooden match. He flicked it with his finger to extinguish it, then let it drop on the ground. I wondered if he did the same thing in a stall full of dry straw.

"The day Gayle was killed, where did you go after Kessler came off the trailer?"

"Another job out at Dunkirk Stables." He shrugged. "Different horses, same shit."

I suppressed a smile. "You see anything when you were driving out of here?"

"Like what?" His eyes narrowed as he blew a stream of smoke up toward the ceiling.

"I don't know. Someone driving out this way. Someone on foot."

He seemed to give it some consideration, then said, "Nope. Nothing."

I nodded. "You ever have anything to do with Jubal Tanner?"

"Not if I can help it. The guy's a loose cannon. Can fly off the handle if you look at him wrong."

"Have you ever done that?"

He frowned and shook his head. "Don't avoid him, though. I can handle him."

"What about his daughter? Can you handle her?"

He dropped his feet to the floor and sat forward, arms resting on the desk. His eyes narrowed. "Sure I can. What's it to you?"

I shrugged. "What about Will? Does he come around here much?"

"Hardly ever see him. Guess he lives in town."

He rubbed his chin, then looked up at me. "You think one of the Tanners did it?"

"Don't see how Brig could have. Wouldn't have been enough time."

Jim frowned.

"Besides, why offer a ten thousand dollar reward?"

Jim's eyes widened. "The old man's got a reward out?"

"For information leading to an arrest."

"Hmm." He smiled a little as though encountering a pleasant thought. Then he cocked an eyebrow at me. "Anything else?"

"I heard that Brig accused you of stealing saddles."

He leaned back in the chair. "So? I didn't do it. He can't prove a damned thing."

"I guess that's why you're still here."

He shrugged.

"Who do you think did?"

This time he almost smiled. "I think the old man shoulda checked under his girlfriend's bed. That's what I think."

"Gayle stole the equipment?"

"Why not? Hell, I don't even like the stupid animals. What do I need a saddle for?"

"You could always sell it."

He made a sour face. "Too much trouble." Then he paused and added, "Lots easier ways to make a few bucks."

When he didn't elaborate, I said, "How's that?"

He gave me an odd look, as though he was debating whether or not to share his wisdom with me. But all he said was, "Turn that radio back on, will ya?"

Elaine was waiting for me in the car when I returned.

"Where'd Cindy go?"

"It's kind of hard to discuss the price of saddles when you just realize you're being considered as a murder suspect."

I started the car. "You think I should rule her out just because she's your friend?"

"No."

"Then what?"

"I don't know. Something she said."

I executed a three-point turn and headed out the driveway without responding. I know better than to rush Elaine.

"It's probably nothing. But she's got kind of a bad attitude toward men."

"What'd she say?"

"I tried to bring up her dad and Gayle, but she got real agitated and said something about Gayle being in over her head. Then she made the observation that men think with their cocks rather than with their brains. Or words to that effect."

"I don't suppose she expanded on that insight."

"Well, not really. I agreed with her, you know, just to keep up the conversation, and somehow we got off the subject of Brig and Gayle."

I thought maybe I didn't want to hear where that went. "So she never told you what that remark about Gayle meant."

"Not really. I came right out and asked her, but then she said her dad wasn't an easy man to love."

"I believe that."

We rode in silence for several minutes. The statement could have been no more than an afterthought on Cindy's part, but I couldn't help thinking about the marksman trophies in the office she shared with her father.

"What do you think I should name her?"

"Who?"

"The horse. Who else?"

"What's wrong with B.J.?"

"It stands for Betty Joe."

I nodded my understanding and tossed some horse monickers around in my head before I suggested Flicka.

"I think it's been done."

"Yeah, but it's a good name. I've got news for you, you're not the first Elaine in the world."

"That's like naming a dog Lassie."

I chuckled. "Our second dog was named Lassie."

"Whose idea was that?"

"I think we voted. She was a collie mix, and we figured if we named her after the big star, she'd act like her too."

"Did she?"

"Hell, no. And I gave her every chance. You know how Timmy would fall down and scrape his knee and Lassie would be standing over him whimpering and sniveling."

"Yeah?"

"Well, I'd clutch my chest as though I'd just taken a direct hit from an arrow, and our Lassie would just kind of glance at me as she stepped over my body on the way to the Gravy Train."

"Maybe it was the Gravy Train."

The conversation degenerated into a discussion of how we both used to sample our dog's food and how Milk-Bones were really pretty good. Then it lapsed into silence that was beginning to feel uncomfortable.

"You got any plans for dinner?" I asked.

"Yeah, let's go to my place."

Elaine had only been in her apartment a few months, but she had a way of settling in quickly. Before her boxes were unpacked, she was hanging pictures. Hell, I'd been in my place almost a year and still hadn't unpacked all the boxes yet. And already she had more furniture than I did. She didn't have any to start with, but we'd hit the monthly Abel County flea market and the place really shaped up fast. She had an eye for a bargain too. She'd see something that looked like a piece of junk to me, take it home, refinish it or paint it, and whammo, she had a great-looking bookcase or table. One nice thing about eating at her place as opposed to mine was that we didn't have to eat off the coffee table.

We stopped at the store and bought a couple swordfish steaks and some teriyaki sauce and indulged ourselves in a half pound of fresh shrimp. While the steaks were marinating, we munched on the shrimp dipped in marinara sauce and tried to resist the frantic cries of hunger from McGee, Elaine's cat.

She had found the animal wandering outside a local restaurant that specialized in seafood. I suspect that location was intentional on McGee's part. He was young but mostly full-grown and friendly. And judging from his size, he was a pretty successful beggar. Though I'm not much of a cat person, I had to admit that the big cat had a personality and knew how to use it. He was fond of jumping at you from corners and grabbing your leg. Occasionally he'd dig his fangs into you in what Elaine called a playful bite, but which had been known to draw small beads of blood. Elaine considered having him declawed, but worried about what it would do to his machismo. Hell, he'd already been neutered. What more could one do?

As I watched him pouncing on his own tail, Elaine said, "You don't really think Cindy killed Gayle, do you?"

"I don't think you can rule it out. She wasn't around when Gayle got the call. I assume the phone in the stable is a different number. She could have made the call."

"I know Cindy pretty well, there's no way she could kill someone in cold blood like that."

"There you go again."

Elaine bobbed a peeled shrimp in the sauce. "I know, but I also know she didn't do it."

I narrowed my eyes. "Okay, anyone else we can rule out? If you've got an automatic innocence detector, I'm going to start charging higher fees." She made a face, and I kept going. "Think of it, we could contract you out, and you could serve as a backup to Judge Wapner."

After a long, cool stare, she said, "I've also got an automatic shit detector, and it's on overload right now." She moved into the L-shaped kitchen and, using tongs, pulled each swordfish steak out of the marinade and placed it on the broiler rack. "Cindy gave me the names of horse people Gayle might have been talking to about that saddle. I'll check them out tomorrow."

"I thought you were going to shop for a computer."

"That's not going to take all day," she replied, then added, "I'm also going to talk to some of the people Gayle worked with."

"Elaine, you're not a licensed investigator."

"No, but if she worked with a bunch of women, they're more likely to talk to me."

I wasn't going to argue.

After inserting the broiler pan into the oven, she picked up her glass of wine and returned to the sofa.

"What are you going to do?"

"See a man about a horse." I said. "A guy named Hines sold Brig the horse even though Jubal had talked to him first. Not a crime, but I wonder if Brig used any special tactics on him." I drank some of the cabernet, enjoying the heavy, woody taste. "I'm beginning to expect that from Brig."

After dinner, Elaine said she had to finish up some work for a graduate student whose thesis she was typing.

"Oh." I didn't try to keep the disappointment from my voice. "I thought we could do some connecting."

She gave me a look that warned me not to take this lightly. "Think about what I said."

I went home and took Peanuts for a long walk by the river. Dogs are so easy to please. This was his idea of heaven—the river at night and the slumbering groups of ducks. I spent about an hour out there with him while he snuffled around, investigating every upturned rock and stick. We were on our way back to the apartment when it occurred to me that when I'd kissed Elaine good-night, it had been on the cheek. She hadn't acted as though she expected more.

Then, because I was tired and didn't want to dwell on Elaine at the moment, I felt entitled to a short glass of Knockando, a liquor I'd come across in my search for the perfect unblended Scotch. When I turned on the TV and stretched out on the couch, I saw that Yul Brenner had just recruited Steve McQueen. *The Magnificent Seven* was too fine a movie to pass up. The bottle's level went down a couple inches as I watched the seven of them defend the lazy little Mexican town from the banditos. By the time their number had been reduced to three, I had decided that maybe I wouldn't look so bad on a horse if I shaved my head and wore black. When the credits rolled, I set my empty glass on the coffee table and switched off the light. The bed was just too damned far.

▽

11

I WAS DREAMING that I had fallen off a dinghy and was drowning in warm water and woke up just as the water was closing in over me. Peanuts was licking my ear. I pushed his muzzle away and sat up. There I was, fully dressed. Nothing like starting the day prepared. My body felt stiff from the contours of the couch, and I smacked at the sour taste in my mouth. I've heard people say that really good Scotch won't give you a hangover. That's just not true. Really good Scotch consumed in reasonable amounts probably doesn't. I guess I'd gotten carried away with the romance of the West. Cowboys never worried about hangovers, did they? And at two bits a shot, the stuff they were drinking couldn't have been all that good.

I dumped water and four large scoops of Stewarts into the coffee maker and clicked it on. What I really wanted was a shower, but Peanuts was insistent, and it was after nine. I opened the door for him, and he stood on the small wooden porch, gazing at me over his shoulder, waiting. "Sorry, sport. Not now. I'd really appreciate it if you'd just take care of your business, sniff out a couple ducks if you really have to, then get back here." He hesitated one more second, then turned and trotted down the steps. I felt like a jerk. All this animal ever asked of me was to throw the Frisbee for him a few times a day. And for that he rewarded me with treasures such as an earful of dog spit. I moved back into the kitchen, rubbing my sore neck and telling myself it was a damned good thing I didn't have kids.

I decided to put off a shave and shower until Peanuts was finished. He hates to be kept waiting at the door. I popped a John Prine tape into the cassette player, punched the replay button, and cleaned up the last couple days of dishes, noting that there were a lot more glasses than plates. When I finished drying the last of them, I opened the door and whistled for Peanuts. The day was overcast, with fat, gray clouds hanging low. When my whistle failed to yield a response, I called his name. Odd. Knowing he got to eat as soon as he finished his business, he usually didn't linger. What was he into now? Maybe some hapless duck had challenged him. But nothing, not even a duck, was more important to my dog than eating.

"Peanuts!" When that didn't bring him, I slammed the door behind me and trotted down the steps. I could feel a knot growing in my gut as I zigzagged across the forty feet of yard down to the river. Maybe he'd gotten into something. Something poisonous. I checked Louise's property first, looking under the porch and around trees, although Peanuts was more an out-in-the-open dog. At the river's edge I scoured the water for anything out of the ordinary. But it was running smooth and slow. I wasn't worried about him following a duck into the river, because his interest in the creatures ended at the water's edge. As I spread my search out from Louise's property, I stood at the river's edge again and looked up and down the river. When Peanuts and I went for walks, it was usually south. I jogged that way, calling his name and scattering ducks along the way. I don't make a habit of running except when I have to, and pretty soon I was sweating and panting. I slowed some, figuring I'd have better luck spotting him if I took more time. I ran into an elderly couple out for a morning walk. She was small and wrinkled and walked slowly as he guided her by the elbow. As I trotted up to them, he looked as though he was ready to shove her out of my path and take me on, but when I asked if they'd seen a short, black-and-white dog, he gave me a sympathetic smile and shook his head. I was almost a mile down the river before I doubled back. This time I went north of my place for about a quarter of a mile, up to Prairie Street, where one of Foxport's two bridges was located. My stomach knotted up tighter. Call me an overprotective parent, but I never let Peanuts anywhere near the street.

The tension eased a little when I saw no sign that he'd wandered this way. I wasn't as concerned about him tearing out into traffic as I was worried that he might try to run herd on a Volvo. As I made my way back to my apartment, I was debating whether to take the car out and look for him or check the neighbors' yards again. It was after ten. I stood in the middle of the yard raking a hand through my hair trying to figure out what happened. He never ran away. It wasn't like him. I shook my head and was digging the keys out of my jeans pocket when I thought maybe he'd come back while I was out. As I climbed the steps, I wondered if I even had a picture of him to use on a lost-dog poster. I also wondered what I'd done to make him run away.

The stoop was empty, but taped to the screen door was a white envelope. Inside was a single sheet of paper with block letters printed in pencil. Just like a ransom letter, which I guess is what it was. KEEP OUT OF TANNER BUSINESS AND YOUR DOG WILL BE OK.

I dropped my fist holding the letter to my side and swept the area with my gaze. I kicked the door. Damn. I kicked it again. Of course Peanuts would be an easy dog to swipe. He was so damned trusting, trotting through life thinking everyone was a decent person. Damn!

I called Louise. If she was home, maybe she'd seen something. I slammed the phone down on her answering machine.

Pacing the room wasn't clearing my head. I sat down and tried to think. Who wanted me off the case? Whoever did the killing. But I didn't have a clue, so what did that buy me? Nothing. Who would want me out of the picture? I'd been hired to keep Jubal Tanner out of jail. Who wanted to see his brother in jail more than he wanted world peace or the Cubs to win a pennant? I grabbed my jacket from the green lawn chair where I'd dropped it the night before.

As I drove toward Windemere, I tried to collect my thoughts, but they were too jagged. Behind every reason there was a dry voice in the back of my head telling me to be logical about this. Whoever took Peanuts figured I might drop the case. Did Brig know about Peanuts? And if he did snatch him, would he stash him at his own house? Not too likely, but it was a place to start. Did Brig Tanner know I was working for his brother? He had to; he knew everything else.

By the time I'd arrived at Windemere, I'd convinced myself that although I didn't know whether he'd taken my dog, he was my best guess, and I was prepared to follow through on that hunch. I had to squelch any doubts and come across with some righteous conviction. Brig answered the door himself, looking more distracted than suspicious. He led me into his study and gestured toward a chair facing a large desk.

I ignored his offer, and before he had the chance to get comfortable in his own chair, I braced both palms on Brig's desk and leaned toward him. "Where's my dog?"

He blinked once. Twice. "What are you talking about? What dog?"

"You took my dog."

"I didn't know you had a dog. And if I did, why would I take him?"

The dry little voice in the back of my head was starting to assert itself. I tried to ignore it. "You wanted me off this case so bad, you swiped my dog."

"What case are you on?"

Sure, I thought, but then Brig smiled like he'd just got the punch line. "You're working for Jubal, then?" He pushed back his chair and stood, forcing me to relinquish my aggressive position. Although he was several inches shorter than me, he was stocky and solid and didn't impress me as the kind that intimidated easily. I was a little surprised that he seemed more amused than angry. Then I remembered that he was running for mayor. "I don't know what happened to your dog, but I swear, I had nothing to do with it."

"I didn't think you'd admit it."

"How can I convince you?" He started to tell me how his dog died last year at the age of fourteen and how he understood my concern. I didn't want to hear any of it. I felt like a fool. I just wanted to leave. This was stupid. Did I expect him to trot Peanuts out of some cage and hand him over?

After a minute, I realized he'd stopped talking and was watching me, curious. He lowered himself into his chair. "Have a seat. Let's talk. How do you know your dog didn't run away?"

"I doubt he'd leave his own ransom note." I lowered myself into a chair, not ready to admit an error, but conceding that I might learn something and, what the hell, I was here.

He raised his eyebrows, which were more tame than Jubal's. I figured he probably had them trimmed. "Why me?"

"You want to see Jubal in jail so bad you're willing to replace the chief of police to make sure it happens."

His jaw shifted and he said, "Ed Carver wasn't doing his job. That's the only reason he was replaced."

I shook my head. "No way. I'm not Carver's biggest fan, but there's no way that Moore is a better cop."

"There's also no reason to believe that Moore is a permanent replacement."

I wrapped my hand around the smooth wood of the chair's arm. "I'll bet if he finds enough to put your brother away, he'll be around for a while."

Brig frowned, as though he hadn't considered that possibility.

"You know," I said, "there are witnesses that place Jubal elsewhere at the time of the murder."

He shrugged it off. "Easy enough for him to hire someone."

"Maybe. Maybe not."

"How well do you know my brother?"

"Better than I know you."

I was sitting across from Brig, who occupied a large leather swivel chair. Between us was a dark wood desk—mahogany maybe—that was bare except for a blotter, a desk set, and some photos. In spite of the mild weather, a small fire crackled in a fireplace with slate trim. I figured that between this office and the one out in the barn, Brig preferred the amenities this one offered. I noticed that soft classical music filled the room without overpowering, offering a pleasant alternative to stark silence.

He pushed himself away from the desk. "I don't know about you, but I can't talk about my brother without something to fortify me." The study was long and narrow and filled with sunlight from large windows that covered one long wall. Spanning one of the short walls was a wet bar, which Brig stepped up to. Instead of pulling out a liquor bottle, he lifted a thermos from one end of the bar. He held it up. "Coffee?"

"Thanks."

He handed me a Windemere mug identical to the one I'd used during my brief encounter with Gayle.

The coffee was rich with a distinctive flavor I couldn't place.

Brig sat back in his chair, placed the thermos on his desk, and breathed in the steam from his mug. "My doctor told me to cut out the caffeine. I compromised. This is half and half."

"It's good."

He chuckled. "It's some Indian blend, I think. Cindy gave it to me for my birthday. Trying to break me of the instant habit. It worked."

He didn't seem in a hurry to get on with the subject of Jubal, and we sat for a minute in a comfortable silence as we drank our Indian blend. I took the opportunity to study the photos that occupied a corner of his desk. Gayle's was among them. A horse appeared to either be biting her ear or telling her a secret. She was laughing. Another photo was of a woman, maybe in her mid-forties, with blond hair that curved under at her shoulders. With her sculpted features and clear, blue eyes, she was a striking woman. I could see reflections of her in Cindy. I touched the picture frame. "Was she your wife?"

"Yes. That's Barbara." There was a trace of reverence in his voice and more than a little regret, as though losing her suddenly had left many things unsaid. When he pulled his gaze from the photo, I saw that his eyes glistened. "I don't seem to have much luck holding on to a good woman, do I?"

"Sometimes things happen," I said, feeling it was inadequate and at the same time wondering why I wanted to say something comforting to this man who had mounted a campaign to get my client sent to jail.

He gave a half shrug and shook his head, then turned toward the windows, squinting.

"Were you and Gayle planning to marry?"

"We'd just started talking about it. Nothing specific. Just feeling each other out."

"How come you're so sure about Jubal?"

"I've known him a long time, McCauley. Give me that." He was leaning across the desk now, the moisture in his eyes replaced with sparks.

"Seems to me you two hate each other so much, you don't see much else."

"Let me tell you a few things about Jubal." He was pointing his finger at me, both angry and defensive. "Maybe you'll understand why he likes hating me so much. Why he'd like nothing better than to see me dead." As he uncapped the thermos and poured himself another cup, he seemed to be using the time to compose himself. And when he spoke again, his tone was restrained but adamant. "I worked hard for what I've got. Damned hard. Nobody gave me anything." He waved his hand at the room's contents. "You think I inherited all this, don't you? Well, I didn't. Sure I started with some money, but Jubal, he started with land. And you know what he did with that land? He pissed it all away, that's what he did." He sat back in his chair, his hand resting on the desk, clutching the mug. "In my family you had to work for what you got. You had to prove you were the best. Jubal could ride better, hunt better, drink better than me and Cody. He was the oldest. So when our folks died, the land went to him. I got some money. Not a lot, but enough to get me started. I opened my first store with it, bought a little land. Pretty soon I had another store, more land. And I went from there." He looked at me with a bitter smile. "So you want to know why Jubal hates my guts. In the end what I had was what counted. Nobody gives a shit if you can plug a twelve-point buck between the eyes at a hundred feet. Money is what counts. I learned how to make it and how to save it and how to invest it. All Jubal knew was how to spend it and lose it. And now he's supposed to be the one everybody feels sorry for." He brushed him off with a wave of his hand. "Well, I'm sorry. I'm just about all out of sympathy for that sorry shit." He seemed finished for the time being.

"Your parents left Jubal all their property?"

"Yeah, but so what?" He raked his hand through his hair with a savage thrust. "They didn't leave me out of the will. Like I said, I got some money. But it was the land that meant everything to my old man, and he left it to Jubal, who managed to lose all but that little piece of dirt he's on now. That land should have been Tanner land for generations. It's what we are. In ten years it'll probably be crawling with yahoos who want to get away from the city but not too far away."

"What about Cody?"

He looked up as though he'd just wakened. "What about him?"

"Where did Cody fit in?"

After a minute, he said quietly, "He didn't. That's why he's dead."

I set my empty mug down on his desk. "Brig, how's Jubal going to keep hating you if you're dead?" I kept coming back to that argument because it made more sense than anything else.

Brig had been staring into the fireplace, and now he turned to me slowly. "That hasn't stopped him from trying to kill me before."

"When?"

"Couple years ago. I don't even remember what his beef was. Anyway, he comes storming in here." He jabbed his forefinger on his desk. "Right here I tell you. And he points a gun right in my face. That old lever action of his, I think it was. Said he was going to do me in right then and there." He paused long enough for a smile to pull at the corner of his mouth. "You know what I did?"

I shook my head, figuring he didn't even need much prompting.

"I grabbed the barrel out of his hands and threw it, butt first, in the fireplace." He chuckled. "You should of seen Jubal beating the barrel with his bare hands, trying to put the fire out. What a sight."

"There's a big difference between what you describe and what you believe Jubal did."

His laughter tapered off, and he gave me an odd look. "What's that?"

"You admit that he must have hired someone to pull this off. Am I right?"

He nodded, waiting.

"Do you really believe he'd deprive himself of the pleasure of watching you die?"

Brig Tanner turned toward the fire and didn't answer me.

▽

12

SOMETIMES I ENVY people who see everything in black and white. It's nice to have things simple. I had descended on Windemere convinced that Brig Tanner had taken my dog and was some hate-driven maniac who wouldn't rest until he destroyed his brother. I thought I understood him a little better now. At least I knew where the hate was coming from. Maybe he'd taken Peanuts and maybe he hadn't. Either way, I wasn't ready to vote for him.

As I drove into town from Windemere, I thought about how Peanuts had made a space for himself in my life. He likes to ride in the car, and more than once he's kept me company on a stakeout. He's come in handy too. It's amazing how you can distance yourself from suspicion if you're in the company of a dog. A closer look at someone's house can appear to be the innocent act of going after your pet when he strays from the sidewalk. Peanuts is real savvy about pulling off that sort of thing. It's almost like he knows exactly what he's doing. I didn't want to get used to doing this alone.

I still didn't have a clue as to who swiped my dog. Brig Tanner had been, at best, the proverbial straw to grasp. Once again I considered dropping the investigation, then realized that my doing nothing was not an option.

I figured I might as well hit all the Tanners, so I headed toward the accounting offices of McRainey, DeFlorio, and Tanner. Will Tanner's secretary, Sandy Charles, was a small, blond woman with short, feathery hair. Were it not for a wicked little smile, she could have played Peter Pan.

"Mr. Tanner's out for the afternoon. Did you have an appointment?"

"No, I thought I'd just try to catch him."

"This close to April fifteenth, that's not real likely." She gave me that crooked smile. "Are your taxes filed yet?"

"Are you kidding? It's not April fourteenth yet."

She made a tiny fist and rested her chin on it. "That's not very smart. You don't seem stupid, so you must like to live dangerously."

"Yeah, well, it's either playing chicken with the IRS or rock scaling." I shrugged. "This way I don't have to leave my house."

"It can get expensive, though."

I think that was the point when I realized she was flirting. Sometimes I'm a little slow on the uptake, but once I get it, I waste no time in reacting. I felt my face get hot. "Ah, do you know when he'll be in?" I wouldn't have blamed her if she'd written me off then, rolled her eyes, and said something like: "It's always a mystery."

But she smiled again and said, "Sure. All day tomorrow." She opened an appointment book and ran her finger down the page. Her hands were a milky white, and her nails a pale pink. "I can squeeze you in between appointments, oh, say around ten."

"Sounds great." I turned to leave, then stopped. "You wouldn't be able to tell me if he had an appointment with John Schaub on Saturday the twentieth, would you?"

"He doesn't usually schedule appointments on Saturdays." She flipped back a couple of pages. "No. He was here that morning but left early."

"Do you remember if that was before ten?"

"I think it was."

"Thanks."

She arched an eyebrow. "You'll be back tomorrow?"

"I'll be here."

"Glad to hear it. Hate to see a guy like you go to jail."

"Thanks."

I probably would have spent more time thinking about Sandy Charles and the way I didn't feel a damned bit guilty about looking forward to returning tomorrow, but I was preoccupied with the knowledge that, despite the tax deadline and Will Tanner's busy schedule, he cut out early on the morning Gayle Millard was killed.

I considered the relationship among Will, his father, and his father's girlfriend as I drove out to Warren Hines's farm. From what I'd observed at the Tattersall that night, there didn't seem to be any enmity. In fact, Will just sat there and watched the game while Brig and Gayle got to know each other better. Will only spoke up when Jubal entered the picture and started hassling them. If he disapproved of his father's choice in women, then what was he doing out for a drink with the two of them? I figured it depended a lot on his relationship with his father. If he wanted to be around him, he'd have to put up with Gayle. On the other hand, if he had a real problem with her, maybe he'd do something about it. According to the man himself, Brig Tanner had a lot of money. Not only did he have the farm and the stores, but he was influential. That usually takes some green stuff. What if Dad were to marry a woman younger than either kid? What would that do to their inheritance?

Warren Hines's farm was farther than Jubal's. I wound up driving through DeKalb, home of Northern Illinois University, where I went to school but only for a couple years. I remember one night at the Candlelight, I was talking to a guy who was on the ten-year-and-counting-plan. All he had to show for it was puffy eyes and a beer belly that all of us undergrads were in awe of. I'd stared into my beer and realized that if I didn't do something drastic, that was where I'd be in ten years. It occurred to me that maybe I needed to find myself. Instead of getting that notion out of my system by enrolling in a psych class, the next day I quit and set off across the country using my thumb for transportation. I got as far as Texas before the army noticed.

The copper peak on the NIU student center had been reduced to a speck in my rearview mirror when I came to Hines's place. As farms go, allowing for my limited knowledge of them, his place seemed to fall somewhere between Brig's and Jubal's. Most of the buildings—the house, a stable, and a shed—had seen a lot of repairs, and it looked as though he was losing the battle with the shed. One side was in a state of collapse. As I pulled off the gravel road into Hines's driveway, there was a large white sign attached to the fence. Painted on it was a riderless horse, legs curled above the ground in a full gallop. All it needed was wings.

I parked in the driveway behind a blue Buick Regal. Hines's house was, unlike most of the farmhouses I'd passed on my way, a fairly new bilevel with an attached garage. I rang the bell and waited.

The woman who answered the door wore jeans and an untucked flannel shirt. She held a pencil in her left hand, and, despite the fact that she looked exhausted, she was attractive. Her chestnut hair was straight and brushed her shoulders, and she had that brown-eyed wholesomeness that used to sell Ivory soap. She was on the heavy side—wide hips and large breasts—with a pretty face and an open smile. Before she could say anything, a black cat skittered past my legs and into the house. She watched its progress, shaking her head and smiling. "He hates to do his business outside." There was a slight lilt to her voice, which reminded me more of central than northern Illinois.

I returned the smile. "I don't blame him." I could hear a dishwasher going and the sounds of two or more children who were either playing or fighting. For the uninitiated, it's hard to tell which.

Apparently oblivious to the commotion, the woman took a moment to study me before saying, "What can I do for you?"

I told her who I was and said I was looking for Warren Hines.

"I'm Nan Hines. Anything I can help you with?" She leaned her hip against the doorjamb and folded her arms over her chest, tapping the pencil's eraser against her chin.

"Well, I wanted to talk to him about Kessler, that Morgan he sold Brig Tanner."

The pencil stopped tapping. "What about him?"

I shrugged. "Just a couple questions." When I saw that wasn't going to be enough, I added, "Like when did Brig approach him? How did Brig know about the horse to begin with? Things like that."

Her brown eyes narrowed. "Why do you want to know all this? There's nothing crooked about the way Warren sold that horse."

"I'm not saying there is. I just wanted to know the details."

"Why?"

I sighed and shoved my hands in my jacket pockets. I really couldn't answer that. I had no reason to believe that the purchase of Kessler had anything to do with Gayle's death, and I was on another of my fishing expeditions. "I guess I'm just curious about the relationship between the two brothers."

She smiled slowly. "Who isn't?" Then she glanced over her shoulder into the house, turned back to me, lowered her voice, and said, "I think Jubal meant to kill Brig, and that poor girl was just in the wrong place at the wrong time."

I shrugged. "You're not the only one."

"What do you think?"

"I really don't know."

I'm not sure whether she believed me or not, but finally she poked her chin in the direction of the barn. "He's in there, working with one of the geldings. But wait a second, I'll go with you. I've got a tax question for him." She made a face. "God, I hate this time of the year." She stepped back into the house, almost stumbling over the black cat, who apparently had important business outside. It tore across the yard.

"I didn't hear you flush," I called after him.

Nan's laugh was deep and throaty, just as I'd expected. "Just give me a second."

As I waited for her, I thought about how maybe it was time to pull my tax stuff together. Nah. Not until Peanuts was back.

When Nan appeared again, she'd thrown a sweater over her shoulders and carried a piece of paper. As I followed her across the gravel yard, she was bemoaning the tax season. "I'm the one who passed algebra, so guess who gets to keep the books? I don't mind, but every now and then he'll sneak a bill or something in on me and I don't know what to make of it." She shook her head and wagged the paper in the air. "This one's not even ours. As if we don't have enough of our own bills."

I recognized the peculiar sound from my limited experience with horses before we stopped in the barn's open doors—the rhythmic hoofbeats echoing off the walls of the barn. A riderless horse passed in front of us at an easy lope. As it made its way around the curve of the arena, past a row of stalls on the right, I saw a man in the center of the circle holding a long lead attached to the horse's bridle. He saw us and nodded, then apparently made some invisible gesture to the horse and clucked at it a couple of times. The animal slowed to a trot and before it made another round had reduced its gait to a walk. The man shortened the lead as he approached the horse, finally resting a big hand on the animal's glistening neck. "At's a boy," he murmured a couple times. The man I assumed to be Warren Hines held his own in the size department when standing next to the horse. He was tall and broad in the shoulders and reminded me of a linebacker ten years after a knee injury benched him for good—muscle going a little soft.

"This is Quint McCauley," Nan was saying. "He needs to ask you a couple questions about Kessler. But first I want to know what we're doing with a bill from Castleton Farms addressed to Tom Erdman?" She pushed the bill under his nose. "Don't we pay this joker enough money for our own bills?" She turned to me. "He's our vet," she said, rolling her eyes.

I might have taken a moment to decide whether her

reaction to the vet was amusement or disgust, but I was too busy noticing how the color had drained from her husband's face as he looked at the paper. "Ah, this . . . this is nothing." He took the paper from her and, still holding on to the reins, folded it in thirds.

"What do you mean nothing? It's for . . ." She hesitated, glancing at me, and finished with, "a lot."

"Uh, I know. But we shouldn't have it. It's not our concern. I don't know how we wound up with it." He finished his short speech as he stuffed it in his back pocket. The horse bobbed its head in agreement and blew air out its nostrils.

"Well, that's what I was hoping you'd say." She smiled at me again. "I'll leave you two to your business. Nice meeting you," she said as she left.

Warren shook his head. "You know anyone who doesn't hate this time of year?" His drawl was the same as his wife's. He waved his hand toward the line of stalls. "I gotta put Mac here up. Mind if we talk while I'm doing that?"

"Not at all." I followed him to one of the stalls, my shoes sinking into the now-familiar feel of the sawdust-and-dirt combination. The pungent odors hit me—sweat, manure, straw, leather—probably manna to the senses if you're a horse person. Me, I could probably learn to live without it.

Hines led Mac into the stall, turned him around, and clipped a rope from rings on either side of the stall to the animal's bridle, effectively keeping him in place. "Don't want you starting dinner yet," he chided the horse.

Though his skin was leathery and the lines around his eyes deep, he had a young full face and a large, drooping mustache. His eyes seemed small beneath thick, heavy brows. "What can I do for you?" He bent down to a plastic box filled with brushes and a few other things I didn't recognize.

"Well, I just had a couple questions about the deal you made with Brig Tanner for that horse, Kessler. I also wanted to ask you about Jubal Tanner."

He straightened and began to work the horse's coat with a brush and long hard swipes. "Why you want to know?"

"Well, I'm working for Jubal Tanner. He thinks he's getting stampeded into a conviction for Gayle Millard's murder. Claims he had nothing to do with it."

He paused to run his thumb and forefinger down either side of his mustache. "I'm sure he does." Then he shrugged. "So?"

"You sold Brig that Morgan, didn't you?"

His eyes grew narrower. "Yeah. What's one got to do with the other?"

"Probably nothing."

The horse shook its head and pulled back against the restraint. Hines had worked his way toward the animal's rear and now he smiled and patted its back. "I know. It's torture, isn't it?"

"That's not a Morgan, is it?"

"No. Mac here's a registered quarter horse." Mac must have heard his name, because he rolled his eyes back toward Hines's voice, flashing crescents of whites and looking like he didn't like anyone talking behind his back. "He's gonna make someone a fine riding horse. You interested?"

"Thanks. Not in the market right now." I moved to the right so I could look directly at Hines without going through Mac. "How'd Brig find out about Kessler?"

"I told him." He stopped brushing and looked at me. When I didn't respond, he waved the brush toward the arena and the rest of the stable. "Look at this place. For the last five years, I've been a half step ahead of the bank foreclosing on me. I couldn't wait for Jubal. He didn't have the money when I wanted to sell, and I didn't see how he was gonna get it in a month. And you know, I might have waited for Jubal to come up with the money if I'd believed he could. I don't know how well you know Jubal, but he's got eyes bigger than his wallet. For all I know those investors he claimed to have were up here." He tapped the side of his head with the brush. "You know any of them?"

"Yeah, I guess I'd heard a few of the names. The last one, though"—he chuckled—"was some old lady Jubal probably had to sweet-talk and promise God knows what."

"You remember her name?"

"Ah, let's see."

"Margaret something?"

"Yeah, that's it. Something like Hepburn, no, Hebron I think it was. Yeah. That's it. Margaret Hebron."

I made a mental note of that and filed it. "Why call Brig Tanner? He's not the only other horse buyer in town."

"Yeah, well, I'll be the first to admit I played on that relationship. I figured the minute Brig found out Jubal had his eye on this horse, he'd jump at the chance to own it. And I knew he'd offer me more too. To tell the truth, McCauley, Brig doesn't know horses that good. I mean, he knows a decent one when he sees it, but he hasn't got the sixth sense that his brother's got about these animals. As soon as he heard that Jubal wanted this one real bad, he figured it had to be something special."

"Was he?"

"Hell, yes. Kessler's a fine animal. His blood's gonna show up for generations."

"So I've heard. How did you come by him?"

"Fellow down in Pekin was having some bad times, had to sell him. I've had him for about a year and a half."

"Brig tells me the horse is worth quite a bit as a stud. People pay big money to have their mares bred with him. Why you give up that income?"

He studied me for a moment, then exchanged the brush for a wire one and began working Mac's mane. "McCauley, how much do you know about animal husbandry?"

"Not much," I admitted.

"There's a lot of work involved in breeding. That's not what I do. What I do is buy, train, and sell horses. I kept Kessler long enough to make some money on him. And then I sold him for a profit. For me, it was a good business deal. That's all."

"You never keep any horses?"

He shrugged. "Nan and me have each got one, and the kids have a couple ponies. Otherwise I'm in the buying and selling business. Boarding too."

"When Brig made you an offer, did Jubal make a counter-offer?"

"He tried, but what difference did it make? Said he'd have it in a month, just like before." He snorted. "It's like Monopoly money to him."

"How long have you known the Tanner brothers?"

He stopped brushing and squinted up at the beams. "Let's see. Fifteen years I guess."

"What can you tell me about their feud?"

He shook his head. "How it got started? Got me. The way I hear it, they've been at each other since they were kids. Everyone kind of figures it's mostly Jubal resenting the way his little brother's a success and he's not."

"It's mutual though. I mean, Brig does a lot of hating on his own."

"Wouldn't you if you'd been hated long enough?"

I asked him a couple more questions about the Tanners, but apparently he didn't have a better fix on them than I did.

As I walked back to my car, I wondered if I'd ever learn the truth about the Tanners, and I also wondered if it would make a difference. I made a mental note to check out a vet named Tom Erdman and Castleton Farms. Maybe it had nothing to do with all this, but judging from his reaction, it was something to Warren Hines.

The black cat was sitting at the door to the Hines's house as I started my car and shifted into reverse, and it watched as I backed down the driveway.

I drove home, in the back of my mind hoping that Peanuts had somehow managed to escape his captor and I'd find him curled up on the porch. But he wasn't there, and it was just as tough to face his dish with food still fresh from the morning. I filled his water bowl and opened a beer, thought about responding to the vague gnawing at my stomach, but nothing in the refrigerator appealed to my appetite. I dropped onto the couch and stared at the wall for a while. The more I thought about the whole mess, the madder I got. And the closer I looked at Jubal's situation, the more I believed that he was being railroaded. As soon as Gene Moore and Brig Tanner could, Jubal would be going directly to jail, without passing go or collecting two hundred dollars. And without much chance of a reprieve.

I opened another beer and grabbed a couple graham crackers just to shut my stomach up. I was thinking how maybe it was time to start curtailing my beer drinking habits when the phone rang.

"It's Carver. What in the hell do you want?"

He caught me off guard. I thought he had another day of nature hiking ahead of him. Deeming the pleasantries weren't called for here, I plunged ahead. "Ah, listen, Ed. There are some things going on here you ought to know about."

"Like?"

"Well." I took a deep breath. "To begin with, and what's probably the main reason we called you is, uh . . ."

"Spit it out."

In my mind's eye I saw Ed Carver clutching the phone, staring out some big picture window at the Rockies, Grand Tetons, or something equally as awe-inspiring, and not seeing a bit of it. His grip on the phone is such that his knuckles are stark white and the plastic is about ready to crack under the pressure of his grip. "It all started when Gayle Millard was murdered." I went on to explain the situation as briefly and as best I could, stressing Brig's role in the whole thing. That was when I hesitated.

"And?"

"Well, Ed, it seems you've been replaced."

There were about ten seconds of deafening silence before Carver said "What?" in a voice that was barely audible.

"At a city council meeting the other night they voted you out and Moore in."

After a sharp intake of breath, he said, "What's your game, McCauley?"

"Game? This is no game." I was about to add "Sorry to say" but changed my mind.

No response from Carver, but I could hear him breathing.

"Listen, Ed, nobody wants to see you patch things up with Ellie more than me. And if you think I'm doing this out of sheer boredom, you've got a really inflated opinion of your ability to entertain me. Now if you want to hear who led the move to get you canned, then say so. Otherwise let's cut this short."

It took a few seconds, but he finally said, "Okay. Who?"

"Brig Tanner." I paused. "You ever have any dealings with him?"

"Oh, yeah." He let it drop.

I decided to throw in a modest plug for my client. "You know, while it might appear that Jubal is the likely suspect, there are other possibilities."

He didn't respond. Perhaps this wasn't the time to push Jubal's case. "Are you due back soon?"

"I am now. But I might have trouble getting the hell out of here." Where in the world was he? Before I could ask, he added, "Listen, don't tell anyone you talked to me."

"No problem."

As if things weren't interesting enough already.

$\triangledown$

13

AFTER TALKING TO Carver, it was easy to justify my staying with the investigation. Jubal Tanner wasn't the only one getting screwed here. Still, I had trouble keeping my mind off Peanuts. I kept telling myself that there was no logic in killing a dog. It wasn't like he was going to identify his captor in a line-up. That didn't comfort me much, so I reminded myself that Peanuts was a scrapper. He could handle himself.

I put on a pot of coffee and grabbed the phone book. For all I knew, Castleton Farms was on the dark side of the moon, but it was a place to start.

Never underestimate the power of the yellow pages and how far honest ignorance will get you. I only had to call two breeders. The first was too busy to talk to some guy trying to find a farm other than his own. But the second was a woman who didn't mind giving me the time. When I told her I was trying to locate Castleton Farms, she said she'd heard the name, but couldn't place it. Without asking me why I wanted to know, she gave me the number of a horse breeders' association. Within a half hour, I was on the phone with the accountant at Castleton Farms, just outside of Memphis.

"Oh, yeah, I hope you can help me out here. My name's Roger Kafka and I'm Tom Erdman's accountant, and he's just about the lousiest record keeper you're likely to find." I waited a second for him to react to the name. Relieved that he didn't, I continued, "Now, his records show that he got a bill from you that he didn't pay. The trouble is, we don't have a copy of the bill, so we don't know what the amount is." I tried a self-conscious chuckle. "To add to the confusion, Tom had a break-in here a month or so back and some of his records are missing. Well, I figured we'd have heard from you if I hadn't paid it, but I just want to make sure."

There was a pause at the other end of the line, and I was starting to worry, but when he finally spoke he sounded more irritated than suspicious. "You don't have any idea when the bill was dated?"

"Sorry, no. I mean he says it was for last year."

I could hear him sigh. "How d'you spell that name?"

I crossed my fingers, realizing I only had one shot. He was bound to be suspicious if I misspelled my employer's name. "E-R-D-M-A-N."

I heard the click of a computer keyboard, and after about fifteen seconds, the guy on other end of the line cleared his throat. "This one woulda been tough to forget. Five thousand worth of frozen semen."

"Ah, yes," I gasped in recognition. "And it's paid?"

"In full. You'da heard from us if you hadn't."

"What's the date on the invoice?"

"October thirty-first last year."

"Well, maybe that explains it. Tom was in the middle of the move then. Is that the Elgin address?"

"Nope. Winfield."

"Okay, yeah, that explains it." I jotted down the address. "That's the old place. The post office wasn't real good about forwarding his mail."

"Then how'd you wind up paying it?"

"Records. I keep really good records."

I could hear him covering the phone's mouthpiece and talking to someone. I was tempted to take the opportunity to hang up but figured I was dealing with a gentleman farmer here.

"Ah, listen," he came back on, "the guy who sold the stuff to Erdman is standing right here. You want to talk to him?"

"No, that won't be necessary."

"What'd you say your name was?"

"Roger Kafka. Thanks very much for your help, Mr. Kinzie. I appreciate it." I hung up.

Okay, what was Tom Erdman doing with $5,000 worth of frozen semen? Could be a number of things, and none of them were illegal. Maybe he bought it for one of his clients' horses. Maybe he had his own horse. Maybe being a vet he just liked having some of the stuff around. Who knows? Finally I asked myself if any of this had anything to do with Gayle's murder. I had no reason to believe that it did. So why didn't I quit pursuing it? Simple. I didn't have anything else to go on.

I glanced at my watch. Two-thirty. Too early to find Will Tanner at home. I was about to head out to the Tattersall when someone pounded on my door. When I opened it, Jubal Tanner was on the other side. He dropped his gaze to the gray wood railing. "Sorry to bother you at home. But I went to your office first, and Elaine said you might be here."

"C'mon in."

He accepted my offer of a beer and made himself comfortable on the couch. I helped myself to some coffee. Then he just looked at me, waiting, like I was the one who'd called this meeting.

"I suppose you're wondering how I'm doing?"

He shrugged like if I wanted to talk about it, fine, but he didn't want to make an issue out of it.

"I'm afraid I don't have much, but someone thinks I do." He raised one bushy white eyebrow. "My dog's been kidnapped."

Jubal froze, beer tilted toward his open mouth. Then he glanced around the room, as though maybe I was pulling his leg. Finally he said, "Someone swiped your dog because you're on this case?"

"That's what the note said."

"Je-sus Christ," he muttered, then focused on me again. "You want to quit, I won't blame you. No way. I'd understand."

I shook my head. "I've thought it over. Believe me, I've thought it over."

"You get one of them ransom notes?"

"I guess that's what you could call it."

"You sure you don't want to call it off?"

"Once they know how to get to you they never stop coming."

He studied me, shrugged, and drank from the can of beer.

I settled into the director's chair. "Gives some credence to your railroad theory, doesn't it?"

Jubal looked thoughtful for a minute, then snorted. "I shoulda seen all this coming. The Carver thing. Brig, he's got most of the city council in his pocket. He makes it his business to know which one of 'em's wearing dirty underwear. You know. Leverage. Blackmail. Whatever you want to call it. Hmm." He considered this while working on his beer. "Then I guess my days as a free man are numbered."

"Not if I can help it." Then to cover the fact that I probably couldn't, I went on the offensive. "Jubal, why did you tell me your horse died of some equine virus?"

He made a pretty good stab at indignant. "He did."

"That's not what I heard. I heard you lost him in a poker game." He worked his mouth a couple times, but nothing came out. "Then you proceeded to lose several mares in the same lousy streak."

Scowling, he said, "Who's telling you that garbage?"

"Someone who's got no reason to lie about it."

He seemed on the verge of protesting again, then deflated, he hung his head.

"Jubal, why'd you lie?"

After a minute he looked up at me. "I figured if you knew what really happened, you'd write me off as a good-for-nothing. I mean, I guess that's what I was, but I swear I haven't touched a card since that night." He waited for me to respond and when I didn't said, "You washing your hands of me?"

I studied him over the edge of my mug. "You lying to me about anything else?"

He shook his head with what I guessed was exaggerated solemnity. "I swear I haven't."

"I hear different, you're on your own."

He nodded again.

We worked on our respective beverages in silence for a couple minutes; then I told him about my trip out to Warren Hines's place.

Jubal listened, frowning, then shook his head. "Why'd you go out there? You think Hines was hiding something? Why were you even checking him out? I mean, I hate like hell the fact that Brig's got that horse, but Hines didn't act different from any other horse dealer I've run into."

"You ever hear of a vet named Tom Erdman?"

"I heard of him. That's about it."

"What about Castleton Farms?"

He frowned and shook his head. "Why d'you think there's a connection between Hines and the murder?"

"I don't have much to go on, so I'm looking under rocks."

"Whatever." He drained his beer and crumpled the can. A human recycling machine.

As I was handing him his second, I said, "Tell me something. I keep asking people why you and your brother don't get along. All I hear is this vague crap about how it's been like this forever and how that's just the way it is. I don't believe it."

He thought for a minute, then shrugged. "That's the way it was though. Raised on competition." He shook his head. "Our old man was a real piece of work." When he saw I wasn't convinced yet, he asked, "You got any brothers?"

"Four."

He raised his eyebrows in admiration. "Then you know something about what I'm saying. There musta been competition between all of you."

I nodded, conceding the point. "Everything was competition. From who got seconds on dessert to who had the highest batting average." Then I paused, recalling the past as I studied Jubal. "But none of us wound up hating the others."

He smiled like that's what he expected me to say. "What were your folks like?"

I shrugged. "Tried to be fair. Made an effort to let us figure out our own interests. Then encouraged us along those lines."

"That's the way it should be. But my old man thrived on competition more than the three of us did. At least at first. Always pitting one against the other. Only natural that one would drop out early on."

"That was Cody?"

He nodded. "I remember the day. The old man took us hunting. Poor Cody. He didn't want to be there. Rather'a been home reading." He shook his head. "Cody, he was the good one." He paused for a minute, then began quietly. "I remember riding home after each of us shot our first buck. Cody was just sittin' there like he'd rather be the one turning stiff in the back of the truck. Didn't say a word, just went up to his room, lookin' all the while like some kind of ghost. Pa and Cody barely talked after that, and the old man stepped up the competition between me and Brig. Like he was trying to make up for losing a son. I felt sorry for Cody. Used to go to his room when Pa wasn't around. Wouldn't go near him when he was." He paused, reflecting.

"Not exactly the Ponderosa, was it?" I suggested.

Shaking his head, he sighed. "He didn't even go to Cody's funeral."

"What do you think happened there?"

He looked past me, toward the blank wall. "Ah, she wasn't worth it, whatever it was. She killed herself. Who knows why? Seemed nice enough, but real, you know, sensitive. Young. A lot like Cody."

"Why'd she do it?"

He frowned and shrugged. "Who knows?" He let the statement hang there.

"What about your mother? Where was she all this time?"

"Oh, she was there. Cody was her favorite. Thing is, she was scared of Pa. Scared to cross him."

"So it was just you and Brig competing against each other."

He nodded. "Thing was, Brig usually beat me. Didn't matter what I did, my younger brother would come along in a couple years and do it better. Tried to tell myself it didn't matter. But it did. It did."

"Why'd he keep beating you?" And why was I beginning to feel like a shrink?

"Luck," he said without hesitation. "He may be smarter than me, but most of it's luck. He's just lucky."

"Is he smarter as far as horses go?"

Jubal smiled. "Could be, but he'll never know."

"What do you mean?"

"Why, Brig, he's scared of horses." He smiled, savoring the way the words fell off his tongue.

"Brig is scared of horses?"

"Oh, sure, he can handle one all right, long as his feet are planted on the ground. But you'll never seen him on top 'a one. Claims it's his back, but I know better." He smiled. "That's always bothered him. You see, everything I have, he wants. Part of the competition thing. Doesn't matter what it is, he wants it. Take my Claude, for instance."

"Claude?"

"Yeah, when I first brought her home, he tried to pull her away. Worked with most women, but not my Claude. Too much sense." He laughed softly and without humor. "Wonder if she's sorry now?"

"What do you mean?"

"He's got everything. What have I got? Claude. And Missy."

"Does it go both ways?"

His pale blue eyes narrowed. "What d'you mean?"

"You said he's got everything. Do you want what he's got?"

He stopped and stared at me for a few seconds that seemed a lot longer. Then he laughed. It was a loud, full sound, but one without much humor. I waited. The laughter trailed off into snorts, and finally he got quiet. "I can want what he's got till I turn blue. I haven't got what it takes to get it." He rubbed his fingers together. "Thing is, everything Brig does works for him. Nothing I do works for me. Not a damned thing. Like the saying goes, you give Brig a bunch of broken eggs, he makes the omelet." He paused. "I just wind up with egg all over my face."

The way he was talking, it seemed like he'd had more than one beer, and I still wasn't sure why he'd come to my apartment. Maybe he was just lonely. He swallowed the last of the beer and compacted the can again. "Well, I'd best be going. Got a few errands to run before Claude'll let me back in the house."

After he left I thought about Brig and Jubal and wondered why I found this whole thing so fascinating. I don't read tabloids, don't watch the soaps, usually don't care much about other families' skeletons. Maybe it was the way these two brothers, more alike than different, were so caught up in this funnel cloud of hate for each other that they were no longer able to objectively interpret a situation. Maybe I wasn't either.

It was like I'd started out feeling one way and wound up not knowing what to think. I had been ready to believe that Brig Tanner arranged for Gayle's murder, snatched Peanuts, hell, it wouldn't have taken much to convince me that he was behind Jimmy Hoffa's disappearance. Now, I didn't know. One thing I sensed was that the person who really deserved the blame for the whole mess of a family was sleeping under a Tanner headstone that probably said something about a beloved father.

I added Jubal's empty beer can to the recyclables and decided to drive into town.

Elaine wasn't in the office but had left me some computer brochures and a note saying she had gone to talk to some of Gayle's friends and coworkers. I hoped she came up with more definitive results than I had.

I was going through a pile of mail that Elaine had sorted when the phone rang.

"I'm looking for a, uh, Quint McCauley." The man's voice was deep and even.

"You found him."

"I understand you're interested in the Tanner brothers."

"Who is this?"

"My name's Ron Miller. I have some information concerning their history that you might find interesting."

"I'm listening."

"No, I'd like to see you in person."

"Why?"

I heard a quiet laugh. "This may be so interesting that you'll be convinced it's worth paying for."

"Give me a sample."

"I know why they hate each other. And, if you're really working for Jubal Tanner, it's something you'll want to know."

I thought it over for a few seconds. If he really knows, it would be worth the trip. "Where?"

"Ever been to Yancy's?"

When I told him I hadn't, he said it was a bar about twenty miles southwest of Foxport. I scribbled directions down on a scrap of paper and told him I'd meet him at seven.

After that, I tried to concentrate on the mail, but the office seemed hollow and empty. Peanuts' empty bed was getting to me. I had to get out of there. In the end I decided to go hassle an old lady.

$\triangledown$

14

MAYBE MARGARET HEBRON had a real good reason for investing in a stud horse, but when I pulled up to her house, I couldn't help wonder why she didn't spend the money on some fix-up work. She lived near downtown Foxport in a white two-story that, fifty years ago, had probably been a handsome home. Now, the paint was peeling, though not quite to the eyesore point, and the green shutters were ragged and a couple were at odd angles. Hanging from the door was a straw wreath with a large blue bow with the words "Welcome Friend" printed on its ends. We'll see.

The woman who answered the door was short and plump with pale red hair that was so thin you could see her scalp through it. She kept the storm door closed until I explained I was working for Jubal Tanner, hesitated a moment longer, then held it open for me. Inside, the hardwood flooring in the entryway was polished to a gloss. As she led me into the living room, I noticed she walked with a stiffness that suggested arthritis.

"Claude mentioned that Jubal had hired someone to help him. I was so glad to hear that, though I can't imagine what you'd want with me."

The furniture in the living room was situated around a slightly threadbare Persian carpet. The couch was old and comfortable, the kind you sink into. A cut-glass dish of pecans sat in the center of the coffee table. I wonder how people can put morsels out for drop-in guests and not clean the bowl out themselves within a day. Guess it takes more self-discipline than I've got. I helped myself to one of the pecans.

"Can I get you some iced tea? I know it's a bit early in the season for most people, but personally I drink it all year around. Except around Christmas. Then it's eggnog." She giggled and patted her rounded stomach. "It takes me the rest of the year to recover from the holidays."

I smiled. "Me too," then added, "Iced tea sounds great."

The floorboards creaked as she moved into the kitchen.

I heard a groan nearby and noticed for the first time a dog curled up in an overstuffed chair. He seemed to be waking up from a rather pleasant dream, stretching his legs and yawning. I figured him to be some kind of mixed terrier breed and noticed as he gazed at me, peering over his shoulder from his prone position, that his beard was mostly white. He wagged his tail slowly, and I moved over and held my hand out to him. He sniffed it without much interest and yawned again.

"I see you've met Frisky." Margaret set a tray with two tall glasses on the coffee table. "He's quite old. About all he does anymore is sleep. Do you have a dog?"

"Yeah," I returned to the couch. "A border collie." I helped myself to the iced tea.

"Oh, they're wonderful dogs, I understand."

I swallowed. "Yeah, they are."

She had settled into an easy chair with lace doilies pinned to its arms.

"Have you and Claude been friends for a long time?" I asked.

"Oh, yes. Since Jubal brought her here actually. Almost twenty years ago now. Just a few years after my husband and I moved here. Before she had Melissa, Claude and I both worked for one of the local ophthalmologists."

"Have you seen her lately?"

"Why, yes. Just a few days ago in fact." Her features clouded over. "She's really quite distraught over this thing with Jubal. I don't think I've ever seen her so . . . so out of sorts, you know?" I nodded. "I think she really believes they'll do whatever they can to send him away."

"They're trying. Tell me, did you offer to invest in that horse as a favor to Claude?"

She leaned over and scooped up a few pecans. "Well, I don't know what you mean. A favor? Not really. Just a good investment."

"You mind telling me how much of an investment it was?"

She popped a pecan into her mouth, chewed, and swallowed. "Yes, I do mind."

I nodded agreeably and she added, "My late husband, Charles, stressed the importance of confidentiality where finances are concerned."

"I see." I drained my iced tea and returned the glass to the tray. "Had you ever invested in horses before?"

She sat back in the chair and crossed her legs. "My husband did. Nothing serious though."

"Morgans?"

"No."

Frisky groaned again and twitched his whiskers.

I smiled and nodded in his direction. "Rough life he's got."

Margaret smiled but didn't say anything.

"I suppose you're wondering why I'm interested in the horse when it doesn't seem to be the point."

"Yes, I do wonder."

I leaned back in the couch and gazed up at the ceiling. "Everything between Brig and Jubal seems to revolve around their hate for each other. The horse was the latest in a long line of contentions." I turned to Margaret. "What's your opinion of Jubal?"

She studied me for a minute before answering. "I think Jubal was a big, handsome man who took Claude by storm. He told her all these dreams he had, and she believed him. He can be charming, but he's also pigheaded to the point where it's destructive."

"Sounds like the Jubal I know."

"As far as I'm concerned, his only saving grace is the fact

that he loves Claude very, very much. It's too bad that she's not always first in his thoughts."

I nodded. "She's a strong woman, isn't she? I suppose she's held him together all these years."

"She has."

"Well." I pushed myself up from the couch. Frisky opened an eye. "I'd better be going. I'm probably keeping you from dinner."

Margaret walked me to the door and hesitated a moment before opening it. "Mr. McCauley . . ."

"Quint," I corrected her.

She nodded absently, then looked up at me. "Please remember that you're doing this as much for Claude as for Jubal. And if you ever start to think that Jubal isn't worth the effort, remember that Claude is."

"I will." I handed her one of my cards. "If you think of anything else, give me a call."

I started my Honda and let it idle a minute while I studied her house. What kind of investment had she made in that horse? Not all investors necessarily came up with the same amount, but she probably had to put up at least ten grand. Ten grand would go a long way in making the outside of that house look as immaculate as the inside. For some reason I just didn't see Margaret Hebron, with her ancient dog Frisky, as the sort of woman to plop down a chunk of money on a long-term, risky investment. Not when there were sagging gutters to replace.

It was almost dark by the time I'd made it out to Yancy's. The bar was southwest of Foxport in an unincorporated area. I guess that was what you call a roadhouse—a big block of a building without much going for it except its location— close to a tollway exit. Each darkened window boasted its own neon sign, hawking some brand of beer. The large expanse of a gravel parking lot was cluttered with cars and pickup trucks, and maybe twenty motorcycles were lined up like horses to a hitching post just outside the building.

I had to park near a barbed-wire fence in the back and managed to squeeze the Honda between a rusted-out Olds and a pickup truck with a large, toothy dog in the cab. Apparently it had been taught to lunge at anything that moved. The truck's window was rolled down about three inches, just enough for the beast to get its snout through, even though it had to twist its head sideways to do it. Its eyes were wide and the whites dominated. The animal would have made a perfect poster dog for the Rabies Foundation.

I stood outside the entrance to Yancy's for a minute, listening to the throb of some country-western song on a jukebox, wondering why this felt wrong. I decided it was my distaste for wild-goose chases. Ron Miller, whoever he was, had offered me information for a price. That wasn't unusual. What would be unusual would be if the information turned out to be worth the price. More than likely, Ron Miller was some guy low on beer money. The music blared as I pulled the door open.

On the inside, Yancy's smelled sour like stale beer, and apparently the stop-smoking campaign hadn't made it all the way out here yet. The gray haze hanging in the air seemed stagnant and unyielding. Mingled with the smoke was the unmistakable scent of grease, probably frying up some potatoes or burgers. I'm always a little ashamed at myself for loving the way that smells.

The place was one big, square room, and the bar itself was an island in the center of this room. I heard the crack of pool balls coming from the northwest corner, although it was too crowded to see a pool table. Like the parking lot suggested, the place was packed with a real assortment of customers. Some looked like they might be farmers, dressed in jeans and wearing either straw cowboy hats or caps advertising some seed company. Then there was the group dressed a lot like the farmers, only their jeans were too dark and their boots too shiny and their skin too smooth for them to be the real thing. Apparently this wasn't the sort of place women went to alone, and the ones without an escort clung together in groups of at least three. Then there was the crowd that I assumed went with the motorcycles—black leather, silver studs, and tattoos. There were only a few women with this group of about fifteen, but it was easy to tell they belonged. One woman wearing a black tank top had tattoos down her right arm to her fingers. I didn't get close enough to read the story.

I jammed myself between two guys sitting at the bar and ordered a beer. One of them rewarded me with a halfhearted sneer, then dropped a full shot glass into his beer. As the bartender drew the beer, I asked him if he could point out Ron Miller. I thought he was going to ignore my question, but as he dipped the glass from under the tap and set it in front of me, he jerked his chin toward a cluster of tables along the back wall of the room. "Middle table over by the wall. Sitting with the big guy."

It wasn't tough to figure why he'd used the big guy as a landmark. He must have topped the scales at something over three-fifty. I paid for my beer and worked my way through the tightly packed tables. The two men watched as I approached, and I had a moment to marvel at the contrast between them. The one was huge in bulk, though probably not very tall. The other was his polar opposite—even when seated, it was apparent that once this guy uncoiled himself, he'd be somewhere around six and a half feet. His eyes were large and his face small and gaunt, and I felt I was being observed by a praying mantis.

"Ron Miller?" I asked him.

He nodded and extended his hand. I set my beer down and shook it. Then he introduced the other man as Artie Fotchke. I said hello, and Artie blinked in response. What set him apart from the rest of the place, aside from his immensity, was his clothing. He looked like he was ready to take his table at La Tour. His suit was a pale gray silk, and I couldn't help but wonder how many yards went into it. He wore a starched white shirt and a red tie with a loud paisley print. His hands were big, smooth, and shiny and reminded

me of cased sausages. The ring he wore on the third finger
of his left hand looked like it was on the verge of slicing right
through the casing. I pulled my attention back to Ron. "You
had something you wanted to tell me?"

"Yeah, let's move over here." He rose slowly, taking both
our beers. Once he'd straightened up I realized I'd been a
couple inches short in my estimation of his height. He waved
me toward an empty table maybe ten feet from where we
stood. As I turned to follow, Artie spoke for the first time.
His voice was so soft I could barely hear him.

I bent down. "Pardon?"

"It raining out there yet?"

"Not yet."

Frowning, he shook his head. "Too bad. We need more
rain."

"We're supposed to get some before morning."

That nugget seemed to make him happy, so I mumbled
something about it being nice to meet him and turned
toward the table where Miller and my beer awaited me.

Either Miller wore a toupee or his hair had one of the
strangest color configurations I'd ever seen. It was dark
around the crown, but his considerable sideburns and the
hair on the back of his head were gray. I wondered how a
person could possibly not notice that his hair was two
different colors. I also wondered how often one was supposed
to wash a toupee.

"How'd you know I was working for Jubal Tanner?"

Miller smiled the half smile of someone who usually has
a cigarette plugged in one corner. "Word gets around."

I studied him over the rim of the beer glass.

"Don't tell me you're tryin' to keep it a secret."

I shrugged. "Just like to know who you've been talking to."

"Well." He leaned back in the chair and looked up at the
ceiling. "I was in Foxport the other day. Stopped in at the
Tattersall." He dropped his attention back to me. "Got to
talking with a couple of the locals about the murder, and
then one of them told me about that set-to between Brig and

Jubal. Your name came up. That's all." He shrugged like that really was all there was to it. I could either believe him or not; that was the only story I was getting.

"Okay, what can you tell me about those two?"

He reached into a black-and-yellow-checked wool jacket and pulled a pack of Marlboros out of his breast pocket, then squinted at me through the smoke as he lit one. "What's it worth?"

"I don't know. You haven't told me anything yet." I lit my own cigarette, did my own squinting. "I need a hint at least."

He nodded. "Okay. How's this? It's got to do with a woman." He smiled again, this time a full smile. His teeth were large and yellow, and I thought of a horse named Scott. "Doesn't it always?"

I studied him through the haze, wondering how much to invest in his knowledge. "What's it got to do with the murder?"

He shrugged. "Maybe nothing. Maybe everything. Depends what you do with it." That smile again.

Sighing, I reached into my back pocket and pulled out my wallet. I gave him a twenty.

He frowned like it wasn't near what he'd ordered. "I had something more in mind."

"I didn't."

He looked at the bill without moving. "I think what I've got is worth more than that. Maybe five times."

I gave him a look that I hoped expressed my lack of enthusiasm. "If you convince me of that, I'll toss in another twenty."

He studied me for a minute, shrugged, and took the twenty, stuffing it into his shirt pocket. "Jubal didn't marry until he was in his forties. Ever wonder why?"

"It never crossed my mind."

"Well, for years he went with a woman named Barbara Zimmer." He raised his eyebrows, waiting to see if I would react. I shrugged. "Doesn't ring any bells?"

I sighed and rubbed my forehead. Either I was developing

a whale of a headache or this guy had discovered a direct route to my irritation center. "No it doesn't, and I thought you were supposed to give me answers, not questions."

"Barbara Zimmer was Brig Tanner's wife." He shot a stream of smoke toward the ceiling. "That's how she wound up anyway."

"What happened?"

"Well, you know, it was more Jubal's fault than he'll ever admit. The two of them, they went together for years. Jubal just never got around to popping the question. While he wasn't looking, Brig stole her away." He shrugged. "Some say it served him right. Maybe that's true. Can't ask a woman like that to wait forever. Anyway, Jubal left town for a while. Came back with Claude. She's a good woman." He blinked his eyes once, slowly. "Better than he deserves at any rate."

"This doesn't sound like a big secret."

"It's not. Though you'll never hear either of them talking about it. Lots of folks know. You just haven't talked to anyone who's been around here as long as the Tanners."

I leaned back in my chair, sighing. "Then what am I paying you twenty bucks for?"

He raised his eyebrows, affronted. "I didn't bring you out here at gunpoint. Nobody forced you."

"Yeah, well, I guess I expected to hear something I couldn't pick up at the local watering hole."

"Now did I say that's all I had?"

"If there's more, you'd better hurry." I lifted my beer, which was half full. "When this is gone, I'm gone. I haven't heard anything worth twenty yet, let alone forty."

"You know how Barbara Tanner died."

"I heard it was a riding accident."

He nodded. "That's true. I always thought that was kind of suspicious. I'm not the only one, either. Barbara was quite a horsewoman. Accidents happen, but . . ."

"You're saying someone broke her neck?"

"It would indicate a pattern, wouldn't it?"

"You're saying Jubal . . ."

"I'm saying nothing of the kind. Only that Brig Tanner's got some real bad luck when it comes to keeping his women alive."

I shook my head. Why had I bothered? "I'd say that information is worth about the price of this beer."

He smiled that yellow smile again. "Sets you to wondering, doesn't it?"

"Not really."

Miller's glass was empty, and he was looking for the waitress. Although I didn't know what the going rate is for an answer, I figured if I was giving him another twenty, I had a few more coming. "You know anything about that horse Brig bought?"

"You want another?" As he was signaling to the waitress, he glanced at my half-empty glass. I shook my head. That task completed, he leaned back in his chair and folded his arms across his chest. "What horse you talking about?"

"The one Brig and Jubal had the fight over."

He gave me a blank stare.

"Surprised you didn't hear about it. Especially if you were talking to someone at the Tattersall."

He chuckled. "So that's what they were fighting about? Doesn't surprise me a bit, to tell the truth. They go at it over the piddliest things."

I nodded, then finished my beer in three large swallows. "Well, Mr. Miller, thanks a lot. I know I'm a better person for what you've shared with me."

Miller shrugged off the sarcasm and held out his hand.

I shook my head. "The way I see it, you owe me change."

Miller shrugged again and went back to his beer.

As I got up, I turned to make sure Artie wasn't going to miss my exit and was surprised to find the table empty and Artie nowhere in sight.

It felt good to leave Yancy's and hit the cool, clean air. After paying for what amounted to a twenty-two dollar beer, I needed it. I'd gotten more out of what Miller had not said than what he had said. Unless I misjudged him, Ron Miller was the kind of man who thrived on gossip. I couldn't believe he'd listen to the details of a Tanner fight and not try to find out what the fight was about. Unless he had been there that night and was going to great lengths to have me think otherwise.

As I approached my car, I was relieved to see that the pickup truck and the devil dog had moved on. Then I realized that my car wasn't there either. Unless it had turned into a black Olds. Wait a minute. I looked up to get my bearings. Where was the fence? I don't get lost in parking lots. I have an uncanny sense of place. I can . . . I heard a dog barking from the row behind me. What the hell? There was the truck and my Honda. At this point, I was still so confident in my ability to find my way around a parking lot, I assumed that someone with a weird sense of humor was playing a joke on me.

Then the car wouldn't start, and I was sure I was the subject of some hoax. That is, until I realized I hadn't pushed in the clutch. I ground the gears a couple times trying to find first and knew I couldn't blame that on anyone but myself. But then I managed to make it out of the parking lot and onto Grover Park Road without any further complications, so I chalked off the confusion to the smoke and grease.

Traffic was light on I-88. We were too far west for any city traffic, and most of the commuters were probably home by now. I went to shift into overdrive, but the shift beneath my palm felt strange. At first I couldn't feel it at all, but it had to be there because I couldn't push my hand down any farther. Then when I finally got a grip on it, it began pulsating beneath my touch. Then it started to squirm. I jerked my hand away and saw that instead of a gearshift, I'd been gripping the head of a cobra, its hood expanded and its eyes shining like black diamonds. A horn blasted in my ear, and I looked up to see I had swerved the car into the right lane, narrowly missing a semi. The guy laid on his horn again, and I dropped back, pulling behind him. The engine was

screaming for a higher gear and I glanced at the shift. It
looked normal enough now. I tentatively touched it. This
time it felt like a gearshift's supposed to, and I slipped it into
fifth. Damn.

I concentrated on the truck in front of me, following its
mud flaps. My car was flying. It must have been because I
felt no bumps in the road. I couldn't even feel the road.
Resisting the impulse to brake, I stared straight ahead at the
truck. It seemed to be holding the road. I was okay for a
minute, then I saw that the truck's back panel had slid up
a few inches and something was starting to pour out. At first
it came out in drops, then a steady stream. I eased my foot
off the accelerator as the liquid began to ooze onto the road.
A car was coming up next to me. I glanced over my shoulder
and saw Artie Fotchke's face filling the window of the car.
His eyes were like slits as he smiled at me, and his face was
grotesque and rubberlike as though he were melting. Then
he waved good-bye and shot ahead. I jerked my head back
toward the truck just as its panel slid up another foot and a
tidal wave of red gushed out. I slammed down on the brakes
as the deluge of blood hit my windshield, blinding me. My
car spun, careened sideways, metal grated against metal,
there was one big flash of white, then dark.

▽

15

I THOUGHT I was waking from a nap—an afternoon nap that left me groggy and unsettled. My nose itched, but I couldn't raise my arms. They must have also been asleep and were waking up slower than the rest of me.

"Quint?"

The voice was familiar, but I couldn't place it in context with the smells—sharp, acrid, and antiseptic. She barely spoke above a whisper. I felt I should respond, but when I tried to open my mouth, it was like someone had glued it together. I could even taste the glue. I said something like, "Mmph."

"It's me. Elaine."

"Good." My nose was driving me crazy and even worse was the fact that no matter how hard I tried, I couldn't move either arm to scratch it.

"Don't try to move too much. You're in a hospital, and they've got you tied down so you won't hurt yourself."

"Huh?"

"You were pretty, um, upset. But it's okay now."

"Upset?" My mind was a huge blank, but it seemed to me, even in the foggy recesses of my brain, that when you wake up in restraints, you've been doing some serious damage either to yourself or to someone else.

"You were in an accident. Do you remember?" I could feel her hand, soft on my fingers. So they weren't numb after all.

"Give me a minute." I worked at opening my eyes and managed to get one working. The other wouldn't budge at first, and then when I finally cracked it, I caught a glimpse of diffused light before the pain forced it shut again.

"You've got a scratch on your eye. You'll need the patch for a few days." The room was bright, and once the vision in my good eye cleared, I saw Elaine's face, drawn and pale. Her hair was pulled back in a ponytail.

"You're going to be okay," she said. "Really."

I did a quick inventory of my body parts and everything seemed to be in working order.

"Other than the eye, you're fine."

"Anything you're trying to break to me slowly?" I mumbled and was rewarded with a tiny smile as she shook her head.

Closing my eye again, I tried to remember. "Anyone else involved?"

"No one else was hurt." Even to my muddled brain, that sounded evasive, but she continued before I could figure out why. "Your car, well, it needs some work."

That was the second Honda I'd managed to trash in as many years. "Guess I gotta stop buying those foreign models." I squinted at her.

"Any word from Peanuts."

She looked confused. "Peanuts?"

"Later."

For several minutes, she just stood there with her arm resting on the metal side rails, which I was tied to. She was being tentative, and that made me uneasy. There was more here, and she didn't know how to say it. "You're sure no one else was hurt?"

"No one."

I squinted at her. "Am I in trouble?"

She shifted her gaze away from me. Bingo. "Um, well, a little."

"Like how little?"

"Well, it depends on what happened before the accident. What I mean is, you were on drugs." Before I could say anything, she rushed ahead. "I told them that was crazy,

that you didn't do drugs, but they said you were definitely
on something."

I tried to force some memories back into my head, but
nothing would stick—just flashes of a tavern and a parking lot.

"Do you remember anything?"

"Just images. Vague ones at that."

"Well, I guess you were acting crazy. I told him it must be
the drugs. . . ."

"What drugs?"

"LSD."

"Jesus," I said.

"I mean, they're not sure, but from the way you were
acting. . . . They said they'd seen it before."

"What was I doing?"

She bent over, resting her arm on the bed rail and her chin
on her arm. "Acting kind of crazy, hallucinating. . ." she said
and rushed ahead with, "The cops said the airbag probably
saved your life."

The airbag. The flash of white. That was when it started
dribbling back. Yancy's, the fat man—Artie—and Ron Miller.

I heard movement in the room, and Elaine straightened
up and turned toward the door.

A tall, thin man wearing a starched khaki shirt and tie
approached the bed. His hands were folded in front of him,
and he eyed me like I was a rattlesnake he wasn't sure was
dead. After the appraisal, he nodded at Elaine like they'd met
before, then introduced himself as Deputy Stevens. "I see
you're back among the living. I've got a few questions." I'll
bet he did.

His nose was long and narrow and he had a deep cleft in
his chin—together, they reminded me of an exclamation
point. "You want to tell me what happened?"

"I don't remember much."

"Start there."

I told him about the phone call from Ron Miller, and as I
told the story, events came back to me—meeting Artie
Fotchke, a rather useless conversation with Miller. The last

thing I recalled was confusion about where I'd parked my car. "I didn't think much of it, though. I don't know why I didn't. I mean, I usually know where I'm going."

"You're saying you only had one beer."

"Yeah. That's all."

"Do you do any drugs?"

Elaine was standing there, arms crossed over her chest. I could tell she wanted to set this guy straight, but her sense of caution prevailed. I was relieved.

"No, I don't do drugs." Not anymore, anyway. I hadn't done drugs for a long time, and even then it was only marijuana, which never agreed with me. Rather than develop a nice mellow buzz, I got paranoid. I knew I wasn't in charge. Granted, with booze you can lose control, but you don't realize it until the next morning. I had never experimented with anything stronger than marijuana. I don't say that with any trace of superiority either. I simply don't like losing control. Seems my grip on things has a tendency to be tenuous. I didn't need anything making it worse for me. I didn't "just say no." I turned down drugs the same way I turned down liver and rap music. I just don't care for them.

"Any idea how you got dosed with LSD?"

"Could someone have slipped something in your beer?" Elaine asked.

I remembered it wasn't a very good beer. Weak and slightly flat. Hell, a dose of LSD probably would have improved the taste.

"Well, at one point this Miller guy took both our beers to another table, and Artie asked me something about the weather. I remember at the time thinking he wasn't the sort of person to make small talk. But I didn't make much more of it."

"Can you describe these guys?" the deputy asked.

Ron Miller's description didn't seem to ring any bells for him, but Artie Fotchke did. The deputy closed his eyes and nodded in resigned recognition. "Sounds like Artie the Slab."

"Artie the Slab?" Elaine almost smiled.

"Yeah." He laughed a little. "You've gotta be careful not to call him Artie the Slob. He's real sensitive."

"Who is he?" I asked.

"Calls himself a horse breeder, though wheeler-dealer is more like it. Raises thoroughbreds. Races some. Sells some."

He snapped a small spiral notebook shut and slid it into his breast pocket. "You happen to know how the LSD got in your glove box?"

"What?"

"I think the next call you make better be to your lawyer."

"This is nuts. You have priors on me?"

"Not for drugs. Though you were arrested for assault and battery."

"Then you also know the charges were dropped."

"Yeah, well, I don't think this is gonna be so easy. Like I said, call a lawyer." Then the deputy nodded to me and Elaine. "I'll check this out. We'll talk again." He left the room.

Elaine rolled her eyes heavenward.

"I suppose you spent most of the night defending me."

"Yeah, I guess. When I wasn't worrying, I guess I was defending."

"Thank you." I gave her hand a squeeze. "Hand me the phone, would you?"

"I'll dial for you. Who you calling?"

I mentioned the name of a lawyer who is also a client, but I couldn't remember his number.

"Never mind," Elaine said. "I'll get it."

Cal Maitlin wasn't in, but with considerable coaching from Elaine, I explained the situation to his secretary, who promised he'd get back to me as soon as possible.

After that I dozed off for a while and dreamed of a blood red landscape covered with short lengths of rope. As I got closer, there were more of them. Then the ropes became snakes, and they were slithering around my feet and ankles—a sea of snakes.

When I woke, my head was clear enough so that the full

impact of what had happened was able to sink in. I felt
alternating flashes of rage and shame and wanted to crawl
out of my skin. I had to get out of the hospital. The doctor
tried to convince me to stay another night, saying that the
drug hadn't worked its way out of my system yet. But I
wouldn't even discuss it, and once I signed a release, he quit
arguing. Elaine brought me some fresh clothes, and my body
creaked and groaned as I changed into them. Just as I was
about to leave, Cal Maitlin called.

"You're really in quite a mess, you know."

"Thanks for telling me. What can we do about it?"

"You claim someone drugged you?"

"Yeah."

"Can you prove it?"

"Kind of hard, isn't it?"

"Well, I think we better concentrate on that right now.
Not only are you facing DUI charges—with an automatic
license suspension—but that stuff they found in your car is
a felony offense. You're not only talking jail time, but you
lose your PI license."

I sighed. "Okay, what's the good news?"

"I'm afraid the only good news is that you've got one
damned fine lawyer on your side." He paused, giving me the
opportunity to agree. When I didn't respond, he continued.
"Come in and see me when you get out of there. We'll work
something out."

I was halfway out the door when I had my final visitor. Gene
Moore was standing in the hall, hands on his hips, staring
at the door. It was almost as though he'd been waiting there
for a while, just willing me to come out.

"Gee, I didn't know they'd posted a guard at my door. How
thoughtful."

Moore scowled as he brushed past me into my room. I
stood by the door, a brown sack with my accident clothes in
it thrust under my arm. "I was on my way out."

"This'll just take a minute."

I shrugged and stepped inside so the door could close.
"What?"

"I hear you've found yourself some big trouble."

"It's not your concern. I believe the sheriff is handling
this. You might want to talk with him, though. Maybe he
could use a consultant."

"Cut the smartass crap, McCauley." Moore was leaning
against the window ledge, watching me. "Any of this got
anything to do with that girl's murder?"

I figured this must be really painful for him. The last read
I'd gotten on him was that he didn't want me within sight.
Now he was actually seeking me out. He must be getting
desperate too. Maybe he deserved a straight answer. "I'm not
sure. At this point I have no reason to believe there's a
connection."

"What were you doing out at Yancy's?" He removed a set
of keys from his pocket and began fidgeting with them.

"Talking to some guy who said he knew something about
the Tanners. Some deep secret. Turned out to be neither deep
nor a secret."

"Heard you were out at Hines's place."

"Yeah. Who told you?"

He stared at me for a few seconds, the keys still, before
saying, "One of my men was out there." I shrugged and he
continued. "I suppose you think there's a connection between the horse and the girl's murder?"

"It crossed my mind."

"You talked to Dworski too."

"Your sources are very reliable."

"Back off."

"Why?"

" 'Cause people don't like you bothering them."

"Don't tell me Dworski complained?"

He ran a hand through his hair, and I noticed a thin film
of sweat at the top of his forehead. "Nobody likes you
breathing down their neck. So just stay out of it. We'll do
the interviewing."

"Whatever you say."

If he was surprised by my compliance, he didn't show it. He bounced the keys in the palm of his hand, then pocketed them. "Don't make me remind you."

Elaine picked me up in a blue Ford Taurus that I'd never seen before. "I rented it," she explained. "Figured you'll need something until your car's fixed."

"Do you know where they took my car?"

She smiled. "The usual place. Tony said it's salvageable."

"Can't wait to see what this is going to do to my insurance rates." I patted my shirt pocket for cigarettes and came up empty.

"There's some in my purse."

"God bless you." I found them and peeled off the cellophane strip.

"You know, this might be a good time to quit," Elaine said, keeping her eyes on the road. "I mean you've gone, what, almost a day without one, haven't you?"

"It's not a good idea to quit if you're under stress." I pushed in the cigarette lighter. "And that's what I'm under." I hoped she'd drop the subject.

"What was that about Peanuts?"

This wasn't much of an improvement. "Somebody swiped him."

"What?"

"They swiped him yesterday morning and left me a note, telling me to stay out of the Tanner business."

"Jesus, Quint."

"He's okay. I know he is. Somebody's just trying to rattle me."

"But . . ."

I had a feeling this episode had been a warning to me and had a nagging suspicion that killing a dog wouldn't be out of character for this person. I responded with more anger than I'd intended. "What am I supposed to do? Jubal's got no one on his side. Should I let him fend for himself because someone got to me? What the hell am I supposed to do?"

After a minute, she said, her voice even, "You're right. It's just that . . ."

"I know."

She drew in a deep breath. "You know, I'm glad you decided to computerize."

"I knew you would be." Grateful for the way she read me so well, I yanked the lighter out, which was barely glowing enough to light my cigarette. I pulled in the smoke and immediately went into a coughing fit.

It must have taken every ounce of self-control for Elaine not to comment, but she continued with the computer subject. "You'll like working with them."

"We'll see." How long before I figured out where this conversation was heading?

She turned onto Main Street and seemed to be concentrating on her driving, but I knew better.

Computers weren't really the subject here, but in order to get there, I should play along. "You find a good one yet?"

"I haven't exactly had a lot of time."

I rubbed the stubble on my chin as I tried to think. Elaine glanced at me. "You look like you shaved with a dull razor."

I pulled the visor down and examined my mangled face and the big white patch over my eye.

"How do you like the beard?"

"Well, right now it makes you look like a bum."

"Why, thank you."

"Either that or a narc."

"Maybe in a few days it'll be really sexy."

"Mmm," was all she said, but it said a lot.

We rode in silence for a few minutes, and as I watched the outskirts of Foxport slide by, I figured I should be looking at it like a man who's gotten a last-minute reprieve. Instead, the colors and shapes reminded me how persistently normal things seem even when you're screaming on the inside.

Elaine broke the silence. "Does your eye hurt?"

"Not really. The doctor gave me some pills in case it does."

I paused. "Think I'll stick with aspirin."

We turned left onto Main Street. "Is Carver back yet?"

She gave me a sharp look. "No. Did you talk to him?"

"Yeah, yesterday afternoon. He said he'd get back as soon as he could, but he wasn't specific." Then I asked, "Where are we going?"

"I don't know. Back to the office, I guess. Why? Is there somewhere else you want to go?"

After a moment, I said, "Yeah. I want to go back to that bar. See if I can find out who this Ron Miller is."

After a few seconds, Elaine said, "You want to go back there, you're going to have to take yourself."

"What's that supposed to mean?"

"Why don't you let the sheriff's department handle it?"

"They're going to handle it by slapping me with a DUI charge and yanking my license."

She took a deep breath. "Tell me about this Ron Miller. What did he look like?"

"Really tall. At least six and a half feet. Skinny. Picture Ichabod Crane with a toupee."

"He wears a rug?"

"Yeah, a pretty bad one too."

"Let's go to the police."

"What a guy does with his hair is his own business, Elaine."

She gave me a sideways glance that said to stop the bullshitting. "How come you didn't give the deputy that detailed a description?"

"At the time I wasn't real clear. Some of it's just hitting me now." We were passing through downtown Foxport and were stopped at a red light. I watched a few pedestrians cross in front of us.

"Quint, you're not thinking of taking this into your own hands, are you?"

I didn't answer.

"Quint, you're not. That's crazy."

I looked at her. "You know what crazy is? Crazy is losing

control. Acting like a goddamned animal. Worse than an animal. They don't go nuts for no reason. God, I cringe every time—"

"You know what makes *me* cringe?"

I didn't answer. Something in her tone of voice made me wary.

"I cringe when I think I might have spent the night at the morgue instead of the hospital." She turned to me, her brown eyes sparking. "You know, I don't want to nag, but I've gotta say this. I worry about you. You scared me to death last night." Someone behind us honked, but she didn't seem to notice. "And you're getting all bent out of shape over making a fool of yourself, when you didn't have any control over it to begin with." Another honk.

"Elaine . . ."

"You really tick me off sometimes, you know?"

"Elaine." The light was quite green and cars were pulling around us. Elaine was oblivious to the nasty looks we were earning.

"I know this sounds selfish, but you know, you're not the only one who gets hurt if you wind up dead or something. I'm sorry to sound this way, but I can't help it." She took a deep breath, like she was fighting back a sob. "I don't know if we're going to make it in the long run, but right now you're my best friend. I need you. You're the only thing I've got that's constant. If I lost you, I'd fall apart."

She seemed to be finished then, so I said, "No, you wouldn't."

"Yes, I would. And here you are agonizing over the fact that you went crazy through no fault of your own." She finally heard someone honk. "Oh."

"Never mind, it's yellow again." She sped through the light as it turned red. "No. I guess I'd like to think you need me that bad, but I'm flattering myself. You don't know how strong you are. Yeah, maybe you're working with a net now, but you don't need it." I sighed. "I wish you did, but you don't."

"I don't think that's true."

"Sure it is. You're a survivor."

She was quiet for a minute, then she said, "I'm sorry. You don't need me dumping on you right now." After another pause she added, "I guess I can understand how you must feel—violated."

I nodded. "That's a good word for it."

"Really, don't go after these guys on your own. But"—her voice softened—"I am glad you had listed my name as the person to contact in an emergency."

She sniffed and dragged the back of her hand across her cheek. I dug a Kleenex out of her purse. It had lipstick smudges on it, but that didn't seem to bother her. "So," she said, "back to the original question: Where to now?"

I told her about the call I'd made to Warren Hines and the invoice to Tom Erdman, which might or might not have anything to do with the case. "I'd like to know a little more about Hines, like who this Tom Erdman is and why Hines goes pale at the sight of one of Erdman's bills." I paused. "I guess I don't exactly feel up to beating information out of anyone today. But maybe Jim Dworski might be able to tell us something."

"Is that the guy who works for Brig?"

"Yeah, he works for Hines too. Maybe he knows something about this Erdman character. Besides, Moore said Dworski didn't like being bothered. That's reason enough for me."

"I'd feel a lot better if you'd just take all this to the police."

"I'm not exactly comfortable taking anything to the police with Moore in charge. I know this sounds out of character, but I think I'll wait until Carver gets back."

We stopped at a pay phone, and Elaine called Cindy to find out if Dworski was there. I stayed in the car. My eye was starting to hurt, so I dug through Elaine's purse until I found a small tin of aspirin. I managed to swallow two of them dry, but their taste wouldn't leave my mouth.

16

Elaine climbed back into the car and snapped her seat belt in place. She took a deep breath. "Well, according to Cindy, Jim Dworski didn't show up for work today, but she says that's not all that unusual. It seems this guy isn't what you'd call reliable."

I nodded. "Maybe he needs a lot of those mental health days."

"No doubt. But I've got his address." She was giving me an odd look. "Are you sure you're up to this? I mean, maybe you should think about taking your own mental health day."

She was wearing her glasses, and I was annoyed with myself for not noticing that earlier. This hadn't been easy on her either, in ways probably tougher. I mean, I got to sleep most of the night—it looked like it had been a while for her. Sighing, she glanced at the scrap of paper in her hand. "Well, we're out. We're in the car. We might as well do it." She handed the paper to me. "Where is this?"

Hidden Valley was the rather quaint name of a not-so-quaint area northwest of Foxport. I gave her directions, and she paused a beat before starting the car.

I should have told her to forget it, let's just go home, but the idea of just sitting there, thinking, seemed tougher than my other options.

As we drove, Elaine began to fill me in on Gayle Millard. She'd questioned some of the people Gayle had worked with at Star Electric. "You know, every one of them said it was a shame and all how she died, but I don't think anyone lost any liquid over her, if you know what I mean. Most said she was pleasant enough to everyone at first, then got to be selective. You know, if the person was in a position to help her get ahead or could make her job easier, then she was nice. But if you're talking, say, lowly secretary or warehouse stocker, then forget it. She was out for herself and apparently made no bones about it. She didn't have many friends and didn't seem to need them." She paused and gave me a significant look. "With the notable exception of her boss."

"Are we talking interoffice romance?"

She shrugged. "According to a couple of the women, Gayle and her boss, Ted Pryor—married, two and a half kids—occasionally took these marathon lunches together."

"Marathon?"

"In terms of hours. And who knows what else. But that cooled real fast when she became involved with Brig Tanner. Lately, she was giving everyone at the company the impression that she was short-term."

We drove in silence for a minute. "Elaine, mind if I ask how you managed to get all these people to talk?"

"I've been in an office situation like that before. Gayle Millard was prime lunchtime gossip material. I took several of the office women out to lunch and just listened." She glanced at me, smiling. "The bill's on your desk."

I was just beginning to understand the advantages of having Elaine on my team and was wondering if maybe I shouldn't just drop out and let her handle the whole thing. In the time she'd dug up some good information, I'd been both duped and doped. Thoughts of early retirement were suddenly appealing.

She continued. "And, you know what else is interesting? Here I was figuring that everyone would be sick of talking about Gayle, what with the police questioning them and all. Not so. Apparently, the police have barely made an appearance. Most of the women I talked to hadn't even been questioned."

"I guess Brig's got Moore convinced that he was the target.

Poor old Brig is sure gonna be disappointed if it turns out that nobody wanted him dead."

We were heading north on Route 41, up a winding two-lane road. Coming out of an S-curve, Elaine had to brake to keep from running up the back of a truck hauling bales of hay. "Damn," she muttered as she slowed to thirty. She irritably tucked a stray lock of hair behind her ear and shook her head. "And then there's the call that Gayle supposedly got. You know, the have-I-got-a-saddle-for-you call. I think I've tried every person in this county who has ever owned a saddle, let alone wanted to sell one. Most have never heard of Gayle Millard. The few who knew her said they hadn't talked to her in weeks. Of course," she mused briefly, "I could have missed one. But I think she never got such a call."

My back was starting to bother me, so I shifted position. "Okay, let's say you did hit all of them. That means that she lied to Brig about the phone call. Why?"

"Well, I figure it's one of two things. Either she had a big surprise for Brig and didn't want to spoil it, or she was sneaking out on him. And the big surprise thing isn't very likely. I mean, if that were the case, someone would have come forward by now."

"Besides," I added, "I don't see Gayle as the surprise type. Unless she were on the receiving end. For whatever reason, this was something she didn't want Brig to know about."

"I think it was another man."

"I'd buy that." I nodded, considering the implications. Brig Tanner seemed awfully possessive. How far would jealousy drive him?

"The thing is," Elaine continued, edging around the truck, then ducking back quickly when a BMW whizzed by. "Why wouldn't Brig kill the man Gayle was seeing instead of killing her? That smacks of cutting off your nose to spite your face."

"Well, even if he is that kind of guy, there is still a physical problem. In order to kill her, he would have to have been in two places at the same time."

"Yeah, but he's got money. Easy enough to arrange it."

I'd thought of that too and admitted it added a whole new dimension to the investigation. A hired killer frequently had no connection with the victim.

Elaine was frowning, and now she shook her head. "I am trying to make this fit Brig Tanner, aren't I?" Before I could agree with her, she continued. "I just don't like the man. I have a bad feeling about him."

"I had a talk with him."

"And?"

"Well, I'm not so inclined to pigeonhole the guy. I think both he and his brother were the product of a father who liked pitting his kids against each other. It's weird. To hear Jubal tell it, Brig was always the winner. But according to Brig that was only the case later in life when the competition expanded beyond the family background." I recalled Brig's distress as he talked about Gayle and Barbara but kept that to myself. "Besides, if we're talking motive here, there are plenty of possibilities. If Brig was going to marry Gayle and write her into his will, then Cindy may have a damned good motive."

"Will would have too," she countered.

"I know. All I'm saying is you can't just rule someone out because you like them. And you can't condemn someone just because you don't." Pearls of wisdom from the crusty, jaded PI. I needed an attitude adjustment.

A smile played at the corners of her mouth as she glanced at me. "You mean that isn't how you people do these investigations?"

"Of course not. We also employ Ouija boards." I saw Dworski's street coming up and told Elaine to turn left at the stop sign.

Hidden Valley was a speck of a suburb crammed between Foxport and Henderson. For years Hidden Valley had been trying to get itself annexed to either one of them, but neither town wanted to claim the little community with its un-mowed lawns, dingy taverns, and homes that some people had the audacity to paint in strange shades of pink and aqua.

The place always seemed more rural than it was, mainly because there was no sign of a convenience store or a sidewalk. The main reason people knew of the place was the Pump Jockey gas station, which regularly undersold its name-brand competitors by five or six cents a gallon. No, nobody wanted to live in Hidden Valley, but lots of people didn't mind going ten miles out of their way to save a few bucks on gas.

Jim Dworski's house was off the main street by about a half mile, down a road in serious need of repairs. The small house had been white at one time, but now its sides were streaked with dirt. It looked like someone had started to wash the house—the lower left corner in the front was considerably whiter than the rest—then given up. The lawn was scraggly with lots of bare patches. One rolled-up news-paper lay across another. It was like the delivery person hit the same spot every day. About seven cars occupied a large patch of dirt next to the house. All were rusted out, missing various parts of their anatomies, and were parked in a random manner so they resembled a herd of bizarre, grazing beasts. Another car, which was rusty but might have enough parts to run, was parked in a narrow, gravel driveway that curved past the house and into the backyard.

There was no doorbell, so I pounded on the aluminum door. From deep in the house, a dog barked. Elaine and I looked at each other. I pounded again. The barking contin-ued, but never got any louder, as if the animal were confined.

"I'm willing to bet that if this guy had a dog, it'd be a rottweiler or a Doberman. That's a Peanuts-sized dog."

The knob moved when I turned it. I pushed the door open. "Dworski? You here?"

No answer from Dworski, but the barking became frantic, and I could hear claws scraping at wood. We moved through the small kitchen and past a chipped Formica table with an open bottle of Scotch and a half-empty glass. The room had a stale, sweet smell, and there was a saucepan half full of something that might have been spaghetti sauce midway

between the liquid and solid state. The scratching came from
the other side of a door in the kitchen, which probably led
down to a cellar. There was whining now; I was sure it was
Peanuts. Elaine stopped me as I reached for the doorknob.
"Are you positive there's a friendly dog on other side?"
Why not ask? "Peanuts?"
The dog hesitated, then went crazy barking and clawing.
I opened the door an inch and a black nose poked its way
out. I threw the door open and forty pounds of black-and-
white fur caught me right in the chest, sending me down on
my knees. I grabbed him and pulled him against me. For
once I didn't mind his dog breath. His tongue scraped against
the stubble on my face.

Elaine had her arm around his neck and gently pushed
his nose away from my eyepatch. When he'd finally settled
down a little, I tried to put him at arm's length. One arm
wasn't enough, so Elaine held him by the collar. "Let's see
how you look, fella." Even though he squirmed and wiggled
under her grip, I managed to run my hand down his back
and his legs. Everything seemed to check out. "Looks like he
ate okay."

"Quint, he's only been gone a day."
I had to run that through my own memory before I
conceded. Elaine smiled. "It only seems like a decade."

Peanuts followed right on my heels as we checked out the
rest of the house. I was learning the disadvantages of having
one eye bandaged. You lost some of your depth perception. I
had to move slowly to keep from running into doorways.

It was a small house with Spartan furnishings. Actually,
it reminded me a little of my place. There were two bed-
rooms, the second a makeshift study with a small bookcase
filled with auto magazines. What struck me was how clean
everything was. Even the bathroom sink, though chipped
and slightly rusted, looked like it was scrubbed on a regular
basis, which made me wonder about the mess in the kitchen.

Elaine cleared her throat. "Um, maybe we should call the
police."

I stepped out into the hall. Something else was bothering me, but I couldn't pin it down. From where I stood I could see through the bedroom window into the backyard and the garage where the rear end of a Chevy Impala—circa '75—protruded. A single light bulb was suspended from a wire attached to the ceiling. I went back through the front room and into the kitchen. A fluorescent overhead light glowed dully. Elaine was watching me. Waiting. "All the lights are on like it's dark out. Only it's a bright afternoon." I glanced at my watch. "It's not even four."

"Yeah? So?"

"Let's check out the garage."

Much to his dismay, we left Peanuts in the house and cut across the yard. As we approached the garage, the sounds of rock music grew louder. The rear of the Chevy stuck up at an odd angle, and as I moved around the car, I saw there were no tires on the front axle. A can of beer sat next to a jack that lay on its side, and sticking out from under the front fender were black high tops, a pair of legs, and the lower half of a torso. "Jesus."

Elaine gasped. I took hold of the fender with both hands and pulled up, but apparently my adrenaline was low. I maneuvered the jack under the fender, and with a smack of my palm, lodged it in place. We both pumped the handle.

As soon as the car rose a couple inches, I grabbed Dworski's ankles and pulled. I wasn't holding out much hope that he was alive at this point but did hope he came out in one piece. He did, but it didn't make much difference in the end. The weight of the car had come down right on his chest, crushing it. Dried blood covered his jaw and neck, and his eyes were frozen wide. At first I thought they were moving, but then I realized that only the maggots were moving. Elaine gagged and turned away. From the smell of things, he's been dead awhile. He wore a dark plaid shirt with the cuffs rolled up. The parts of his arms closest to the ground were a bluish purple. The discoloration resembled a bruise but was probably caused by his blood, no longer in circulation, responding to gravity. I slid my hand under his wrist and lifted his arm to see how much movement there was. When I released him, I realized I'd been holding my breath. I took in a quick lungful and slapped my sleeve over my mouth and nose. As I stepped away from him, I was thinking there were worse things than being drugged and busted up.

Elaine's hand on my shoulder brought me back. "Quint, maybe now we should call the police." This time I had to agree.

A squad car from the Abel County Sheriff's Department responded in about fifteen minutes. I put Peanuts in the car to keep him out of the way. The deputy was around my age and thick around the middle. He introduced himself as Mike Keenan. Aside from a slight grimace, he didn't seem fazed by the sight of the corpse. As he knelt for a closer examination, I saw Gene Moore and Henninger coming up the driveway. Why wasn't I surprised?

He nodded to the deputy, then walked around the Chevy to take in the full spectacle. After a glance at Dworski's body, he turned to me, his mouth twisted up like he'd just sucked a lemon. "You'd never get me under a ton of metal with just a jack supporting it. No way." For a change, I had to agree with Moore.

"Heard about this and thought I'd come take a look. May be related to a current case of ours," he said to Keenan, who nodded and moved away to consult with his partner.

Moore ran his thumb and forefinger down the corners of his mouth. "Thought I told you to keep your nose out of this. This is police business. What we call an ongoing investigation. What the hell were you doing out here?"

"We were going to ask him if he'd do a few chores around the house." Elaine nodded toward me. "He's got so much to do with the business, there's no time."

I was constantly impressed with Elaine's ability to tell a good story. Lie. Whatever.

Moore regarded her for a moment. "What did you say your name was again?"

She tried not to act pissed, but only partially succeeded. "Elaine. Elaine Kluszewski." Then she spelled it for him. Both parts.

"You think pretty fast, don't you?" He glanced at me. "You oughta take a few lessons."

"Maybe we both should," I said and proceeded to explain how we'd entered the unlocked house and found Peanuts locked in the basement.

"Somebody swiped your dog and you didn't report it?"

I sighed. "Well, you folks seemed to have your hands full."

"You got the ransom note?" I detected a touch of sarcasm.

"At home."

"What's it say?"

"It warned me off the Tanner case."

"We'll have to take a look at it."

"No problem."

Moore turned to Henninger. "I want you to see what you can turn up here. If he did kill that woman, he had to do something with the gun."

"Gee," I said to Moore, "you think maybe Jubal Tanner didn't do it?"

He stared in my direction, chewing his gum. "Easy enough to hire somebody."

"Maybe. But Mr. Dworski's not talking anymore."

Moore removed his sunglasses and squinted at me. "We'll see about that."

As we drove back into Foxport, Elaine said, "You think Jim Dworski was hired to kill Gayle? Or Brig?"

"I don't know."

"You sound kind of doubtful."

"Well, I guess I am. Not sure why." Peanuts' breath was on the back of my neck. "I guess it's partly because I have a hard time believing Peanuts would get in the car with Jim Dworski. He's got a pretty good sense of character." There was more that bothered me, but I was still trying to work it out.

"No offense, but I think you're giving your dog too much credit."

"I'm serious. He left the room whenever Bush gave a State of the Union address."

"Uncanny," Elaine murmured.

"When I talked to Jim Dworski at Brig's place a couple days ago, he was pretty vocal about his opinion of Gayle. It wasn't very high. Somehow I doubt he'd have said all that if he'd just killed her. Intentionally or otherwise."

"Maybe you're right."

We drove in silence for a few minutes. Peanuts had settled into the backseat.

"Will you come back to my place with me? And stay?" I didn't want to wake up alone.

"Sure." She barely hesitated.

We had to park behind a couple cars in our driveway. Louise must have had company. "I swear, that lady entertains more than I do." That wasn't saying much, but it was nice of Elaine not to agree.

"That's because she knows everyone in town."

Peanuts bounded ahead of us up the stairs. Elaine walked with me, her arm around my waist. It felt so good, I wanted to drop my head on her shoulder and fall asleep midstep. Peanuts' nose was in the door before it was open more than an inch, and he pushed the door out of my hand. He made a dash for the food dish and halfway there came to a skidding stop. I was two steps into my apartment before I saw why.

Three men were sitting in my living room. One of them stood. At first I didn't recognize him, but then I never thought I'd live to see Ed Carver out of his uniform.

$\triangledown$

17

WHAT WAS IT about Ed Carver and his accusatory posture that made me feel like a dog caught lapping water out of the toilet? I knew he was on his way back to Foxport, and in the back of my mind a little warning bell should have been clanging. I guess I hadn't figured that when Ed Carver left his connubial paradise, the end of his journey would be the couch in my apartment. I suppose these feelings of paranoia date back to one of our early encounters, during which he professed his undying disdain for me and his desire to nail my privates to the wall. First impressions have that indelible quality. Since then our relationship had improved somewhat, but gut-level responses are persistent, and the situation with Elaine had put a new spin on things.

I didn't need Dr. Ruth to tell me that Carver uprooting himself in the midst of a marriage encounter, or whatever they were engaged in, didn't bode well for the marriage. It also meant that he'd probably soon be just another one of us lonely bachelors. I've never thrived on competition and didn't look forward to dueling with him for Elaine. I could see it now—pistols at forty feet—maybe Elaine would shed a few tears over my bloodied torso. Then she'd get up, wring her hankie, and walk right into Carver's arms. With thoughts like that keeping me company, it's a wonder I don't slip while shaving.

I refocused on Carver. He really wasn't as tall as he looked. Maybe he had a couple inches on my six feet, but he was bony and angular with sharp features and a tendency to slouch. He reminded me of a hawk—keen-eyed and ominous, though a little less so in his crewneck sweater and jeans.

Jeff Barlowe was the other person on the couch, and my director's chair was occupied by a man with blond hair and a ruddy complexion. I knew he was a cop, but I couldn't place him.

I nodded at Carver. "When did you get back?"

"Late this afternoon." He shifted his stance, appearing vaguely uneasy and not at all familiar with the sensation.

I really wanted to sleep, but I could tell from the expressions on the three wise men that I'd have to put sleep on the back burner for a while. Peanuts turned his pointed nose up toward me, and the look was so human I almost laughed. It was like he was saying "And you call this being rescued?" Peanuts, being a sensitive dog, picked up on people who weren't immediately bowled over by his charm. And, being a reasonably bright dog, he kept his distance from them. Now he hung his head and quietly retreated into the kitchen. Carver had that effect on animals. Some people too.

Elaine, never one to let a conversation lapse, crossed the room and stepped right up to Ed. Elaine is tall—five eight or nine—and I had to admit that they complemented each other—each possessing their own brand of strength. "I'm sorry we had to call you. It's just that we thought . . ."

He held his hand up to stop her. "I'm glad you did. You were right, and it's worse than you knew."

I was still getting my bearings, something I didn't feel I should have to do in my own apartment. I felt the stirrings of hunger and recalled that I hadn't eaten much at lunch. For Peanuts it had been longer. I put food out for him, and he seemed grateful for the distraction. Then, as I stood in front of my refrigerator, empty of everything except a shriveled apple, a quarter slab of Velveeta wadded up in its foil, and a six-pack of beer, I wondered if Peanuts would be willing to share.

"Is anyone hungry?" I asked. Carver shrugged and returned to the couch. Elaine perched on the arm next to him.

Jeff jumped up and headed into the kitchen. "God, I'm starving. We helped ourselves to your beer, not much else was worth taking." And the other cop cocked his head and nodded. "I could eat."

Jeff stood behind me gazing into the open refrigerator. "Well, gang," he said, "how does pizza sound?"

As everyone murmured their assent, Jeff said, under his breath, "I hope you're not planning on sleeping for a while." Then, as though noticing my battered condition for the first time, added, "What the hell happened to you? Looks like you went head-on with a train."

"Later," I said.

"Give me a hint. Is this"—he waved his can of beer at my face—"related to the current state of Foxport's police department?"

"I sure as hell hope so." I hated to think there might be two separate situations to deal with.

Momentarily satisfied, Jeff frowned and nodded, then retreated back to the living room.

Carver introduced the other cop as Darryl Rush, one of his sergeants. He wore dark-rimmed glasses and flashed a wide gap between his front teeth when he smiled.

Jeff got the consensus on topping preferences and placed the order. I heard him tell them to throw in a couple six-packs of beer. When he hung up, he made a show of consulting his watch. "Thirty minutes and counting." Rubbing his hands together, he returned to the couch. "Well," he began, turning to Carver and pausing as he made a note of Elaine's proximity to Carver. "Why don't you go first?"

Carver took a deep breath and crossed his arms over his chest. "Well, I guess the long and short of it is, I'm being sent up the river."

Jeff nodded in agreement and waited for Carver to continue.

I stared at Jeff in utter amazement. I never thought I'd see the day the two of them shared a couch, let alone an opinion.

Rush shook his head. "It's pretty bizarre."

Elaine sipped from her can of beer and returned it to the Cubs coaster on the scarred end table.

Carver took a long drink out of his beer can, then nodded at Rush. "Why don't you tell them what you told me."

Rush crossed his right ankle over his left knee and paused for a minute, apparently collecting his thoughts. "Right after the Millard murder, next day I think it was, Brig Tanner showed up at the station to talk to Moore. They had this long, private talk, and when Moore walks out of his office, you know things have changed. I don't know what happened in there, but it was like one day Moore's using a corner of Carver's desk and the next day he's spread out over the whole thing."

"How was Brig acting when he left the meeting?" I said.

"All I can say is he left in a better mood than the one he came with." He turned to Carver. "Like I said, if I'd had your number, I'd have called you right then myself." I watched Carver as Rush told us how Moore had effectively split the police department, convincing a number of officers that they'd be better off if he were in charge on a permanent basis. Rush avoided Carver's gaze when he said, "I guess it was easy for him to convince some of these guys to write letters of complaint."

Carver twisted his mouth into a bitter smile. "Some things you can count on. Guys who slack off'll take any chance they can get to stick it to you."

It wasn't difficult for me to see how Carver might alienate some of the people who worked for him. He had no patience with laziness or ineptitude and had no qualms about dressing someone down in front of an audience. Usually his recriminations were deserved, but he sometimes had trouble discerning the line between ineptitude and an honest mistake.

"Anyway," Rush continued, "as you know Carver was demoted to sergeant at the last city council session. The motion was, of course, introduced by Brig Tanner. Some of us spoke up on his behalf, but Moore's crowd, well"—he glanced at Carver—"they had a few tricks up their sleeves."

Carver had leaned forward, elbows on knees, and was staring into his folded hands. Elaine remained impassive but attentive. "Like what?" I prompted.

"Well, they brought up Ellie." Carver's jaw clenched, but otherwise he didn't move. "They said, ah . . ." Rush hesitated, shifting in his chair.

Carver continued to stare into his hands as he spoke. "They said she's got a reputation for wandering and that was a good way to compromise a cop. They also said I was looking the other way when it came to some businesses." He sighed and glanced at me out of the corner of his eye. "One in particular. The Outback Inn?"

I nodded. How well I knew it. It was a little dive east of town and also the place where I inadvertently picked up Ellie Carver. I say "inadvertently" in the sense that I didn't know she was married to the police chief or to anyone else for that matter. There was nothing, however, inadvertent in my action. It was when I'd first moved to Foxport, and I was pretty lonely at the time. Ellie had been sweet and funny, and I'd found talking to her the easiest thing in the world. Much later I learned that Ellie only got conversational after four or five manhattans.

Carver cleared his throat and continued. "They're saying I'm turning my back on certain 'improprieties.' " He turned to Rush. "Was that the word they used?" Rush nodded. "Anyway, they're saying I'm turning my back on all the improprieties that are going on there because Ellie's one of them."

"Is she?"

Carver scowled. "I don't know. I haven't asked. I don't think so, but . . ." He rubbed his forehead. "What the hell difference does it make anyway? Nobody from the Outback Inn or anywhere else has ever gotten a favor out of me."

I didn't ask Carver to get specific about the complaints against Ellie. At this point it didn't matter. And while I believed Carver when he said he'd never look the other way, everyone in this room, including Carver, knew how much appearances counted here. He continued. "And then there's this crap about that DUI thing. You add all of it together with the whiners on the force and that horse's ass Moore, and I guess it was enough to convince the city council to give me the boot."

No one spoke for a minute, and I began to wonder if I was the only one in the dark concerning DUI things. I had to ask. "Ah, excuse me. What's this DUI stuff?"

Carver shifted uncomfortably, glanced up at Elaine, then back to me. Sighing, he crossed his arms. "About eighteen months ago I got pulled over in Hillcrest. Blood-alcohol level was borderline DUI. It was right after they lowered the level too. Legal limit's one-point-oh. Mine was one-point-oh. Barely." He rubbed his hand over his mouth and took a minute before finishing quickly with: "I have some friends over there. Let's just say a few records were slightly altered. I didn't think anything would ever come of it."

"Am I safe in assuming that not everyone in Hillcrest's police department is a friend?" I asked.

Carver managed a grim smile. "Guess you could say that. They can't prove anything, but it sure raised some questions." He finally worked up the nerve to glance at Elaine, who gave him a little smile and patted his shoulder.

Rush spoke up again. "All this might add up to nothing more than a power play, but there's been some evidence suppressed in this Millard investigation." Carver eased back into the couch as Rush continued. "For one, Tanner suspected this stable hand of his, Jim Dworski, of theft. Seems that in the year he'd been working for him, a couple expensive saddles and a few other pieces of tack had turned up missing. I guess Gayle Millard was pretty outspoken about the guy's guilt. Said she'd seen him loading some stuff in the trunk of his car. Dworski denied it, told Tanner the woman was lying." He paused and shrugged. "Tanner couldn't prove it either way, so he didn't fire him, but I guess Dworski didn't take it quiet. He didn't exactly say anything to Tanner, but behind his back he did plenty of bad-mouthing about him and the way he ran his business."

I glanced at Elaine, then Jeff. "You may be suppressing that, but it's no secret. I asked him about it myself. He said it was a bunch of crap."

"Wait," Rush said, "I'm not finished. When they were going through Millard's apartment, guess what they found?" He nodded. "Three saddles and five bridles. More than you'd expect one person who doesn't even own a horse to need."

"What'd Brig say?"

Rush smiled and shook his head. "Well, I wasn't there to see it, but he claims he never saw any of it before." He paused. "I bet Dworski would find this interesting."

"Not anymore," I said. "Elaine and I just came from his house. Seems that Dworski was working under a Chevy when the jack slipped." Jeff winced.

"This just happened?" Carver asked.

I shook my head. "I'm still trying to work this out, but if I'm thinking straight, which there can be no guarantee of right now, someone's trying real hard to make sure the big neon finger points to Dworski."

"How can you be sure?" Elaine was looking up at me, arms wrapped around her knees, puzzled.

"Well, I'm not. But hear me out. Yesterday morning someone snatched Peanuts." I got up and went into the kitchen.

"What?" Jeff's eyes were wide. Carver looked vaguely amused.

"Yeah, I let him out and he never came back. After I came back from looking for him, I found this." I presented the dognapper's note.

"This is nuts," Jeff said. Carver still seemed amused.

"When Elaine and I got to Dworski's house, we found Peanuts locked up in his basement." Elaine nodded. "If Dworski took Peanuts, he would have to have been alive yesterday morning."

"Move over Sherlock Holmes," Carver muttered.

"Dworski would have to have died last night, but he couldn't have."

I sat down and took a drink of beer, hoping that my logic wouldn't fail me in the middle of this explanation. "First, I figured he must have been out there at night—his house was lit up like a Christmas tree. But he didn't die last night. Two reasons. First, there were two days' worth of *Tribunes* in his front yard." Carver rolled his eyes, and I held up my hand to stop him. "You'll be relieved to know that's not the big reason. Now, Ed, you be sure and correct me if I'm wrong here. Rigor mortis starts to set in about five or six hours after death. Eighteen hours after he died, he should be stiff. Now, I'm not saying I did a thorough examination, but his arms were not stiff."

Elaine nodded, paling at the recollection. "He's right."

"We found him around four P.M. If he died at any time last night, at least parts of him should have been stiff."

Carver shifted on the couch. "So you're saying he died the night before last and had already thawed out."

"Exactly. Now, I saw him the day before yesterday late in the afternoon. I think it happened when he went home that night." I hurried on. "Another thing. Now, I'm no expert on insects, but I do know he was dead long enough for flies to lay eggs and for those eggs to hatch into maggots." Jeff made an unpleasant face. "I don't know how long that takes, but an entomologist could tell us."

"I didn't realize it was warm enough for flies," Jeff said to no one in particular.

"All it takes is a day or two of mild weather," Carver informed him.

Rush frowned, nodding, his arms crossed over his chest. "Sounds like we need a new suspect."

Jeff looked thoughtful for a moment. "Would Peanuts hop into anyone's car?"

"How the hell do I know? Blame me. I never gave him a talk about climbing into cars with strangers."

"Barlowe," Carver said, assuming his patronizing tone,

"it's not like the dog weighs in at a hundred and fifty and has a bite that'll snap your arm in two. It's supposed to herd sheep, for God's sake."

"So you're saying he'd be easy to pick up and toss in the trunk." I was surprised at the calm way Elaine spoke, as though he weren't in the next room. Probably trembling in the corner.

Carver shrugged. "Yeah."

"Okay," I decided to change the subject, "what else is the police department suppressing?"

Rush cleared his throat. "You know that phone call Gayle Millard got? Well, we know who made it."

Jeff drained his can of beer, then turned to me with that greedy newshound look of his. "Guess."

"Boris Yeltsin. How in the hell am I supposed to know?" Jeff shrugged good-naturedly.

I turned to Rush. "Please tell me."

"Will Tanner."

Jeff couldn't contain himself. "Gayle and Will had something going."

"You know that just because of one phone call?"

Rush shook his head. "No, it was more than a phone call. I don't know how Moore's people found out, but they were seeing each other behind Brig's back."

My eye was starting to smart, and I pressed on the bandage. I could feel a tear escaping. "So you're saying that she was having an affair with both Brig and Will Tanner? Father and son?"

"Yep."

"Did Brig know about this?"

Rush continued, "That I don't know. Actually I don't know much more than the fact."

"How did you learn all this?" I asked. "Don't tell me you were one of the cops Moore kept informed."

"I sure wasn't." Rush smiled. "Thing is, Moore's got a lot of faults. One is that he assumes those he's taken into his confidence want to be there."

We were interrupted by a knock at the door. Elaine jumped up. "Pizza's here. Does anyone have any money?"

We all looked at each other like we thought the other guy had brought the ball, then dredged our pockets and managed to pool enough to get the pizza out of hock. Elaine found some plates and napkins, and we took a break and dug into the two large pizzas—one with pepperoni and mushrooms and the other with sausage, green pepper, and extra cheese.

Elaine gave up the arm of the couch for the floor, but only after waving off Carver's offer of his seat. Now she was situated at the end of the coffee table between Carver and me. I decided not to dwell on the significance, if there was any, and concentrated on the pizza and beer.

Peanuts returned to the living room, the desire for pizza overcoming his fear of Ed Carver. He kept the coffee table between them and only begged from Jeff, Elaine, or me. Rush offered him a pepperoni, but he would only accept it after he'd set it on the carpet. Then he moved in, grabbed it, and was back before I could blink. Must be the uniform.

As I split the crust with Peanuts, it occurred to me that an obvious inconsistency hadn't been explained. "Ed, since Moore's such a horse's ass, how come you put him in charge?"

Carver finished chewing and swallowed. "I asked my other lieutenant, Sturgis, if he'd do it. Thing is, he's just coming off a bad divorce, and he didn't figure he was up to it." He shrugged. "Hell, I've never been wild about Moore, but up until now he's never done anything to me. Well, I guess he heard about Sturgis, so he came in and asked if he could be my replacement. What was I supposed to do? Tell him I was going to have one of the sergeants fill in?"

"Boy," Elaine said, "this guy sure knows how to milk an opportunity." She plucked a pepperoni and offered it to Peanuts, who snatched it so fast, she paused to check her fingers.

"Jeff, has the *Chronicle* reported any of this?"

Carver snorted. "What do you think? Nothing like a

character assassination to boost circulation figures."

Jeff stopped chewing and stared at Carver. After a minute in which Carver gave no indication that he knew he was being stared at, Jeff swallowed and cleared his throat. "Look, Ed. It's nothing personal. I don't give a shit what kind of conspiracy you think the media are involved in. That council meeting was public record. What do you think we do? Pick and choose items according to how well we like someone?"

Carver seemed to be ignoring Jeff, and before Jeff could launch into one of his freedom-of-the-press sermons, which were usually long-winded but oddly inspiring, I interrupted. "Are you going to run any of what's been discussed here?"

He nodded. "What we can prove. Tomorrow we're running a story on some of the withheld evidence—Dworski's grudge with Tanner for starters. Right now we haven't been able to verify any of the business between Will and Gayle. Will Tanner hasn't exactly been returning our calls." He pulled off another slice of pizza and snatched a loose pepperoni off the cardboard. Peanuts watched as he popped it into his mouth. "We're not going to start quoting anonymous sources in the police department. Not yet anyway. Still, with just the suggestion of a cover-up, the shit's gonna hit the fan." He bit off a chunk of pizza and chewed happily.

I was looking forward to getting the *Chronicle* tomorrow. "I'd like to be a fly on Moore's kitchen wall when he's sipping his morning coffee and opens the paper."

"You know," Jeff continued, "it's not like we're out to get Moore or anything like that. But he's not exactly playing by the rules here. I've been trying to get in to see him, but no dice. He's the chief of police, for God's sake, and he won't talk to the media. Can you believe that?" He glanced at Carver, who didn't offer his well-known views on journalism run amok. "I even tried calling him at home." He turned to Carver and added, in mock sincerity, "You know I'd never do that unless it was my last resort." He shrugged. "But forget it. His wife's like a human pit bull. No way I can get past her. Besides," he said as he wiped a smudge of tomato sauce from the corner of his mouth, "she's bigger than I am."

I polished off my last slice of pizza and leaned back into the lawn chair with my beer. Jeff seemed to be finished, and both he and Carver were watching me, so I figured it must be my turn. "Well," I began, "I guess my client was right. He is getting sandbagged. And I've got the messed-up face to prove it."

Then I told the rest of my story, stopping only to clarify points and to ask if they knew the people I was talking about. Artie the Slab was the only familiar one. "The guy's a real operator," Carver had sneered, then added, "Or so he thinks." By the time I finished, all but two slices of pizza had been consumed. I wedged the beer bottle between my legs and scratched Peanuts' head and neck while waiting for the crowd reaction.

After a minute, Jeff said, "Moore didn't show up at the hospital?"

"Yeah, he was there." Then I added, "Didn't have much to say, though I've gotta admit I'm surprised he made the effort."

Carver shifted on the couch. "For all you know, this Miller guy, or whoever he is, has got a grudge against you from way back." He took a pull on his beer and added, "You can have that effect on some people, you know."

Elaine had been listening to Carver. Now she turned her face up toward me, waiting.

"I don't know. Maybe there's nothing. It's just that this horse thing happens just before all hell breaks loose. I don't know. I guess it could be a coincidence."

"Right now, I don't see how it could be anything but," Carver added.

No one spoke for a minute, then Elaine said, "Well, even if there is no connection, it's not like you can ignore it. There's definitely something wrong." She patted my knee and chuckled to herself. "No kidding, huh?"

I put my hand over hers before she could remove it. "Well," I addressed the others, "about the only positive result I've gotten is on this horse semen thing. For whatever it's worth. Maybe I'll pay Mr. Hines another visit."

"I'm gonna keep my ear to the ground," Rush said, then glanced at Carver. "I'll let you know what I hear."

I turned to Carver. "Does anyone know you're back in town?"

"No. And I'd like to keep it that way. At least until I can get a handle on a few things."

I nodded but didn't say anything. This must be bugging the hell out of him. If anything, Ed Carver's main fault was becoming too involved in an investigation, not delegating, giving the impression that he didn't trust any of his officers to do it as well as he could. I think that was probably the case too. Carver's a perfectionist. Must be hell to be married to that. I wondered if Elaine shared my opinion.

We talked for maybe fifteen more minutes, discussing strategy and basically deciding we'd each pursue our own line and keep each other informed. Since I had the most mobility, figuratively speaking, seeing as I didn't work for Moore, I was going to be busy. But then, I was getting paid for it. Then Jeff got up to leave, and Rush asked Carver if he wanted a ride home.

Carver sighed and pushed his fingers into his hair. "I'm not exactly welcome there." I felt Elaine's hand on my shoulder.

"Ah, Ed," I said, "if you need a place to stay tonight, you can crash on the couch." Elaine squeezed a little harder. "I mean, until this gets straightened out. You can stay here." I could tell from her sigh and the fact that the circulation to my shoulder had been restored that I'd scored a whole shitload of points, and I could tell from Carver's resigned appreciation that he wasn't any happier about the situation than I was but understood there were few options.

What with my delicate condition, I didn't figure I should have to surrender the bed. Besides, Elaine might still be staying. Though I doubted it.

She followed me into the hallway to get some blankets.

"I think I'd better go home," she whispered.

"Why?"

"He's feeling awkward enough as it is."

"Elaine, tell me something."

She turned to me, and suddenly I decided I didn't want an answer. "Never mind."

She gave me a kiss—not a passionate one, more friendly. Sisterly. Great. I took small consolation in the fact that she only said good-night to Carver. She said it real nice though.

I showed Carver where the coffee was and told him to help himself to what was in the refrigerator. After a glimpse of its contents, Carver said, "What do you eat for breakfast?"

"Usually nothing. Coffee."

He looked at me like I'd just said "raw oysters."

"Breakfast is the most important meal of the day. It's the foundation."

I shrugged. "I'll make a run up to Mac's."

He nodded as though maybe that would be okay. "I like the one with the sausage."

This had the makings for a long haul. Not only was I playing host to Ed Carver, but it was an Ed Carver who was under house arrest.

I watched as he threw a sheet on the couch and a blanket over it.

"Ah, Ed, are you and Ellie splitting up?"

He removed his shoes and lined them up under the coffee table. Then he sighed and regarded me for a few seconds before saying, "Looks that way."

"Sorry to hear that."

He shrugged. "What about you and Elaine?"

I couldn't tell where he was coming from, so I just shook my head. "Don't know."

It felt good to be in my own bed staring at the familiar patch of moonlight on the wall. Peanuts was sprawled across the foot of the bed, forcing me to sleep on the diagonal. I didn't mind.

Part of me thought I was the world's biggest jerk for not

appreciating a good thing when I had it. Another part of me was a little more forgiving—you can't force something that's not there. Why wasn't it? What in the hell was wrong with me? If I wasn't looking for someone who was smart, funny, and great looking, then what in the hell was I looking for?

Somewhere deep inside me was a nagging suspicion that Elaine felt the same way but, like me, was reluctant to let go of the known in exchange for the unknown.

I grudgingly had to admit I'd be less reluctant if I didn't believe that once I let go, she'd go straight into Ed Carver's arms. Elaine had an affinity for wounded animals. I ought to know.

$\triangledown$

18

IT WAS ALMOST nine when I cracked open my good eye and let the daylight filter in. My body ached, especially my back, which wasn't used to being slept on all night. Sitting up took more effort than usual, and it was a minute before I could focus on the *Chinatown* poster that hung on the wall next to the door. I peeled the bandage off my right eye, blinked a couple times, and decided it had healed enough to manage on its own. I smelled coffee—maybe that's what woke me—and it was a couple minutes before I figured out who was responsible—my new roommate. I pulled on a pair of jeans and ventured out of the bedroom.

Carver was on the couch, feet propped on the coffee table, and Peanuts was curled up on the living room floor, in dangerously close proximity to the dog-kicking former chief of police.

"You wanna go out?" Peanuts' ears perked, and he started to get up.

"He's already been," came the voice from behind the newspaper. "I figured if he had to wait until you got up, I'd have to teach him how to use the toilet. Opening the door seemed easier."

I found a can of Alpo for Peanuts, and his head was in the dish before the food got there. Being kidnapped apparently hadn't spoiled his appetite.

"You find the shower okay?" I rummaged through a kitchen drawer looking for the plastic wrap, wondering why I'd asked a rather obvious question, seeing as my apartment wasn't exactly Buckingham Palace. I've never been good with small talk.

"No problem." He was back behind the paper.

"What's the story in the *Chronicle*?"

He turned the paper so I could read the headline: SOURCES POINT TO POLICE COVER-UP.

I whistled softly. "Moore's probably doing cartwheels right about now."

"Yeah, well, he's hiding from the press. That's for sure. They can't find him to quote him. Wonder how he does it." He opened the paper again and folded it in half, then in quarters. I hate reading a newspaper that's been origamied to death.

Showering made my face sting, and I debated whether or not to shave. But one look in the mirror convinced me that a little pain was preferable to scaring small children.

As I stared myself down in the mirror, trying not to slice up my face any more, I thought about Ed Carver and tried to imagine what he was going through right now. It wasn't easy because I first had to try his shoes on, and I wasn't at all comfortable in them. Ed Carver must be one hell of a lonely place. Carver expected loyalty as a natural part of the job. He dished it out, and he expected to get it back. He did his work because he loved it and because it was important to him. It might be all that was important to him. He didn't expect favors, though apparently he accepted them on occasion, and he didn't expect anyone who worked for him to seek favors. That was fine, but he was also damned stingy with compliments and praise—quick to criticize and slow to praise. Those qualities didn't tend to engender loyalty. The bare fact was that most people weren't single-minded the way Carver was. Most need more than the satisfaction of a job well done. If he carried those habits over to his marriage—hell, I had trouble figuring out how he made the time to court a woman, let alone marry her—then that marriage wouldn't stand much of a chance. But just when I think I've got the guy figured out, he takes a month's leave to try to make things work with Ellie. She must have stipulated that he have no contact with Foxport while they were trying to patch things up. There was no way I could imagine that scenario being a dream vacation for either one of them. Carver must have been like a junkie going through withdrawal. He was possibly relieved to get the phone call. Maybe Ellie was too.

I had just changed into a clean pair of jeans and a cotton shirt when someone pounded at the door. Carver looked up from the paper but didn't move.

"Anyone besides the gang from last night know where you're staying?"

He shook his head. "Just Ellie."

I opened the door, and a man in a navy blue jacket over khaki chinos looked me up and down. He had a soft, pudgy face and an oversized nose. "Are you Edward Alvin Carver?"

"Nope." Alvin? I was deciding whether or not to play dumb when I heard someone behind me.

"I am."

"I'm serving you with these papers on behalf of Eleanor Carver."

Carver clenched his jaw and blinked his eyes a couple times, then took the papers and threw them on the coffee table. "Get lost," he said.

The guy looked at me as though anticipating another slam, shrugged, and left. I guess he didn't expect to be thanked.

Carver stood at the window overlooking the river, hands tucked in his back pockets. It was foggy and the trees on the opposite bank looked ominous, like giants in the mist. "You and Ellie just got back yesterday, didn't you?"

Carver nodded.

"That's awful fast work, even for a starving lawyer."

He glanced over his shoulder at me. "Not if your old man's a lawyer who hates his son-in-law's guts."

"I see," I said and added, "Then that explains the interesting timing."

"No shit."

"Be sure you get a lawyer." I didn't know why I pursued this. Carver hadn't indicated that he wanted my advice. I guess it just seemed insensitive to gloss over the fact that the guy had just been served his divorce papers.

"Lawyers," he muttered with the same tone he usually reserved for journalists. "They're the only ones who make out here, aren't they?"

"Sure seems that way."

"Vermin."

Some of my best clients are lawyers. I was hoping a lawyer would save my ass right now. So, what would that make me? I kept my mouth shut. That was when I noticed the partially consumed coffee cake on the kitchen counter. I pulled off a chunk. "Where'd this come from?"

He turned to see what I was talking about. "Oh, that. Louise brought it up."

I poured myself a mug of coffee and held up the pot to offer Carver a refill. He hesitated, then shook his head. "No thanks. That stuff's caffeinated, isn't it?"

"Ed, it's nine-thirty. Not even a zealot has to drink decaf until after three P.M." I drew up a swallow, noting that Carver made a weak pot of coffee. "What's the purpose of coffee, anyway? To wake you up. Decaf is an abomination."

"You don't own any. So what do you drink after three P.M.?"

"Scotch. Or beer. Helps me sleep." I cut a larger slice off the slab of coffee cake and dropped it on a paper towel, then proceeded to lick a dab of frosting off my thumb. Carver made a face as though I'd offended his sensibilities. I noticed he was wearing another sweater—he owned at least two of them. This one was navy blue with a little red fox over his heart. Nice touch.

"Last night," I began, "was it Louise who let you guys in?" I'd assumed that immediately. My friend and business partner had a soft spot for Ed Carver. I think she also likes professional wrestling.

Carver nodded. "Yeah. Barlowe was camped out on your porch so she had to let him in too." As he spoke, he was looking around the living room as though he was thinking about decorating. "What's it cost to rent a place like this?"

I told him and added, "She cuts me a pretty good deal, though. I was paying a third more across the river at River's Edge Apartments."

Carver whistled softly and shook his head.

"Foxport's an expensive place to live."

"No shit."

"River's Edge isn't a bad place if you like boxy rooms, surly management, and don't try to sneak in a dog." I'd probably still be there except for the pet clause. One more reason to be grateful for Peanuts. Elaine had a small but nice apartment over on East Locust, but I didn't mention it.

I was about to ask him about his kids. I knew he had two—a boy around eight and a girl in junior high or high school. From what Louise had told me, having two mostly absentee parents—Carver with his job and Ellie in other ways—had turned the girl into a mother to her younger brother. I assumed Ellie would want custody but could have imagined Carver fighting it. Before I could ask him, though, we were interrupted by a knock at the door. Probably just as well.

To the delight of both of us, it was not another process server, but Elaine.

"Hi guys," she said cheerfully and thrust a white bag at me. "I brought doughnuts." She dropped her purse on the counter next to the coffee cake. "Oh, someone beat me to it."

"That's okay," I said. "We're growing boys."

After pouring herself a cup of coffee, she dropped onto the couch. I couldn't help but notice that she'd omitted the part where she gives me a kiss. She nudged Carver's divorce papers with the toe of her sneaker. "What's this? It looks official."

"It is," Carver said. "Official word from Ellie."

Elaine looked at him as though she could read the implication on his face. "Oh," she said, her voice small and, I thought, sincere, "I'm sorry, Ed."

He shrugged. "No surprise."

"Did she come back with you?"

"Yeah." His gaze drifted out the window again, and he added, "Long trip."

"Hmph. She sure knows how to kick a guy when he's down, doesn't she?"

"She's always had that talent."

I broke in. "Well, as much as I'd like to stick around and eat doughnuts and drink caffeine with you guys, there's people I've gotta see." I knew I was being ornery but couldn't help myself. Maybe I was even a little offended when no one seemed to notice.

"Yeah." Carver braced his hands on his knees and pushed himself up. "Think I'll pay a visit to the chief of police."

"You think that's a good idea?" Elaine's eyes were wide with concern. "I mean, he doesn't even know you're in town, does he?"

He flicked the document on the table. "If this guy knows I'm here, anyone who cares knows."

"Yeah," I agreed. "Probably the last person Moore wants to see is the guy he replaced. I think you should go for it."

Elaine shrugged, apparently buying the logic. "What about me?" Her ankle was crossed over her knee and she was studying the heel of her shoe.

"Aren't you supposed to be turning my office into the office of the future?"

"I need to go over some stuff with you. How about this morning?"

I shook my head.

"Okay, then why don't I try to find out something about this Ron Miller?" She seemed intent on prying a tiny, encrusted pebble out of the heel.

"No," I said quietly, "Miller's mine."

She dropped her foot to the floor and gave me the look she reserves for my more inane moments. Carver snorted. "Great idea," he said. "You don't even know if there's a connection between that mess and the one Tanner's in. Besides, how are you going to prove that he doped your drink?" He raised his eyebrows to emphasize his point. "It's his word against yours."

"I don't care. Besides, who says I'm involving the police? I've got other things in mind." Fortunately, that shut him up. Truth be told, I wasn't sure what I'd do once I was nose-to-nose with Ron Miller. Maybe pray for a bolt of lightning. I turned to Elaine. "See if you can find a computer that has some good games on it. You know, for the slow days."

Elaine gave me a sour look.

"For my mental health. All work and no play . . ."

"Thank you for explaining your priorities," she said dryly, reaching for last week's copy of *Time*.

I drank some coffee and leaned back into the couch. Why was I intentionally goading Elaine? You'd think I wanted her out of my life. She was watching Carver as he scratched Peanuts' head. This guy would do anything to impress her, wouldn't he?

"Something else is bothering me," I began and waited until Carver gave Peanuts one final pat and looked up at me. "The other day I talked to Margaret Hebron. She was putting up money for Jubal to buy Kessler. She's also a friend of Claude's. Now I don't know how much she was investing, but she just doesn't strike me as the sort of person who would make a risky investment. Not one like that anyway."

"So, what're you saying?" Carver asked. "You think someone gave her the money?"

"It crossed my mind."

"Who?"

"Don't know."

"Are she and Claude close friends?" Elaine asked.

"Seem to be."

"Then if she had the money maybe she'd do it as a favor to a friend?"

"It's a pretty big favor. Margaret Hebron doesn't live like she's got money to spare."

"Maybe her friends are more important than her money."

"She doesn't even like Jubal."

"Doesn't matter," she said with finality as she flipped her way through the magazine, pausing every few pages for a longer look.

Elaine probably was the kind of person who would give a friend her last dollar. No questions asked. I drained the mug of coffee. Maybe the reason I was pushing her away was because I knew I didn't deserve her. As I watched Carver pull his jacket on, I took small consolation in my estimation that he probably didn't either.

19

I FIGURED THAT a roadhouse like Yancy's wouldn't be open at 9:30 A.M., so I focused on the horse semen and a vet named Erdman. I got no answer when I called his house, but when I called his office in Winfield, things got a little interesting. The woman who answered the phone said he wasn't in and asked me if I had an appointment that morning. Then she made some excuse about Erdman being on an emergency and he'd get back to me, but she sounded agitated. I asked when Erdman had been there last, and she responded by asking who I was. I made up some name and told her I'd call later. Interesting, but still probably nothing. Maybe what I needed to do was get more specific with Warren Hines.

As I pulled out of the driveway, I wished that dogs could talk so Peanuts could just come out and tell me who snatched him. Then I wondered if they'd still be man's best friend if they could talk.

I made a detour on my way out to Hines's farm. While I was in town, it seemed a good time to visit Will Tanner. After all, I did have an appointment. Even if I was a day late.

I showed up at his office hoping Sandy would take pity on my mangled face and find a slot for me.

Today she was wearing a pale blue sweater with white sheep bounding across her chest. I walked in and she removed a pair of round, pale blue glasses. Apparently she could still see pretty well, because she knotted her eyebrows and peered at me. "What happened to you?"

"Just a little accident. No permanent damage. Any chance

I can get in to see Mr. Tanner? I only need a minute of his time."

"Does your face have anything to do with your not showing up yesterday?"

"Everything."

She gave me that crooked smile again. "Did you bring your tax forms?"

"If it'll help me get in there, then sure."

After regarding me for a minute, she looked down at the appointment book and ran her hand down the page. "Let's see. His next appointment isn't due until ten-thirty." She glanced up at the wall clock. It was ten-fifteen. "Maybe he can give you a few minutes."

"I'd really appreciate that."

She disappeared into his office and a moment later emerged with a guarded smile. "Just a few minutes."

Will Tanner looked up from his desk. "I'm going to have to keep working while we talk."

"That's fine." He did resemble his father—same build and cut to his jaw—but he lacked the abruptness of his father's gestures, and his eyes, framed in narrow-rimmed tortoiseshell glasses, were softer, less belligerent. He wore a white, oxford-cloth shirt open at the collar and a purple flowered tie with its knot pulled down a couple inches. "Have the police questioned you yet concerning Gayle Millard's death?"

He opened his mouth to respond, then stopped. "Are you with the police?"

"Well, not exactly. I'm a consultant, but not for the police."

He stapled two forms together and placed them on an open folder. "Good. Then I don't have to talk to you."

"No, but it might be a good idea."

"I doubt it." He started punching some numbers in on a calculator. "Have you filed your taxes yet? I didn't think so. People who owe something wait until the last minute, and people who can't get their shit together wait until the last minute. That's most people. As busy as it is today, it'll be seven times this in two weeks." He stabbed the total button and jotted down a figure. "I think you can understand why I don't have time right now." Another column of figures went into the machine. His hands were large and square and seemed better suited for shipbuilding than numbers crunching.

"Don't you use a computer for all this stuff?"

"Yep, everything's computerized." He hit the total button again and frowned.

"I see. You're just keeping your finger limber."

He looked distracted, then puzzled, then cracked a self-deprecating smile. "I don't like to be surprised by a computer."

I nodded my understanding. "So, you don't trust them suckers either." His smile deepened a little, and he shrugged. Then he resumed his totaling.

Unlike his father's desk, Will's was devoid of photos, and the office was apparently without personal touches. Even the pictures—landscapes that blended in with the wall and furniture—looked like something selected by a decorator.

"Are you aware that the police know you're the one who called Gayle the morning she died?"

He froze, finger poised over the eight key. "What?"

"That call she got. The one that prompted her to borrow Brig's car and head off into town. The cops know it was you."

He moved a form from the top of one pile to another and forced a small laugh. "That's nonsense." After punching the clear button on the calculator, he entered a couple more digits, then stopped and looked at me, waiting.

"Not according to a source at the police department."

"Who?"

"Can't say. But, believe me, they know."

He pulled at his shirt collar and shifted in his chair. "I—" He broke off and looked away. I run into a lot of accomplished liars in my business. Many of them can easily put me to shame. This guy wasn't one of them. I found his lack of skill kind of refreshing.

Will rose from his chair and stepped around the desk.

After a quick check of the outer office, he gently closed the door. Then he turned to me, arms folded across his chest. "Well, if they think I set Gayle up, then why doesn't someone arrest me? Or just ask me about it?"

"Good question."

"Look." He returned to the leather chair, elbows resting on its arms as he faced the window. His tone had lost its harshness and was almost matter-of-fact. "Whatever there was between me and Gayle is none of your business. If the cops want to talk to me, they can try, but I've got nothing to say to you."

"Kind of makes you wonder why they're not asking, doesn't it?"

He glanced at me, then returned to his window vigil. "Does my father know?"

"Not as far as I know. And he won't hear it from me if you're willing to open up a little here."

Scowling, he grabbed a pencil and began rolling it in his hand. "Just apply a little pressure, that's how you guys like to operate, isn't it?"

"Whatever it takes."

Will threw the pencil down on the desk, and we both watched it roll off the edge. I picked it up and returned it to a leather pencil holder. "Look," I tried, "I'm here because I think there are some machinations going on to make Jubal Tanner the scapegoat in all this." He seemed to be watching the course of a silver Camry as it made its way down the busy side street. I continued. "The only reasons for this that I can figure are either your father killed Gayle himself and he's trying to cover up, he's afraid you did it and he's still trying to cover it up, or he hates his brother so damned much that he wants him convicted of a murder regardless of whether he did it or not. Now, I can understand the motives behind theories one and two, but my gut tells me it's behind door number three, and I can't figure for the life of me why these two guys hate each other so much."

Will sighed, hands folded across his midriff. After a

minute he said, "I don't know either. It's something that goes way back."

"You know, that's what everyone says. Someone's got to know more." I sounded angrier than I'd intended, but if Will was moved by the display, he didn't show it. "Was it your mother? I understand that Jubal dated her."

He shook his head and turned the chair so he was partially facing me. His eyebrows met above the bridge of his nose in the famous Tanner V, and he seemed to be giving my statement some consideration. Finally he said, "No, that wasn't it. At least I don't think so. When I was a kid I remember Jubal coming over for dinner with the rest of the family—Grandpa, Grandma, Uncle Cody. The two of them looked out for Uncle Cody."

"Jubal and Brig?"

He nodded. "I barely remember Cody, except that he was always smiling and spent a lot of time trying to keep Jubal and my dad from killing each other."

"I thought they got along back then."

"Oh, yeah, they got along all right. The same way a couple of male wolves in the same pack get along. Each was always looking over his shoulder, making sure the other wasn't sneaking up on him. But, yeah, they were close. Competitive, but close."

"Who was Cody closer to?"

"Hard to say." He chuckled. "I guess that was up for grabs too. I mean, why not? They competed over everything else, why not their little brother?"

"When did all this neighborly business stop?"

"Near as I can figure it was after Cody died." He shook his head in remembered disbelief. "Like I said, that's what's really strange about this family." He removed his glasses and rubbed the bridge of his nose, then dropped his hand to the desk. "Damn, isn't that something? You grow up in a family and you get protected from its own history. And they never stop. It's like you're always a little kid." He shifted in the chair. "I don't know. I guess I was around seven at the time.

All I remember is my mom saying that JoEllen had died in her sleep, and then a couple days later, Cody died of grief. Guess it's sort of true." He sighed deeply. "It was years before I learned what really happened, and then I heard it from some kid at school. If it had happened now, I suppose I'd have gone through grief counseling or something like that. Back then you dealt with something like this by suppressing it."

"Yeah, it's no wonder we're spoiled and repressed and score lousy in math." Will chuckled, and I added, "You know, that's not unusual. These days, it seems like scandals are about as common as people who want to hear about them. You air them out on national talk shows. Back then, family secrets were kept in the family. And then only on a 'need-to-know' basis." Will nodded in agreement. "I've got an uncle who served twelve years in prison back in the forties and fifties for armed robbery. I didn't know it until the old guy's funeral about five years ago. The minister said something about Uncle Fred embracing God when he was in prison. I thought my mother was going to slap her hands over my ears. I've got news for the minister. Uncle Fred only embraced God so Aunt Helen would embrace him."

Will smiled and nodded. It was hard to tell whether he was acknowledging this affinity or just being polite.

"So, Jubal stopped showing up after Cody died."

"As I recall."

"Was he married to Claude at the time?"

He shook his head. "No, that was strange. Jubal kind of went into a . . . I don't know, I guess you'd call it a depression after Cody died."

I nodded.

"Then I guess it was in the late sixties, early seventies he just went off for a while. Year or two maybe. Nobody heard a word from him. Then all of a sudden he's back in town with a wife. Starts trying to be respectable." He shrugged. "Who knows? Maybe someday he'll get there."

"You don't have any contact with him now?"

"No. Though Cindy does. I guess it figures, she's got the

horse fever the same way Jubal does." He shrugged. "I've got nothing against him, though. I remember I used to like him real well."

"How long had you been seeing Gayle?"

He hesitated, then said, "Couple months."

"Was she going to leave your father?"

"Probably not."

"Then what was the point?"

He smiled wryly. "You don't know my dad and his history with women. He likes them young and makes them think they're something special." He paused. "Until the next one comes along, that is."

"Who did Gayle replace?"

He consulted the ceiling. "Actually there was a gap. The last one took a job offer out east somewhere. Dad was without a love interest for, oh, maybe a month or two. Long time for him."

"He doesn't sound like the kind of man who'd be the most faithful husband."

"I wouldn't know about that." From his clipped tone and the ominous look he gave me, I figured this wasn't an avenue to pursue. Not if I wanted to keep him talking. Besides, there were other places I wanted to go.

"I don't get it. If Brig was showering Gayle with gifts and affection, why was she wandering?"

"You'd have to know Gayle." I waited. "She came from nothing. Her father deserted her and her mom, and then her mom died when Gayle was eighteen or nineteen. Security was real important to her. That's what Dad gave her. For maybe the first time in her whole life she wasn't scared of winding up on the street."

"And then you came along."

He nodded. "It just sort of happened."

"So you were just biding your time until he got tired of her?"

"Exactly."

"Wasn't he talking marriage?"

"It wouldn't be the first time. He had a talent for getting distracted at the last minute."

"That morning you called Gayle at your father's. No offense, but she didn't seem any too thrilled at the prospect of sneaking off to meet you."

"That was for Dad's benefit."

"I see. Gayle Millard was a woman of many talents, wasn't she?"

"She was a survivor." He caught himself. "At least she thought she was."

I was beginning to wonder if maybe Will wasn't a more accomplished liar than I'd thought. I also suspected that Gayle being his father's love interest made it all the sweeter for Will, but doubted that he'd admit it. Coveting neighbors' wives must be some kind of weird sport with the family.

"What if she had dumped your dad and taken up with you? What would that have done to your inheritance?"

"She wouldn't have done it."

"Yeah, but what if?"

"I guess I could have kissed it good-bye."

I stared at him for a minute, but his gaze remained fixed on the pencil holder or something just beyond it.

"That scene in the Tattersall. Did the three of you go out together a lot?" I figured that had to be one of the all-time awkward situations.

Will chuckled. "No, that was Dad's idea. I figured it was just the two of us who were gonna be there. But then he shows up with Gayle." He shook his head. "She didn't know I was gonna be there either."

"Sounds like maybe your dad has a sense of the dramatic."

He regarded me curiously. "You think he did it on purpose?"

"What if he had his suspicions? How better to test them out than to see how you two behaved? You were lucky you had a Bulls game to watch. Gayle had to make small talk with your dad."

He tapped his nails against the side of the calculator and

stared out the window. A Canada goose was strutting across the lawn, pecking at the decorative pebbles surrounding the bushes. Will sighed. "He can't know. He just can't."

"He won't hear it from me. But then I'm not the only one who knows." Will conceded the point with a shrug and a nod.

I stood to leave. "Well, thanks for your time." I paused and added, "Sorry to ruin your day."

"Yeah," he said as the goose was joined by another.

As I thanked Sandy for letting me in to see Will, she wagged a finger at me. "Don't forget to file those taxes."

"Sure," I said without much enthusiasm.

"I'm serious. Trust me. You don't want those IRS folks after you."

"They're going to have to get in line."

▽

20

I DECIDED TO make one more stop before heading out to Warren Hines's place. I'd given my "if dogs could talk" musing some serious consideration and decided to bring Peanuts along with me. Now, I knew he wasn't going to point an accusing paw at the guilty party and start barking, but he might tend to act a bit skittish around someone who hustled him into a car and dumped him in a basement. Or maybe not. Either way, he usually enjoyed the opportunity to get out of the house.

Though it was still early, the day was sunny and promised some nice, mild temperatures. I pulled up alongside a battered pickup truck in my driveway. Claude Tanner emerged. She smiled as she approached my car, fingers tucked in her jeans pocket. "Is it true? Did this Jim Dworski kill Gayle? My Jubal's been cleared?"

She seemed so happy and relaxed that I hated to tell her otherwise. "I'm afraid it's not quite that simple." I climbed out of my car.

Her shoulders dropped a couple inches. "Why not?"

"Well, there are some inconsistencies. I'm thinking maybe whoever did kill Gayle also killed Jim and set it up so it looked like he's the one." I faltered under her stare and finished with, "But I could be wrong."

"What inconsistencies?"

"Well, there's my dog." I explained about Peanuts and how I didn't think Dworski could have taken him.

She walked toward me, her arms folded across her chest.

The gravel sounded harsh beneath her boots. "Do the police know this as well?"

"I'm not sure. But once they do the autopsy, they ought to get a better fix on the time of death."

It was hard to read her expression as she leaned against my rental car, looking past me toward the river. "You have a nice view here," she said.

"Yeah, I like it." Then when she didn't respond, I added, "You want to talk, we can go upstairs." I gestured toward my apartment.

"No. Thank you. I was just in town on some errands and I heard about Mr. Dworski."

"Where?"

"Pardon?" She finally pulled her gaze from the river, slowly focusing on me.

"Where did you hear?" I shrugged. "I was just wondering."

"Oh. The newspaper. The *Chronicle*." She paused. "Is your dog all right?"

"Oh, yeah. He's pretty sturdy. Peasant stock."

She nodded and shifted, but she made no move either to leave or to continue the conversation.

"Claude, is there something else? You seem a little, uh, distracted."

"Oh, it's Jubal. I worry about him. If they send him away, he'll die. I know he will." The last few words were whispered.

"Jubal's a long way from being sent away for this. Even if they suspect him, how can they prove it? If Jim Dworski was hired to kill Gayle, or Brig, then killed to shut him up, they're still going to have to trace him back to Jubal. And if there's no link, they can't do it. They can suspect all they want."

"But Jubal needs his name cleared. You understand, don't you?"

"I do. And I'm doing what I can."

She squeezed her eyes shut and pressed her thumb and forefinger against the bridge of her nose. "All that he is depends on this." Abruptly she dropped her hand and opened her eyes. "Do you think sixty-three is too late to start over? Do you?"

"It's never too late." I wished that something less trite had come to me, but I seemed to be fresh out of wisdom.

"I think sometimes it is." Again, she spoke so softly that I barely heard the words. As I watched her try to keep her emotions in check, I noticed that the last couple weeks had taken a toll on her. The spray of lines around her eyes seemed to be etched deeper. It occurred to me that there are those who cause the trouble and those who take on the worry. One of nature's little mysteries is how these two types often wind up married to each other.

She took a deep breath and released it slowly, then managed a smile. "What happened to your face?"

I told her and she listened, shaking her head. When I'd finished, she said, "This is all Brig Tanner's fault. Everything."

"What do you mean?"

"If he hadn't bought that horse, Jubal wouldn't have caused the scene that night at the Tattersall. That's why he's a suspect." She buried her face in her hands. When she spoke again, the words were muffled. "This is all Brig Tanner's fault. He probably doesn't even realize it."

"Claude, why don't we go upstairs? I'll get you some coffee or something." I put my hand on her shoulder—just trying to make contact—and she abruptly pulled away, wiping her face.

"No, I don't want to keep you from what you are doing. I'm sorry I bothered you."

"It's no problem," I said, but she was already climbing back into her truck.

Nan Hines's eyes widened when she saw my face. "What happened to you?"

"I missed a car payment."

Her mouth dropped an inch, then she snapped it up and eyed me for a few seconds, before smiling. "Yeah, I guess it's none of my business. You looking for Warren?"

"Yeah." Then I added, "I was in an accident."

"Ouch." She made a face. "Glad to see you didn't fare any worse than that."

"Me too." Before I could ask for Warren, Nan noticed the dog standing slightly behind me.

"And who is this?" She crouched down as though Peanuts were a small child who might give her a shy answer.

I introduced them, and Peanuts gratefully accepted her affections. Clearly, Nan was not a dognapper. Either that or Peanuts liked it and wanted more.

"Is Warren around?"

"Oh," she gave Peanuts one more pat on the head and straightened, "I guess you didn't come here to show off your dog."

"It's good for his ego."

"I've got a feeling that dog's got a healthier ego than most of us." She flashed me her dimples. "To answer your question, yes, Warren's in the kitchen trying to figure out what's wrong with the coffee maker." She took a step back from the door. "Maybe you can give him a hand."

"That's about all I can give him."

She laughed a little and closed the door behind me and Peanuts.

Warren Hines was sitting at their kitchen table, the dismembered coffee maker and several screwdrivers scattered in front of him. He glanced up at me, then did a double take.

"What the hell happened to you?" He didn't seem so much concerned as alarmed.

"Got between my car and a guardrail." Now he seemed more confused than anything, and I decided that was a good place to keep him for a while.

"Did you hear about Jim Dworski?"

"Yeah." He set the screwdriver down and looked up at me, interested. "What a way to go, huh? I'll tell ya, I never liked working under a jacked-up car. No way."

"I think it was probably old hat to him. He had a half-dozen cars, most of them didn't have tires."

"Still. Sounds like a good way to get yourself killed."

"Apparently it is." Nan was standing behind me, resting her hips against the kitchen counter. "He worked for you, didn't he?"

"Yeah. For about six months. Not a bad worker. Not real sociable. Why you asking?" Peanuts was almost within petting range of Warren, and he had to lean out of his chair to reach his head. The dog accepted the gesture but didn't move any closer to him.

"Well, there's some talk that he might have been involved in Gayle Millard's murder. Did he ever mention her?"

Frowning, he considered the question for a minute before shaking his head. "Don't think so. Like I said, he didn't talk much. Did his work," he said, pausing, "real slow sometimes, but he did it."

"You notice anything missing lately? Saddles? Something like that?"

"No. And believe me, I'd notice. We keep pretty close track of equipment." He chuckled. "What equipment we've got."

"Did he say anything about Brig Tanner giving him a hassle at Windemere?"

"No." His chair creaked as he leaned back. "Though lately he was talking about telling Brig what he could do with his job. Acting kind of cocky."

"When's the last time he was out here?"

"Oh, when was it, Nan? Three days ago?"

"Day before yesterday, I think. He was out here for a while in the early afternoon."

It finally occurred to me that Warren was going out of his way to look at anything other than my face. Even with the nicks and cuts, it wasn't that bad. "You ever been to a place called Yancy's?" I asked.

Nan snorted. "Not for a while." She crossed her arms over her chest and stared at her husband as she added, "Have you, dear?"

"Ah, no. It's been a while. Quite a while."

She glanced at me again. "You hang out at places like that, you're asking for it."

"Well, believe me, I wasn't asking for this."

"What happened?" Nan patted the back of a cane chair. "Sit down and tell us. I'd offer you some coffee but . . ." She trailed off, sounding both regretful and optimistic. "I'm holding out hope for Warren fixing this machine. I guess we could always get another, but this one makes such good coffee. You know how long it takes those new ones to develop character."

Warren watched as I lowered myself into the chair.

"How about some instant?" Nan was inspecting a cabinet shelf, pushing cans and bottles aside. "Or we've got some tea. Let's see. Earl Grey?" She glanced over her shoulder at her husband. "Where on earth did we get something you're supposed to drink with your pinkie crooked?"

"Probably your mother," he said without much enthusiasm as he picked up one of the screwdrivers and began rolling the handle back and forth in the palm of his hand.

"Instant sounds great. My pinkie doesn't crook very well."

Nan filled a saucepan with water and put it on an electric burner. "So, tell us what happened."

"I got a call from some guy who said he had information on the Tanners. When I got there, I had a beer with him, didn't learn much of anything. Then on the way home I learned the hard way that he'd slipped some LSD in my beer. It was a minor miracle that nobody else got hurt."

Nan's eyes were wide as she leaned against the counter. Warren continued to work the handle like he was molding clay. His expression remained impassive.

"So, who was the guy?" Nan asked.

"Well, he said his name was Ron Miller, but I kind of doubt he used his real name. He's real tall, skinny, with a prominent Adam's apple. Oh, and a bad toupee."

"Warren, that sounds like Tom." She turned to me and added, "The second you said bad toupee, I knew it. . . ."

Warren had stopped working the handle and was working on silencing his wife with a sharp look. Nan stood at the counter, a teaspoon of instant coffee poised over a mug. Then she caught Warren's glare. "What?" she said, cutting the word off with a razor. "I don't know who you're trying to protect. That sure as hell sounds like Tom."

"Tom Erdman?"

Now I had Warren's attention.

"How do you know Tom Erdman?" he asked.

"He's the one who bought five thousand dollars' worth of frozen horse semen."

There aren't many times in this business when you are absolutely positive you've struck pay dirt. When it happens, it feels so damned good you want to bottle it.

Warren threw the screwdriver down on the table, and it skittered across its surface. Peanuts had been lying quietly next to my chair. Now he jumped up to see what the action was about.

Warren stood, his finger pointed at Nan. "You keep out of this, you hear? It's none of your business."

In what seemed a defensive reflex, Nan stepped back, then just as quickly regained her position and then some. She was nose-to-nose with her husband. Well, more like nose-to-chest. "What are you saying, it's none of my business? What's going on? You're up to something with Erdman. I know it. Did you have anything to do with almost getting this man killed?" She jerked her head in my direction. "Did you?"

Warren raised his hands so they were a scant inch from his wife's shoulders. There they hovered for a few seconds. "No, I didn't, hon." He touched her shoulders and she backed up like she'd been scalded. Raising his hands to show he had nothing up his sleeve, he said, "You know I don't tell Tom what to do."

"But why do you do anything he tells you to? That's crazy, you know. You don't need him. You don't work for him. He works for you." She gestured toward me again. I felt kind of like a visual aid and decided that was okay for now. "You know something about this, don't you?"

"Just get off my back, Nan." He turned and marched out of the kitchen. Seconds later I heard the front door slam.

Nan heaved a disgusted sigh and grabbed the pan of boiling water from the stove. Both Peanuts and I backed up a step. She filled a mug, sloshed the coffee around, and set it on the table in front of me. "We'll be right back," she said and followed her husband out the door.

After a minute, I approached the door, hoping to hear some of the discussion. Peanuts watched me intently. No sound came from the other side of the door. Either they argue quietly or they'd gone somewhere out of hearing range. I looked at my dog. "What did I do to Tom Erdman to make him want to kill me?"

Peanuts sat down and wagged his tail.

"I've never met the guy, only uttered his name once." We returned to the kitchen. "So, it's got to be the phone call." The coffee had a bitter taste, but drinking it gave me something to do. After a couple swallows, I decided it needed some milk. Pinned to the refrigerator with colorful fruit magnets were childlike crayon drawings of horses. Some with riders and some without. One was a pretty good depiction of a big brown horse that with a little stretch of the imagination could have been Kessler. I sat at the table, drank my coffee, and stared at the drawing.

Fifteen minutes later Nan and Warren returned, and if Warren had a tail, it'd be between his legs. Nan sat across from me at the table, folded her hands in front of her, and looked me straight in the eyes. "You should have kept out of this."

"But I didn't. And if this has anything to do with Gayle Millard's murder, you two would be smart to start talking."

"It's got nothing to do with it." Warren stood behind his wife. He kept clenching and unclenching his fists.

"Well, I don't know how you can be so damned sure. Even so, it has got something to do with almost getting me killed. So, I think I've got a right to know."

Warren opened his mouth again, but Nan cut him off with a subtle movement of her shoulders. "No. You don't. Why don't you leave?"

I took a sip of the coffee, which was lukewarm by now and barely drinkable. "You know what I think? I think you sold Brig Tanner a sterile horse, didn't you?"

Nan's features remained frozen, implacable. Then I looked up at Warren and was rewarded with his mouth dropping open and face paling a few shades.

Nan broke the silence. "I don't know what you're talking about. There's not a damned thing wrong with that horse."

"Never mind." I finished the coffee and set the mug on the table. "I guess he can be tested."

"That's an older horse," Warren interjected. "He doesn't come with guarantees."

"Whatever." I stood and Peanuts' claws clicked against the tile as he followed me up. "I'll let you and Brig hash it out. What I do take offense to is an attempt on my life. I intend to report it, and you're probably going to wind up as an accessory."

He started to protest, but I kept going. "You won't be able to prove you're not, and I've got a feeling that Tom Erdman isn't going down all by himself. Even if he deserves to."

"I had nothing to do with it."

"With what? My busted-up car or the great horse fraud?"

He didn't answer.

Nan got up and moved around the table toward the counter. "All right. My husband did a stupid thing, but that doesn't make him a bad person."

"Convince me." I turned toward Nan and was somewhat surprised to see that she had managed to put her hands on a gun, which she was pointing at my head.

"We don't want this leaving the room."

"Oh, that's a good idea. At this point all he's guilty of is horse fraud. You want to make it murder too? You think you've got problems now, try getting rid of a body."

What followed was a very long minute during which I sweated and, I assume, Nan weighed her choices. Or tried to decide where they could stash me and my dog.

Finally, Warren spoke. "Never mind, Nan."

"We can't let him go."

"Like the man said, what're you gonna do? Shoot him? Don't be stupid."

"I could do it."

"Forget it, Nan." This time there was more authority in his voice.

Nan dropped the gun on the counter and brushed her hand across her cheek. "Shit, Warren. That was a stupid thing to do. I wish you'd never met that goddamned Erdman. Him and that god-awful rug. Damn."

Warren put his arms around his wife's shoulders, and a few seconds later she buried her face in his chest. He turned to me and said quietly. "Why don't you leave now?"

"Just tell me if I've got this right. Kessler is sterile."

Warren swallowed, then nodded.

"How long?"

"Six months maybe."

"You've been selling some other horse's semen as the real article. Some horse who wouldn't get two thousand a shot like Kessler."

"Yeah."

"Brig Tanner doesn't know this, does he? He thinks he's getting a fully operational stud, or whatever he's called."

Again, he nodded.

"Doesn't the horse have to take some kind of test before he's sold? A sperm count or something?"

"Yes. That's it. A sperm count," Warren replied without much enthusiasm. Nan's sobs got louder.

"But then if the vet's in your pocket it's not real tough to fix that, is it?"

"Do you know how much I sunk into that animal? I couldn't afford to take a loss. No way." He brushed the top of his wife's head with his lips. "Besides, it's not like Kessler isn't a fine animal. I've never seen a better trained animal, though I can't take claim for it."

"Yeah, I know. You can play the *William Tell* Overture in his ear and balance a glass of water on his head at the same time. But that's not why Brig Tanner bought him, is it?"

"No." He barely whispered the word.

"So, tell me. Is your little secret worth killing someone over?"

"That wasn't my idea."

"That makes me feel a whole lot better."

"Tom figured it was you who called that guy at Castleton. He said he was just going to scare you off."

"I don't think so. It felt too much like he was trying to kill me."

"I . . . I guess he was scared about his reputation. Maybe scared of what some folks he's had dealings with might do if they thought he was, you know . . ."

"What?" I said. "Does he make a habit out of this?"

No one answered me.

"Look," I said, "he's not doing you any favors, so why are you covering for him?"

"Tell him, Warren." Nan's face was still buried in her husband's shirt, so her voice was muffled.

"I don't have any of the specifics, but I know that I'm not the only breeder that Erdman's helped out."

"No shit." Nan pulled away from him and was drying her eyes on a shirtsleeve. "If you put all the breeders that man's 'helped out' in one room, you'd have to rent an auditorium. Of course"—she managed a wry smile—"Artie would take up half the room."

Warren shot his wife a look that silenced her.

"Artie Fotchke?" I asked.

"You didn't hear that name in this house."

"Whatever," I shrugged. "You're saying Erdman's done this phony semen business with other horses?"

"Not only that." Warren thought it over, then shrugged as though he'd come so far, why not go for it. "There's a lot of horses out there that claim to be out of champions but are really out of common stock."

"How does that work?"

"Well, you know, it's kind of like with humans. It's easy to prove a baby is not some guy's son. All you have to do is show the baby doesn't carry his blood type. But it's not so easy to prove the opposite—that a baby is his son. You know what I mean? It's all done with blood types. You do a little doctoring of a blood sample and you can make a foal look like it came from some pretty impressive stock. Hell, I know of one really fine brood mare that was, according to registrations, popping out foals a year after she died. Dead-mare foals they called them. The fact is, breeders' associations can't investigate every foal that's born. And they don't unless there's a lot of complaints."

"What would happen to Erdman if he were caught?"

"They'd yank his license so fast he'd spin."

I liked the way that sounded.

Warren bowed his head. "I never woulda let him talk me into doing that with Kessler except the horse set me back so much I just didn't see any other way to dig myself out."

I nodded, letting it sink in. "So when Brig bought the horse, Jubal really got a lucky break, didn't he?"

He looked up slowly. "What do you mean?"

"Jubal almost bought him, didn't he?"

"Yeah, but Jubal knew."

"He knew Kessler is sterile?"

Warren looked puzzled for a second, then laughed dryly, shaking his head. Nan was watching him closely. "Shit yes," he said. "The only way he'd keep his mouth shut was if we sold Kessler to his brother. I guess he thought it would be pretty funny for Brig to spend a bunch of money on a horse that turned out to be worth only a fraction of what he paid."

"Especially if the reason is because it's sterile," I added.

I stood, slightly dazed with this new knowledge. I went over events from the beginning with this new angle. "That night at the Tattersall. Did you have anything to do with Jubal getting whacked in the parking lot?"

"Not me. That was Erdman. He figured Jubal was a loose

cannon. Poppin' off like that in the bar. What in the hell was he trying to do?"

"Maybe Jubal figured Brig needed one more sales pitch."

"Whatever. Erdman had had it up to here with Jubal."

As Peanuts and I passed the Hineses on our way out the door, I said, "He's not the only one." I was beginning to wish I'd stayed for another beer that night. Even a green one.

$\triangledown$

21

By THE TIME I got to Jubal's I'd reduced my level of anger to a simmer. I did this by telling myself that rage and raw emotions weren't going to serve me. Deep breathing helped too. I would not improve the situation—my situation—by killing Jubal Tanner. Logic was really important here. It was simple. I would tell him I was off his case. He could keep his horse. Perhaps I'd suggest what he could do with his horse. As I left, I would recommend that he not use me as a character reference at the trial. All this would take approximately two, two and a half minutes, during which time if Jubal were to speak, I would not listen.

It didn't quite work out that way.

Perhaps Bear sensed my bad intentions, because he approached my car barking and baying. The other two just watched. Then Peanuts started and tried to jump into the driver's seat, which would have been easier if I weren't occupying it. I ordered him into the back and managed to squirm out of the car and get the door shut without him escaping or getting his paw smashed.

Jubal was walking around toward the house from the barn, and when he got close enough he must have read something ominous in my expression, because he hesitated, then mustered up a halfhearted smile and pretended to be pleased to see me. "McCauley, must be some powerful news that brought you out here. They haven't cut off our phone service. Not that I know of anyway."

"Jubal, we've got to talk." I tried to keep my voice even.

He lost any pretense of a smile. "Bad news?"

I didn't answer.

Nodding as though he understood, he said, "Yeah, sure. C'mon in."

Claude was sitting on the couch, knees together, face buried in her embroidery. She was jabbing the needle into the stretched fabric with an intensity that was almost vicious. The harsh red of the roses had blossomed across the white material. The muscles in her neck tightened as she watched me.

I heard the clatter of dishes in the kitchen, and a moment later Melissa emerged, pulling her hair back and capturing it in a bright red piece of elastic. She wore a gray jumper-type dress over a white blouse. "Hi, Mr. McCauley." Then she looked up at Jubal. "Who's taking me to the hospital? Or can I take the car?" There was a restraint to her manner that hadn't been there two weeks ago. I suspected she'd aged quite a bit in that time.

"You just wait a minute, okay?" Jubal sank into the chair, waiting. Melissa perched on the arm of the couch. She glanced at her mother's embroidery.

"So," Jubal said, crossing his arms, "what's the news?"

"I just came from Warren Hines's farm."

He hesitated, glancing at Claude. She didn't appear to have heard me. "Oh?"

I stepped back toward the window so I could keep an eye on all three of them. "Yeah, he was in a real talkative mood."

Jubal didn't respond, and Claude kept right on stitching. Melissa was watching me, her curiosity dulled by a stronger emotion.

"You never intended to buy that horse. Did you?"

He puffed his chest up. "The hell I didn't." Claude hesitated but picked up the pace again.

"What possible good could that horse be to you?"

"What're you talking about?"

He suddenly remembered his manners and waved his hand toward the couch. "Have a seat. Take a load off."

I ignored him. "Kessler is sterile."

His mouth dropped, and he gaped at me for a moment. Claude had stopped, needle poised above the fabric. "The hell you say."

"Don't give me that crap, Jubal. You know damned well that horse was worthless as a stud. You just pretended to be interested so your brother would buy him."

"Where the hell'd you hear that?" He ventured a nervous glance at Claude, who was watching him now.

"If you'll excuse the expression, I heard it from the horse's mouth. In this case the name's Warren Hines."

"That lying son of a bitch."

"I don't think so, Jubal. He's got no reason to lie about your involvement."

Claude's embroidery was on her lap and she stared at her husband, her expression oddly impassive. Jubal waved her off. "Oh, don't give me that, honey." His shoulders sagged, and he looked up at me, avoiding his daughter's expression. "Well, I didn't say I ended up wanting to buy Kessler. But I started out wanting to buy him." Like that made it all right.

"Dad—" He cut Melissa off with a raised hand.

"How did you find out he was sterile?"

He regarded me for a minute, perhaps running down his options. Finally he sighed and said, "Well, I never trusted that Erdman character. Though I always liked Hines." He paused, reconsidering. "At least I used to. Anyway, I picked a day when both Warren and Nan were away from the farm and nobody else was around and"—he gave a half shrug— "went and got my own sample." Simple.

I really wanted to know just how he managed that but didn't want to deviate from the issue. "So you just pretended to be interested in the horse, knowing that if your brother was true to form, he'd go after it."

He smiled, proud of himself. "Worked like a charm."

Claude placed her embroidery on the cushion next to her and stood slowly, hands folded in front of her. "You never intended to buy that horse?" she asked.

"Sure I did. Like I said. At first, anyway."

She stared at him long enough to get him squirming. "Why didn't you tell me?"

"Well, we never made a big deal outta these things. I . . . I guess I didn't think you'd be interested. That's all."

She put her hands to her face, took two deep breaths, then said, "I can't believe this, Jubal. My best friend was willing to invest money she really couldn't afford. You deceived her."

Jubal shifted in his chair. "Not really. I mean, it worked out. Never had to use Margaret's money."

When she dropped her hands to her side, I saw that her eyes were dull and flat—if eyes are the windows to the soul, right then hers was empty. Her voice cracked when she spoke again. "You just don't get it, do you? It's all a big joke to you. Do you know . . ." She stopped herself, turned, and walked up the stairs, her pace slow and measured. I could hear the floorboards above us creaking and then a door closing.

Jubal watched her retreat, frowning. When he saw me watching him, he shrugged and forced a laugh. "She'll get over it. She's just hyper these days." He leaned over and patted Melissa's knee. "Isn't that right, honey?" She pulled away from him like his hand was a hot iron.

"Don't you start now."

"I can't believe this, Daddy." Melissa was standing, looking down at her father. "Is this true?"

His eyes widened as he looked up at her. "I didn't do anything but a little horse dealing, honey. Don't start crying over it."

"You lied."

"I didn't lie. I just didn't tell you the whole truth."

Melissa crossed her arms over her chest. "You're a liar."

Jubal stood, towering over his daughter by at least four inches. "Don't you call your father a liar."

"Well, you are." She held her ground. "This is incredible."

"You go to your room and wait until I'm ready to take you to the hospital."

After a couple deep breaths, Melissa said, "No. I'm going without you. I'll get there myself. All these years you've been talking about what a miserable person your brother is. Well you're the one who's miserable." She paused and swallowed hard. "I know you think Jim Dworski is going to take the blame for all of this. Well, he's not. He didn't do it and I know. You know how I know? I knew him. I knew him real well. Better than I've ever known a man." Jubal's eyes were wide and his face red, like someone had just slapped him. "That's right. For you and Mom, his dying was really convenient. Well, it meant a whole lot more to me. Because I loved him. I slept with him."

Jubal backed up a step. "You better be making that up."

She raised her tear-streaked chin a couple inches and said, "I'm not like you. I don't lie." Then she spun on her heel and walked out the door, barely pausing to grab a sweater and a purse from the coatrack.

Jubal stood in the living room, fists clenched, staring at the closed door. Abruptly, he charged the door, throwing it open. Then he was on the stoop, slamming the storm door shut behind him. It sounded like a gun report. He hollered after her, his face red against his graying hair. "That's right. You go. And good riddance. Get the hell out of here. You go and you better find someplace else to come back to. 'Cause it's not gonna be here." He stopped, maybe waiting for a response, then raised his voice another level. "You hear me, Melissa? I don't know you anymore." After a moment, he stepped back inside, drained. He barely glanced at me as he sank into his chair again. I felt like I'd walked into a Eugene O'Neill play and had forgotten my lines.

Jubal sighed and shook his head, then muttered, "Ah, the hell with 'em. The hell with both of 'em. I don't believe any of that. Do you?"

"If I were you, I'd listen to her."

He studied me for a moment, then said "Bah" and shook his head in disgust, dismissing the whole scene. Then, abruptly shifting gears, he leaned over and patted the empty couch. "Now you sit here and cool off a second. Then we'll talk."

"No more talking, Jubal. I'm outta here too."

As I turned to leave, Jubal was on his feet. "What did I do?"

His disbelief was so genuine that I stopped.

"You screwed over one too many people, Jubal. You can't keep doing that and expect to have people pulling for you."

He held his arms out. "This is all that damned brother of mine's fault."

One hand on the doorknob, I delivered what I hoped would be my exit speech. "You're sick, Jubal. You hate your brother so much you can't see straight. And all he's been is your excuse. You've managed to make a shambles of your own life, and you've got nobody to blame but yourself. Not your lousy luck, not your timing, and not your brother."

I had the door open and one foot out when he said, "I hate him because he killed our little brother."

I hesitated, then slowly turned toward him. He was watching me, waiting. "He shot him?"

"He might as well have." He squared his jaw and added, "He loaded the gun."

I'd waited a long time to hear this. Closing the door behind me, I said, "You'd better tell me, Jubal. Or I'm going straight to the cops and I'm telling them about Kessler. I don't know if it ties you to the murder, but it sure as hell doesn't do much for your credibility."

He mulled that over for a few seconds, then disappeared into the kitchen. I heard the clinking of bottles, and when he returned he brought a fresh bottle of Scotch and two glasses. He gestured toward the couch as he took his chair. This time I accepted the offer. I watched as he methodically cracked open the bottle, poured a generous amount in the glasses, capped the bottle, and set it aside. He took one glass and handed me the other.

He stared into the amber liquid for almost a minute, then took a large swallow. Mine was much more conservative. He sat back in the chair, glass resting on his chest, and said, "Cody, he was supposed to marry this girl who worked for one of the town's two lawyers. JoEllen was her name." I'd already heard this part but let him set his own pace. When he continued, his gaze was focused at a point just past me. "She was a pretty little thing, but I never thought she was good enough for Cody. She was from a town out west, even smaller than Foxport. Hell, Foxport musta seemed like the big city to her. And she came here, wide-eyed, believing good things were gonna happen to her. And, at first they did. Cody took to her and she thought he was big time." He paused and smiled sadly. "She was really Cody's first woman. He was always sort of a babe in the woods, if you know what I mean."

After taking another drink, he continued, "Thing was, I guess Cody wasn't as manly as what JoEllen had in mind. But he courted her and she let him. I guess maybe she loved him. Some. Cody, he had it bad for her. But once she got a whiff of Brig, it was all over. Now Brig was married at the time to the best woman Foxport had to offer. But that didn't matter." He frowned and shook his head. "Brig's got to know he can get to any woman. So he came on to her, and she fell like a sack of rocks. But that was all he wanted, just one night. Just to know that he could have her if he felt like it. Well, JoEllen, she figures he's gonna leave Barbara and all, but that's not what he's got in mind. And he tells her to go ahead and marry Cody, because that's all she was to him. She wasn't used to it. Didn't know anyone could be like that. I guess she couldn't face Cody anymore, so she sliced her wrists." He emptied the glass. "Brig might as well have done it himself."

"Did Cody know why she killed herself?"

After staring into the bottom of his empty glass for several moments, Jubal said, "Cody figured she just couldn't bring herself to marry him. He wasn't good enough. Man enough. Once she figured out that he was no good at hunting and fighting, she wanted nothing to do with him. She was the one who wasn't good enough. Couldn't tell him though. Figured dying was better."

Blinking back the moisture from his eyes, Jubal settled back into the chair. "I miss him. It's been almost thirty years, and most days it feels like it was yesterday. I still talk to him, you know. I go out there and we talk."

I took one more swallow and set the glass on the floor, close enough to Jubal in case he wanted the rest. When I left, Jubal was staring up at the horse's painting. I thought I'd never seen a man so old.

My curiosity had been sated, but in its place was a dulled depression, as though the death of a young couple thirty years ago had affected me personally.

As I pulled out of Jubal's long driveway, the crunch of gravel beneath tires somehow satisfied. As I accelerated, it occurred to me that I missed the Honda. It's got a manual transmission, and I work out kinks in my mental state by shifting gears. Then I felt Peanuts' cold nose at the back of my neck. That helped some.

I'd got about a quarter of a mile when I saw Melissa leaning against a white fence, pulling apart a blade of grass. When she saw me, she moved toward the road. It was like this was a prearranged pickup. "Hey, Mr. McCauley. Can you give me a lift?" She wasn't crying anymore, but neither had her buoyancy returned.

"Hop in."

Before settling into the seat, she gave Peanuts a little attention, stroking his neck and cooing over him. "This is a cool dog. Is he a mutt?"

I'm never offended when someone thinks he's a mix. That's one of the things I like about the breed. Nothing pretentious. "No, he's a border collie. They're used to herd sheep. His name's Peanuts."

After fussing over him for another minute, she gave him a final pat, kissed him (I'm not sure, but I think that kissing animals is a female trait), then settled into the seat. She yanked the band that had been holding back her hair and shook it loose. Then she produced a pink plastic comb from her purse and began running it through her hair. "Can you take me to Abel County Hospital?" Although she'd put it to me as a question, the tone was the kind you use with a cabdriver.

I didn't disappoint her. "No problem."

She switched on the radio, tuning it to US99, a country-western station. After a few bars of "Here's a Quarter, Call Someone Who Cares," she began humming along, then abruptly stopped. "I work there, you know."

"I think Cindy might have mentioned that," I paused. "She says you want to be a psychiatrist."

Melissa nodded, sighing. "Sometimes I think it's the only way I'll escape this family curse." She looked at me. "They're all crazy, you know."

"I don't know. Stubborn, pigheaded, illogical maybe, but crazy? I don't know."

"I do," she said softly, swallowing.

When the song was over, I said, "Your dad gonna let you back into the house tonight?"

She heaved a disgusted sigh. "Who says I want to go back?"

"It's not like you can stay at your boyfriend's anymore."

I felt her turn to me. Slowly. "I didn't sleep with him, you know. I just said that."

I was sort of touched by her need to tell me that but wasn't sure how to respond. "That's probably best."

"I don't know." She spoke softly as she pulled hair out of the comb's teeth and carefully wound it around her forefinger. "I do know that Jim didn't kill anyone. He didn't take your dog either."

I knew that too, but she seemed pretty convinced herself, and I wanted to know why.

Now she sniffed and wiped tears off her cheek with the back of her hand.

"How do you know that?" I wished I had something other than a used handkerchief to offer her, but I didn't.

"He found a gun. It was hidden."

"Where?"

"In the barn. Our barn. We were in there one afternoon
about a week ago. You know, just fooling around. And it was
behind some hay bales. I was so scared. I mean, not at first.
I didn't think anything of it. But then Jim said 'Why would
Dad be hiding his gun in the barn?' and we got to thinking."
Her voice was choked and she had trouble getting the words
out. But they came. "And Jim said not to worry. He'd take
care of it. He'd get rid of it. Nobody would ever know."

"And did he?"

"He said he did. But I don't know where. I didn't want to
know."

"You can't be sure that's the gun that killed Gayle then."

"It's not."

"How do you know?"

"I know my dad. He may be crazy and ornery, but he's no
killer. It's not in him."

"What about your mother?"

After a moment, she said, "I thought about that, but
there'd be no reason. She barely knew Uncle Brig. Never met
Gayle. No reason."

"Did your mother know you were seeing Jim?"

She made a face. "Probably. My big-mouth cousin probably told her."

"Cindy?"

"Yeah."

"But your dad didn't know."

"Yeah. That's the weird part. Can't figure out why Mom
wouldn't tell him."

"Why would she?"

She gave me that look that teenagers of every generation
have managed to perfect. It said: You are as dumb as mud.
"Because the less he thinks of me, the more he thinks of her.
She's probably thrilled that I'm out of there now."

This probably had something to do with Oedipus, but I
wasn't sure. "You and your dad are pretty close, aren't you?"

She didn't answer and slouched down in the seat.

"Put your seat belt on," I said.

"Why? Are you planning on crashing this thing?"

"Only if the mood strikes me."

She gave me an odd look but did as I'd told her.

"Are you close to your uncle?"

She shrugged and sniffed, her eyes blinking rapidly. "Not really. I mean, I don't hate him. He's really kind of a jerk. You know, thinks a lot of himself." She turned her attention out the window and watched the newly tilled fields slide by. Eyes still fixed on the passing scenery, she said, "Did you know that woman he was seeing?"

"Not well. Did you?"

She shook her head, then after a minute said, "Cindy didn't like her."

"What about Will?"

"That's why Cindy didn't like her."

"Cindy knew about Will and Gayle?"

"Yeah. I don't know." She sounded far away. I waited for her to come back on her own. When she turned to me after a couple minutes, her eyes were shiny. "My dad's in a lot of trouble, isn't he?"

I figured any way you looked at it, Jubal was in trouble and probably deserved to be, but I wasn't convinced they'd be able to make this murder rap stick to him. But a little dry voice in the back of my head told me to play this close to the vest. "He might be."

"Are you still working for him?"

I paused a beat. "I don't know. I don't like being lied to."

"I know what you mean." She found a tissue in her purse and blew her nose. "But you know, as mad as I am at him, and right now, that's real mad, I really understand him. At least I think I do. He just does it so he'll look better. So people will give him a break."

I kept quiet.

She emitted a frustrated sigh and began running her thumbnail down the tines of the comb. "I know something," she said quietly.

"What?" We were coming into town, and I slowed for a

yellow light I might otherwise have run.

"It's about Will." She paused. "He was seeing Gayle."

"I know."

"She was dumping him."

"How do you know?"

"I heard him. On the phone with her. Sometimes I go to his office, you know, to help out. Filing. Stuff like that. Sandy's real nice." I waited. "I heard him that morning asking Gayle to see him one more time. I know that's who he was talking to because he used her name once. I don't think he knew I was there. Sandy was on a break and I was in that chair by his door, sorting some papers. His door was open a crack and I heard him. He was real upset, saying stuff like 'You can't do that' and 'He won't believe you.' And then he was begging her to see him." She paused. "Finally I guess she agreed."

"When was that?" I held my breath.

She turned to me, her eyes clear, focused. "The morning she was murdered."

The car in back of us let me know that the light had changed. As I moved into the flow of traffic, I asked her, "Why didn't you say anything before this?"

"I told Cindy. She already knew about them. She didn't say, but I could tell."

"Who else did you tell?"

"Nobody." She looked away and added, "I'm not a snitch, you know."

"So, you'd hide a weapon that might have been involved in a crime, and you wouldn't reveal some important evidence. Have I got that right?"

"I didn't want Will to get in trouble." She paused, then added, "He's nice."

"Melissa, Will couldn't have killed her. Not if he made the phone call from his office like you said. Gayle left right after the phone call. There's no way he could have gotten from there to the woods out by Windemere in time to shoot her. It's physically impossible."

She was silent for a minute, then said, "Yeah, I guess you're right."

"Did you tell the police?" When she didn't respond, I added, "I need to know because if you didn't, that means I still have to find out who did."

"Yeah," she said in a small voice, "I called them. Didn't leave my name though." She sighed. "I didn't want to get him in trouble or anything like that. I just was worried about Jubal. You know?"

"Yeah, I know."

"Do you think he did it? Killed her?"

"No," I said, then lapsed into silence. How convoluted was this whole thing? Hard to tell when you've got some of the cops doing the convoluting. I had just turned onto the hospital's access road when I asked Melissa, "You said you and Jim found the gun. Which one of you actually spotted it first?"

"Jim did."

"Had you two ever, uh, used the barn before?"

"Well, no, I mean we hadn't been seeing each other that long."

"Whose idea was the barn?"

"Jim's. Why?"

"Just wondered." I like things simple, and the scenarios I was putting together were anything but. I had a different one for every story I'd heard.

I slowed and pulled up in front of the hospital.

"Thanks, Mr. McCauley." She smiled at me, her eyes wide and uncomplicated. If I closed my mind to the fact that Jubal was her father, it was easy to believe every word she said.

22

ON MY WAY back to the office, I stopped at the Tattersall for a burger and a Guinness. Both tasted great, especially since it was almost five and I hadn't eaten since the massive sugar doses at breakfast. Peanuts spent most of the meal with his chin on my leg, drooling. The fact that I didn't make him lie down under the table and even gave him a few bites was a good sign that I hadn't forgiven myself for his ordeal. It kept nagging at me too. If Dworski didn't take him, then who did?

I wasn't exactly comfortable leaving Jubal in the lurch either, but I reasoned that I just couldn't work with a client I couldn't trust. Even if his reasons for lying were good ones. But there'd probably be a message from him when I got back to the office, and I'd probably be back in it again up to my knees before I knew what hit me. But for a half hour, it was nice to enjoy the burger, the beer, and my dog.

Elaine was sitting at my desk when I got back to the office. Spread out across the desk were brochures hawking various brands of computers. Here we go.

Her greeting to me was lukewarm, and Peanuts didn't fare much better.

"Something wrong?" I poured myself a mug of coffee.

"Ed just left." She sighed.

I wanted to ask if he just left for the Australian outback, but I stifled the urge and said, "How'd his trip to the station go?"

"Not good. Moore wouldn't talk to him, and the officers

who are on his side were afraid to." She shook her head. "This is killing him." She was fiddling with a pencil and staring at a black-and-white glossy of a monitor with a split screen.

I studied her for a minute, wondering how Ed Carver could evoke that much sympathy. I mean, was this the way you act when a casual acquaintance is in trouble? She turned her attention to the computers, sorting the brochures into three piles.

I took a swallow of coffee. Unlike Carver, Elaine made a nice, strong pot. She was wearing her hair the way I liked it—loose and full so that it fell soft against her shoulders. Even on a gloomy day like this with the sun just about to give up the fight, her hair blazed with streaks of gold. I wondered how long it had been since I'd noticed.

It was a moment before I realized she was looking at me and had said something. "Sorry, just taking a twenty-second vacation."

To her credit, she didn't roll her eyes and shake her head. "Actually, he came here to see you. He managed to learn a couple real interesting things. First, they found a rifle at Dworski's house that has been positively identified as the murder weapon."

What a surprise. "Anything else?" I asked.

"They also found a large amount of cash stashed in a closet."

"How large?

"Ten grand."

"Reward money?"

"Well, Moore is calling it hit money."

"Figures. What about the coroner's report?" I propped my feet up on my desk.

Elaine looked like she was about to tell me I had ten months to live.

"What?" I prompted.

"You're not going to like this."

I took another drink, thinking a shot of Drambuie might

help both me and the coffee right about now. "There's not going to be an autopsy."

"Well, not as of this moment. According to Moore, and I think these were the words Ed said he used, 'With a ton of metal sitting on his chest, only an idiot would wonder what killed him.' "

I slammed my feet on the floor and the mug on the desk. "Damn. Double damn. That's not why we need an autopsy, for shit's sake. We need to know when he died."

Elaine held up her hands. "I know. I know."

"I know you do." I started pacing the small area. "Without proving time of death, they're not going to have any trouble pinning this on Jubal." I stopped dead in my tracks. "And why the hell do I care?"

"Is Jubal trying your patience again?"

"Trying isn't the word. More like abusing."

"Well, all may not be lost. As far as the autopsy goes, that is. Ed is using what pull he's got left to get someone to intervene." She wiped up the coffee I'd sloshed and added some to the mug. "Here, drink this and tell me what happened." I just looked at her. "Sit. Talk to me."

I did, starting with Warren Hines and finishing with Melissa's story.

As Elaine listened, she leaned back in my chair, one leg crossed over the other, rocking slightly. She didn't say anything for a minute after I finished, then sat up, arms folded on my desk. "Wow" was all she said at first. "That family's really got the skeletons, don't they?"

I nodded.

"Do you think that rifle Jim and Melissa found is the one that turned up in his house?"

"Doesn't make much sense, does it? Stash a possible murder weapon in your bedroom closet?" I shook my head.

"Maybe he was hiding it for Melissa."

"Maybe," I said, unconvinced. Elaine was giving Dworski the benefit of the doubt, but then she'd never met him.

"Are you through with him? Jubal, I mean."

I took a minute before answering. "I doubt it," I finally said.

I grabbed the local phone book and thumbed through the yellow pages for accountants. Will wasn't in his office, but Sandy asked if I had plans for later.

"Uh, yeah, I do have something on for tonight."

"Are you sure? I make the best lasagna in the western suburbs."

"Oh, yeah, I'm sure." I swallowed and ventured a glance at Elaine and saw that she was slightly amused. Or intrigued. Either way, she was a long way from jealous.

"Well," Sandy said, "maybe some other time."

"Yeah. Sure."

When I hung up, Elaine arched an eyebrow and said, "What are you doing tonight?"

"Don't know yet. What about you?"

"I may have plans."

Miraculously, the phone rang.

"Uh, McCauley, this is Jubal." Miracles are overrated.

"Hello, Jubal." I managed to keep my voice even. Elaine suppressed a smile.

"Uh, listen, are you still working for me?"

"I'd rather not be."

"Yeah, well, that's what I figured." But he kept going. "I need some help here. See, they've got me over at the jail. You know, on Second Street—"

"I know where it is, Jubal," I interrupted. "Why are you there?" There was a befuddled, almost bewildered quality to his voice that seemed out of character.

"Well, they say I killed Gayle."

"They've been saying that for a while now. What's different?"

"I don't know. Probably nothing." He paused. "I don't know. I just got here. You're my phone call."

"Why me?"

"Nobody else to call."

"I'm calling you a lawyer."

"I hate—" he began.

"I don't care if you hate them. You need one. Do yourself
a favor and don't say anything until he gets there."

"I got nothing to hide."

"Nothing. Say nothing."

I heard him sigh. "This murder charge. It's bullshit."

"That's what you keep telling me."

When I hung up, Elaine said, "This guy's really got your
number, doesn't he?"

I raised my hands in surrender. "What can I say?"

"Did he say it was the gun they traced back to him?"

"He didn't say. But I've got a feeling that's it."

"You still don't think he did it, do you?"

I shrugged and lit a cigarette, wondering if I'd missed this
one by a country mile.

I made a couple calls, finally tracking down Cal Maitlin
at his home. I figured he'd be the least objectionable of the
species to Jubal. At first he thought I was calling about my
own situation.

"No, no," I said, "we'll get to that later. You know Jubal
Tanner?"

Fortunately, he did, and he also knew about the situation.
Chuckling, he said, "That man's a wild one." In spite of, or
maybe because of, that he agreed to go see Jubal. "You
coming along?"

I glanced at Elaine. "I'd rather take a pass. There's a
couple people I need to track down. Why don't you give me
a call at home after you've had a chance to talk to him?"

"You're going home?" Elaine asked after I'd hung up.

"I need some thinking time." I stretched out in the chair
and propped my feet on the desk.

"You're worried about him, aren't you?"

I thought about that for a minute. "I don't know. He
might have put one over on me. I wouldn't put it past him."

I patted one of the brochure piles. "You pick one out yet?"

"Working on it." She smiled, then added, "I love spending
other people's money," and went back to the pile of computer
information.

"You seeing Carver tonight?" I didn't mean to hit her out of the blue like that, but I knew if I gave the question too much thought, I'd never ask it.

She tapped her pen against one of the brochures and without taking her eyes from the black-and-white glossy said, "I guess I would like to go out with him." Sighing, she lifted her gaze up to me. "I just don't want to lose you."

I nodded, unable to speak because of the lump that had materialized in my throat.

Then she added, "You're my closest friend."

I swallowed hard and moved my hand so that my fingers barely brushed hers. "I don't know. Maybe we're better at being friends than anything else."

She seemed to relax a little. "I think maybe you're right."

"I hate it when I'm right."

She patted my hand. "Thank God it doesn't happen often."

Smiling, she began to straighten the brochures. When I continued to stare, she folded her hands on the pile. "What?"

"Regarding you and Ed . . ." I hesitated, then continued. "Just a word of warning."

She arched her eyebrows in that suspicious way she has. "Just one word?"

I nodded. I could do it in one word. "Rebound."

At first I thought she was going to let me have it, but then her eyes softened and she said, "Thanks. I'll be careful."

As soon as I got home, I took Peanuts for a run by the river. I even stole a few minutes to toss him the Frisbee. That's the one way to relax—watch a dog who really knows what he's doing shag Frisbees. When we returned to the apartment, I was planning to open a beer and wait for Cal Maitlin to call but decided waiting didn't suit me. Tom Erdman clearly had the advantage over me. No one was going to admit seeing him slip LSD into my drink, and it was a pretty safe bet that he wasn't going to confess. Maybe he just needed to be flushed out of the bushes.

"Yancy's." The guy on the other end of the line sounded like he had a two-pack-a-day habit.

"Yeah, is Tom Erdman around?"

"Ah, hold on." He dropped the phone on something hard. I winced and waited while I heard him holler Erdman's name a couple times. After a minute, he came back on. "Nah, not here yet."

"Thanks." I started to hang up, then thought of something. "Hey, is Artie around?" I couldn't dredge up his last name.

"Artie?" He was starting to sound interested, which meant he was probably suspicious.

"Yeah, uh, the Slab." What kind of thug lets himself be called that?

After a couple beats, he said, "Who's calling?"

After a brief brain scan, the best I could come up with was, "His accountant."

"Thought you were calling Erdman."

"Yeah, well, I work for both of them."

He must have bought it, because he dropped the phone again. A couple minutes later, Artie came on.

"Yeah, Leon. What's the problem?"

"Here's the problem, Artie. This isn't Leon. It's Quint McCauley. In case you haven't heard, I'm not dead yet. Now here's a little advice. If you keep surrounding yourself with losers like Erdman, your reputation is going to suffer. You won't be able to sell one of your nags to a glue factory." Horses probably weren't used in the glue process anymore, but I figured he'd get the point.

He let loose with some colorful, although unoriginal, expletives, and I hung up, feeling both exhilarated and stupid. Yanking Artie's strings sure felt good, but what was it going to buy me? That all depended on how important Artie's opinion was to Erdman.

Peanuts was stretched out in front of the TV. "Sometimes you just gotta poke the hornet's nest." He raised his head, regarded me for a second, then dropped it back to the rug. I turned on channel nine and caught the end of a "Cheers" rerun and "The Golden Girls" while I drank my beer. The seven o'clock movie, *The Wild Bunch*, was just starting when the phone rang. Just as well.

"You're not going to believe this." It was Cal Maitlin. I wasn't sure I wanted him to continue.

"Try me."

"Jubal Tanner escaped."

Though I'd braced myself, I was completely unprepared for that. I worked my jaw up and down a couple times before saying, "The hell you say."

"Yep." I could hear voices in the background, some of them loud as though yelling orders. "Apparently he gave them the slip, as they say."

I could get to enjoy this. "Oh yeah?" I tossed Peanuts a biscuit. He took it over to the carpet. "How'd it happen?"

"Well, as you can imagine, they're a little reluctant to discuss it, but apparently one of Moore's minions left him alone in the interrogation room and forgot to lock the door. He just sort of strolled out."

That struck a sour note. "You think they let him?"

"Well, I wondered that myself. But I just saw Mr. Moore. He looks like a man who would feel a lot better if he could just strangle someone."

"Did you get a chance to see Jubal?"

"Yes. It was the strangest thing. Moore showed him a gun and asked if he'd ever seen it. Before I could counsel him otherwise, he said it was his and what did it have to do with anything. Moore said it was the murder weapon. Jubal didn't believe him. Finally I asked for a few minutes alone with him, during which time I advised him of our alternatives. He sat there, not speaking or asking questions and certainly not listening. Finally, he interrupted me and said, 'I did it. I killed her.' Just like that.

"I asked him how he managed to be in two places at once, but he didn't have a good answer. All he said was he wanted to make a confession. Was quite adamant about it. I left to

find Moore—there was an officer at the door. Before you
know it, Jubal is gone and the officer is locked in the
interrogation room. God knows what his story will be."

Cal continued on about the inadequacies in the department. I half tuned him out, trying to make sense of what
he'd just told me. Or rather, trying to make sense of my own
stupidity. Then I realized, from the silence, that Cal had
asked me a question. "Sorry, what was that?"

"Don't suppose you'd have any idea where Jubal might go?"

"I'll have to think on it."

"Please do. I realize it's a little late for damage control, but
it would help ease a bad situation if the cops didn't find him
first."

"I'll try. Are you staying there?"

"For a while." He laughed softly. "I'm really rather enjoying the turmoil."

I lit another cigarette and noticed that there were only two
left. Jubal Tanner was hazardous to my health. Where the
hell was the son of a bitch? He wasn't the type to grab the
first plane out of the country. You need a credit card for that.
Think, McCauley. I flashed back to something he'd said in
our earlier conversation. It was a long shot, but then the way
my luck had been running lately, I was way overdue for a
payoff.

Eight P.M. isn't one of the best times to visit a cemetery.
Trust me on this. As I pulled off the road into its gravel
entrance, I could feel the hair on the back of my neck rising.
During the day these little rural cemeteries are idyllic
patches of green with lots of just plain folks sleeping eternity
away. But once the sun drops, these "plain folks" get restless
and figure, what the hell, let's kick some mortal ass.

The cemetery was small, just over an acre, and was
surrounded by a wrought-iron fence and dotted with oaks
and pines and little scrub bushes. Fortunately, there was no
lock or even a gate to speak of. I've been told that gates on
cemeteries are to keep out the body snatchers. But I wonder.

The sky had cleared for the time being, and the moon was almost full, coating the land in white light and drowning out the stars. But a bank of clouds moving in from the west promised the clear, bright night would be short-lived.

Out of the shadows, I spotted a mangy pickup parked off the road in the northwest corner of the cemetery. I pulled in behind it.

Jubal wasn't far away. He was standing over a group of graves sheltered by a huge oak. Though I wasn't trying to be quiet, he gave no indication that he heard me approach him. But when I cleared my throat, he looked over his shoulder, only slightly interested to find me there. He smiled and nodded, not like he was expecting me, more like he didn't mind.

"How'd you know I'd be here?"

"Lucky guess."

"I knew I'd hired a good one. Come hell or high water, he can find his client."

I smiled, conceding the point. "What can I say? It's a gift."

He stood, head bowed, gripping the brim of his cowboy hat in his hands, like he was about to say a few final words.

Stepping up to the tombstone, I read the inscription:

> Cody William Tanner
> Beloved Son and Brother
> b August 8, 1934
> d June 4, 1964

Jubal looked over his shoulder, taking in the rest of the cemetery. "I like it here," he said. "Quiet. You can almost hear the worms crawling around. Five generations of Tanners are buried here." He paused and regarded the Tanner patch of tombstones. "But I don't know. I'm not crazy about worms having a field day in my carcass. Know what I mean?"

"Exactly."

Jubal squinted at the moon as its light etched shadows in his face. "You know, I want them to cremate me and then

have some airplane spread my ashes over my land." He
looked at me. "Sort of like a full circle, know what I mean?"

"Yeah," I said, nodding, then tried and failed to suppress
a smile.

"What's funny about that?" He spoke quietly, more
curious than hurt.

"Nothing. Not a thing." I shook my head. "It just made
me think. I've always figured I'd want my ashes mixed with
limestone and used to paint the third-base line at Wrigley
Field."

Jubal chuckled, then looked up at the moon again. "It's
gonna be a clear day tomorrow." He moved his right hand,
and I saw that in addition to gripping the hat, it also held a
.38 special.

"Tell me," I said, "how'd you break out of jail?"

"Oh, that," he said as though I'd asked him how he
worked a simple card trick. "After that lawyer went to find
Moore, I told the cop outside the door I had to use the can.
I don't know. He didn't have his gun out or anything. When
he stepped back to let me out of that little interrogation
room, I just pulled him in and got the hell out of there. I
slammed the door shut and I guess it locked. He was
hollering, but those walls in the room are concrete. Guess
his voice didn't carry too far. I just walked out like I wasn't
in any hurry. Nobody stopped me. Didn't even look at me
twice." He paused, took a deep breath, and blew it out slowly.
"They'd picked me up in town, coming out of McDonald's.
You know, the one by the station. My truck was still there.
Really no big deal."

I pictured Gene Moore, red-faced, eyes bulging, but
couldn't savor the image for long. Jubal looked down at the
gun, lying dark and dull in his hand. "I was gonna use this."
He paused and added, "Still might."

"That's no answer, Jubal."

He waved off my protest. "Who's looking for answers? I
just want some quiet." Dropping the gun to his side, he said,
"Thing is, you know what?"

"What?"

"I don't know that I've got the guts."

"That's not what it takes."

"Sure it is." He turned back to his brother's grave and nudged a clump of grass with the toe of his boot. "Funny. In the end, he's the one with the guts."

"I don't get it. Why does your family equate everything that defines what a person is with either violence or conquest?" After a moment, he turned to me, confused. "For God's sake, Jubal, we're practically into the twenty-first century. If the Tanner family were running the globe, we'd have blown ourselves to hell and gone a long time ago."

He shrugged as though maybe that wasn't a bad idea.

"I mean, no offense to Cody, but people have lived with worse things happening to them, you know."

"Now, you listen here." He stepped toward me, angry.

"He had choices. But what did he do? He chose the only option that he figured his family would understand." I paused, waiting for an outburst. When none came, I added, "You guys are anachronisms. Pure and simple."

"What?"

"You're living in the wrong century."

Jubal snorted. "That's for goddamned sure." He put on his hat, pushing it back on his forehead. Then he lowered himself into a crouch over his brother's grave. He cradled the gun, almost lovingly, as though he were reading the answers in it.

"Yeah, I guess that's the way you people deal with things, isn't it? You either blow out your brains or someone else's. Shit, it sure beats facing the music."

He shook his head and laughed softly. "There's something I didn't mention this afternoon," he said.

"What's that?"

"Cody knew about Brig and JoEllen."

"How?" I figured I knew the answer, had known there was something like this at the bottom of all the hate. But I had to hear it from him.

"I told him."

"Why?"

He sighed deeply and began to clear away some dead leaves from his brother's grave. "You know, I thought maybe it'd help if he knew. After JoEllen died, he just seemed so close to the edge, like he thought he'd driven her to it. I was afraid he'd go right after her. Figured if he knew it wasn't him, if he knew she did herself in because of Brig, well, maybe he'd quit blaming himself."

"And start blaming Brig."

"I don't know. I thought at the time I was doing the right thing, but now . . . I don't know. Don't know anything anymore. Nothing. All I know is that this mess is where it's all going to end up."

"Did you kill Gayle?"

Without looking up, he answered, "I'm afraid so."

"I don't believe you."

He took his time standing up, and when he faced me again, I saw that he was smiling. In the moon's glow he looked slightly deranged. "I know. Why'd you think I hired you? You talk about anacro . . . whatever. You know what you are? You're worse. You put your money on the bandy-legged horse 'cause you feel sorry for him. You think you're this tough-ass detective with these great instincts. You're as bad as me, only different."

"I hope there's no charge for the evaluation." He waved me off in disgust.

"How could you have killed her if someone spotted you in the grocery store?"

I waited one minute, then two. He straightened slowly. "I hired someone to do it. My first mistake. She wasn't supposed to die, and she never would have if I'd handled it myself."

"Who'd you hire?"

He ignored the question.

"Why would you deprive yourself of the pleasure of seeing your brother die?"

He frowned and shrugged. "Not that big a deal. Bottom line's the same anyway." Sighing deeply, he added, "Just so long as he's dead."

"But he's not."

"I know."

"So why not try again? Where's that famous Tanner persistence?"

Shrugging, he didn't hurry to answer. Finally he said, "Not so easy now. He's expecting something."

"Why now?" I nodded toward Cody's grave. "Why not thirty years ago?"

"I was younger then. But the years pass and things add up." He regarded me for a moment, then added, "He took everything I ever had. Everything I ever wanted. You understand?"

"What about your family. Did he take them too?"

He looked away.

"Who you protecting, Jubal?"

"What d'you mean?"

"Did Moore tell you where they found that rifle?"

He didn't answer.

"I've got a feeling that's the one that Dworski and Melissa found in your barn."

"Missy?" Staring at his brother's tombstone, he barely whispered her name.

"Who are you covering for, Jubal?"

He turned and confronted me, gun pointed at my head. "Don't—"

The gunshot came like a blast out of the dark, and the bullet came so close to my neck, I could feel the breeze. Jubal spun backwards and went down. As I began to turn, expecting to come face-to-face with a rescue effort, a second shot took a chunk of bark off the oak. I hit the ground. So much for the cavalry theory.

▽

23

Jubal coughed and stirred, then started to raise himself
up on his left elbow. I pushed him back down. "What
the . . ." His voice cracked.

"You okay?"

He responded with a noncommittal grunt.

"Welcome to the duck shoot." I squinted into the distance
and could make out only shadows, none of them moving.

We were sheltered on one side by the oak, but that left the
other three wide open. The clouds moved steadily toward
the moon, but it would be several minutes before I could
count on darkness.

"Who the hell is out there?" Jubal touched his left hand
to his right shoulder. I assumed he'd been hit but couldn't
tell how bad.

"You tell me. You're the one with all the friends." As I
studied the shadows, I thought one of them moved. "Give
me your gun," I whispered, holding out my hand.

He started to hand it over, then stopped. "Where's yours?"

"At home."

"At home?"

"Look, Jubal, I was on my way to a cemetery, not the
gunfight at OK Corral."

Snorting his disgust, Jubal eased his weight off his right
arm and took the gun with his left hand. "You think I'm
handing this over, you're dumber than I figured."

I calculated the odds of making it to Jubal's truck while

remaining in cover, then glanced up at the clouds again. Almost there. "As soon as that cloud blots out the moon, let's try to get to your truck. You got the keys?"

As an answer, he rolled over on his left side. "Hold on." As he dug for the keys, I heard a twig pop about twenty feet beyond the tree. Before Jubal could protest, I snatched the gun out of his hand and twisted toward the noise, firing off a round. I didn't expect to hit anything, just hoped whoever was stalking us would back off and we could buy a couple minutes. At first it seemed to work. I didn't hear anyone running away, but he wasn't coming any closer either.

"That was real smart," Jubal said as I settled back down next to him.

"What?"

"You just used up all our ammo."

"What?"

"I was gonna blow my brains out, what the hell do I need two bullets for?"

"You've only got one bullet in here?"

"Don't have any now." He paused and added, "I don't like to load my weapons unless I'm planning to use them."

"That's . . . that's. Shit." I pounded my forehead against the cool grass. "You got more in the truck?"

"Yeah, in the glove box, but we're a long ways from there."

"You got a better idea?"

Jubal didn't answer, but he handed me the keys. They felt slippery. "Tell you what," I said. "I'll get to the truck, load the gun, and start blasting away. You use the cover to get there. All you have to do is jump in." No response. "You up to that?"

"That's the dumbest thing I ever heard. How do you know where he is to shoot at him?"

"All right. Let's hear from the critic."

He muttered something under his breath.

The cloud bank edged its way in front of the moon. I estimated we were thirty feet from the truck and there were no tombstones to use as cover. Half the moon was gone now.

"You do what you gotta do, just quit trying to rescue men who want to sleep."

Three excruciatingly long minutes later, we lost the rest of the moon's light. It was like somebody flipped a switch. The cloud made it difficult for our assailant to see us, but it worked the other way too. God, it was dark. We were out in the middle of the country—the city's glow never reached this far. I could barely make out the hulk of Jubal's truck, and I had no idea where our friend was. But once I opened the truck's door, he'd know exactly where I was. The truck bed was covered by a cap, which would provide some protection . . . if I could get there.

"Is the truck unlocked?"

He grunted something that sounded more like yes than no.

"Can I get to the back from the cab?"

Another affirmative. "There's a window."

"Could I fit through it?"

"I guess. It's a slider."

"Don't go anywhere." I patted Jubal on the back and began crawling toward the truck. It was impossible not to make some noise, and I'd only gone ten feet when the first shot came, missing me by only a couple feet. That motivated me to cover the rest of the distance as fast and as low to the ground as possible. Two more shots were near misses before I made it around the far side of the truck. The door stuck at first, and I cursed under my breath, thinking Jubal had locked it after all, then I yanked hard and it gave, opening with such force I almost knocked myself over. Two bullets shattered the windshield and I climbed in, pulled the door shut behind me, and jammed my palm against the glove box lock. It didn't give. I pushed it with my thumb. Damn. The sonofabitch had locked it. Shit. The door took another hit, then another. I shoved the sliding window open and dove through. Well, it was somewhat less clean than a dive, and I had to suck my gut in to work my torso through. My legs were still flailing behind me when he started shooting through the door. I somersaulted onto the truck bed.

He fired two shots before stopping, paused for about thirty seconds, then put another two through the door. I crawled the length of the truck and found the cap's handle. Holding my breath, I turned it and pushed it up and open, praying the whole while that Jubal oiled the hinges every now and then. It lifted without a sound. Getting out without the truck bobbing was another problem. It was dead still outside, almost like the night was waiting for something. I felt around the truck bed and found a box filled with stiff brushes and curved metal objects. Horse paraphernalia, no doubt. I gripped a brush, aimed at the window I'd wormed my way through, and lobbed it into the cab. While he fired into the door again, I lowered myself out over the truck's flap. I eased down slowly, so the truck didn't give much. Then I waited. After almost two minutes, I heard the click of the door latch. By the time the light went on in the empty cab, I was right behind him with Jubal's gun at his ear.

More than anything, it was his height that gave him away—his height and the smell of smoke and stale beer that rose off him.

"God damn you, Erdman." I pressed the barrel into the back of his ear and reached around him for the magnum he'd tried to do me in with. He hesitated a moment before releasing it. "Wise move," I said in congratulations, pocketing Jubal's empty gun. I wondered if he'd gotten here on his own, then figured it wasn't likely he'd level with me anyway. If he was with anyone, it was probably Artie. We'd hear him coming.

"Jubal," I hollered. "Jubal, you got any rope?" I pushed Erdman's face down on the driver's seat and twisted his arm behind him. Then I found the headlights knob and pulled it on.

Gravel crunched, and Jubal staggered into view. He was squinting into the headlights and gripping his shoulder. "Who you got there?"

"Your buddy, the vet."

"Erdman, you piece of shit."

"He knows about the horse, Tanner." Erdman's voice was muffled by the seat.

Jubal snorted. "You dumb sonofabitch."

"You got any rope, Jubal?"

He hesitated, taking a moment to sneer at the back of Erdman's head, then walked past me to the back of the truck. His jacket's shoulder was torn and there appeared to be some blood, but I couldn't tell how bad he'd been hit. "You okay, Jubal?"

"I'll live," he muttered, apparently none too pleased with the prospect.

I heard him rummaging around in the truck for a minute; then he returned with a couple yards of good, strong rope. While Jubal held the gun, I looped Erdman's arms through the steering wheel and bound his wrists together good and tight. All the activity had skewed Erdman's rug so that it resembled a badly placed squirrel pelt. He wet his lips nervously as he watched Jubal with the gun. Finally he said, "Tanner, are you nuts? This guy knows about the horse. It gets out and you've had it. You want that asshole brother of yours to win?"

"Shut up, Erdman." I sensed where he was going with this and wanted to cut him off before he got much further.

He kept going. "Brig Tanner's spent his whole life making an ass out of you. You know it. He knows it. The whole goddamned town knows it. If it gets out about Kessler and your part in it, you can kiss the horse business good-bye. You're finished. He wins big time. The game's over."

Jubal was watching him, listening. But the magnum was still pointed at Erdman.

"Jubal," I said, "what're you listening to this guy for? He just shot you."

"It was a mistake." Erdman was quick on the uptake. "I was aiming for this troublemaker." He nodded at me, and his toupee slipped another inch.

"Yeah, right. And when you clubbed Jubal in the parking lot on St. Patrick's Day, who were you aiming for then?"

He kept talking to Jubal. "I don't know what this guy's talking about." He was pulling at the rope that bound him to the car. "What about Brig? Is he gonna keep making you the laughingstock of Abel County?" His Adam's apple bobbed up and down as he swallowed. "And what about that daughter of yours?"

Jubal cocked his head and narrowed his eyes. "What about her?"

"Don't listen, Jubal. Give me the gun." I took a step toward him, but he backed off and flashed me a look that kept me from moving any closer.

Erdman smiled and licked his lips. "With Brig's taste for those young things, kinda makes you wonder, doesn't it? Especially when that young thing belongs to his brother. Oh my. How sweet it is."

I took him by the collar and slammed him up against the steering wheel. "Don't listen to this garbage he's spouting, Jubal."

"You know what I'm talking about." Erdman's face was inches from mine and I could smell the beer on his breath. "Why don't you ask that daughter of yours why she spends so much time at Will Tanner's office?" He paused long enough to gauge Jubal's reaction. His smile grew, baring long, crooked teeth. "Didn't know about that, did you?"

I released Erdman and turned to Jubal. "Don't listen to this idiot. You know better." I extended my hand. "Give me the gun and let's get out of here."

Jubal stared at me for a full minute before he said, "Give me your keys."

"What?"

"You heard me. I want your keys."

"Shoot the sonofabitch," Erdman interjected.

I didn't move.

"Look," Jubal said, "I guess you figure I'm not going to shoot you over this, and you're probably right. But I'll do whatever I have to do to get those keys of yours."

"Jubal—"

"I'm through talking."

I decided I believed him and dug into my jeans pocket for the key ring. "Here," I said. "Just don't do anything stupid. Melissa's not involved with your brother. If you don't believe me, ask her. You owe her at least that."

He took the keys without a word and left Erdman and me with his bullet-ridden truck. A minute later I heard him start up my rental car and head into Foxport.

Erdman's chuckling brought me back.

"What's so funny?"

"Don't read folks too well, do you McCauley?"

"Neither do you if you think you've got something to laugh about."

I used Jubal's keys to open his glove box and was pleased to find that, true to the man's word, there was a box full of bullets.

Erdman stopped laughing. "Hey, what're you doing?"

"You're worried about me?" I spoke as I loaded the gun. "I think Artie's the one you're going to have to answer to. How many Kesslers does your fat little friend have?"

He didn't answer but was doing a lot of swallowing as he watched me. When I patted down his pockets for his keys, he began to sputter. "Hey, what the hell you doing? You can't steal my car."

I ignored him and he cursed me. I left him tied to the truck, his angular body twisting and contorting against the restraints. I was tempted to relieve him of his rug, but decided he looked worse with it on backwards.

Erdman's protests faded as I made my way down to the road to where he'd parked. He drove a Cadillac equipped with a radar detector and a car phone. Convenient.

I tried calling Cal Maitlin at home, and his wife said she was expecting him at any time and she'd have him call.

I was at least ten miles out of town and a long way from Windemere, which was on the other side of Foxport. I placed my faith in the radar detector and my own ability to see on this darkened stretch of highway and stepped on the gas.

I couldn't get rid of the image of Jubal Tanner bowed over the grave of his little brother, dead some thirty years. And then there was Brig, more culpable than anyone, and he goes on and makes a success of himself. Jubal was mainly guilty of opening his mouth—for whatever reason—and he goes on to make a complete failure of his life. I guess it all has to do with personal ethics and being able to live with yourself when they're breached. Brig might have the claim of respectability, but Jubal had the corner on decency. I was hoping he had enough of it to keep from doing anything stupid right now. He had to believe that someone he was close to killed Gayle, and though I had trouble placing either Claude or Melissa in that role, the possibility was all too real.

The shrill beep of the phone brought me back. As I picked it up, I hoped I wouldn't find myself talking to Artie Fotchke. Maybe my luck was changing; it was Cal Maitlin.

"I found Jubal," I told him. "He was out at his brother's grave. Burnhill Cemetery. We were ambushed, you might say, by a veterinarian named Thomas Erdman. He also happens to be the guy who slipped me the LSD."

"Burnhill? That's sheriff's jurisdiction." He paused. "Is Jubal with you?"

"Ah, no. Not exactly." I described the events of the last hour. When I finished, Cal was silent for a minute. Finally, he said, "Well, needless to say, we have to find Jubal. If he didn't kill the woman, he must think he knows who did. The gun they've identified as the murder weapon is almost definitely Jubal's. It has a burn mark on the butt." He paused. "I have to question why Jubal would not hesitate to identify the murder weapon as his own if he knew it was the murder weapon. But subtlety is lost on this crowd."

"You say there's a burn mark on the butt?"

"Yes, it's rather distinctive."

"That's interesting," I said, recalling an earlier conversation with Brig. "I wonder if it's any coincidence that Brig

Tanner caused the burn mark? Unless I'm mistaken, that's
the one he told me he tossed into his fireplace. Butt first.
And what's even more interesting is the fact that I believe
that's the gun that Melissa and Dworski found." Once
again, I told him about the discovery in the barn. "I've got
the feeling Mr. Dworski decided his love for Melissa Tanner
wasn't worth ten grand."

"Well, there's one thing I can add to that. I've learned
that the ten thousand they found in Dworski's closet did
not come out of Jubal Tanner's bank account. That isn't to
say, of course, that it wasn't a cash transaction. Seems
much more likely that it was Brig's reward money." Cal
paused. When he spoke again, he sounded frustrated. "I'm
not sure where that leaves us. Any idea where our client
might have gone?"

"I'm not sure. I'm hoping he'd want to talk to Melissa.
She's at the hospital. The thing is, I doubt he'd be dumb
enough to march right in there. Same with his own house if
he wanted to see Claude. Moore's got to have both places
staked out." I hesitated, not wanting to get Cal involved any
more than he had to be, but I was desperate, so I went ahead.
"You think you can get hold of Ed Carver? He might be at
my place or, uh, maybe Elaine's." I gave him her number.
"Have him meet me at Windemere."

"I can do that. Then I suppose I should give the sheriff
a call. Unless you'd rather I forgot and we just let Mr.
Erdman enjoy the elements tonight. Feels like we might get
some rain."

"What does my lawyer recommend?"

"I'll give them a call."

I disconnected the call and lit a cigarette. Initially I'd
decided to go to Windemere because I figured Jubal would
eventually wind up there, and that was where he could cause
the most trouble. I was still heading to Windemere, but now
I had my suspicions about Brig. What if you wanted to make
sure the rifle gets traced back to Jubal? Use a distinctive one,
maybe with a charred butt. Who knew about the charred

butt? The guy who was responsible for it. Who else? Who
was likely to have ten grand lying around? Someone who
could easily fork over 125 grand for a horse. Who was trying
his damndest to see that his brother got convicted? And
then, hadn't Elaine wondered if you know your girlfriend is
cheating on you, why not kill the guy she's cheating with?
Not so easy when he's your son.

▽

24

THE SHARP REPORT sliced through the cold night air and hung in the stillness like an unspoken echo. I'd just pulled up next to the Tanner house and was sure that Jubal had beaten me to his brother and set into motion the worst of all possible scenarios. But as I got out of the car, I saw a figure silhouetted on the porch beneath the glare of the outside light. At first I thought it was Brig, but as I approached I recognized Will Tanner's voice. Then I heard the sound again and, with some relief, recognized it as a door slamming shut.

"Whoever said honesty was the best policy never spent five minutes under this roof." He spoke loud enough to be heard through the door, which remained closed. I stopped at the base of the steps, apparently unseen by Will, who shifted uncomfortably and pinched the bridge of his nose with his thumb and forefinger. Then he sighed and kicked the door. "At least give me my damned coat, okay?"

Several seconds passed, then the door opened and a jacket flew out, missing Will and settling on one of the bushes that rimmed the porch. "I've had it with you and with him and all of you men who think with your dicks instead of your brains and then blame a woman when the bottom falls out." At first Cindy was hollering at her brother, but then her voice dropped to a level I could barely hear. "She was an opportunistic little tramp, but nobody put a gun to your head or to Dad's and forced you to fall into bed with her." This time she closed the door with hardly any sound at all.

Will sighed and shook his head, then turned to retrieve his jacket. That was when he saw me. "What're you looking at?" He made no effort to go around me as he plowed down the porch and into the night. Presumably, his car was out there somewhere. As I made way for him, I noticed his face was red and his jaw clenched. Before the dark swallowed him up, he turned. "You oughta keep your nose out of other people's business. This whole mess"—he waved his hand at the house—"is your fault."

I didn't respond, figuring it was useless to defend myself against someone who blamed three generations of a classically dysfunctional family on a guy who'd never met any of them until two weeks ago. Instead, I climbed the porch steps and knocked on the door. If Cindy figured Will was still standing out here, I could be in for a long wait.

It took her almost a full minute, but she finally pulled the door open a few inches. Judging from her expression, I was not a welcome addition to the porch. She didn't say anything.

"Is your dad around?"

"Why?"

"I have to talk to him."

She looked tired and made no effort to shake off the lock of hair that had fallen in her face. "He's not in the mood."

"Neither am I, but then life's just full of things we don't want to do."

She opened the door a little farther so she could rest her hip on the jamb. When she spoke again, she sounded reflective rather than angry. "You know what? I'm writing both of them off. Who needs them?" I assumed she meant her brother and her father, and I was inclined to agree with her, but before I could, she continued. "You know, I thought now that she's dead the two of them would get over it and we could go back to a normal life. But that's not the way it is, is it? She's causing as much trouble dead as she did when she was alive. Nothing's ever going to be normal again." As she stood there, chewing on her lower lip as she watched me,

I wondered what she was telling me. She continued, "I mean, who cares who killed her?"

"Jubal does."

Smiling as though that suddenly amused her, she nodded. "Yeah, I guess he would."

"Will told Brig he'd been seeing Gayle?"

Instead of answering me, she said, "He thinks Dad's the forgiving kind. I wonder whatever gave him that idea." She stared through me for a minute, probably not seeing anything but her own thoughts.

In the distance, I heard a car leaving the Tanner property at full throttle. Suddenly I felt sort of sorry for Will. People who damn the consequences and do the right thing deserve a lot of slack. "I suppose he won't actually be welcome here anymore."

"What did he expect?"

I nodded. "I see. You're going to make sure that the old Tanner family tradition doesn't skip a generation."

She stood up straight and gave me a quizzical look. "What's that supposed to mean?"

If I had to explain it, there wasn't much point. I shook my head. "Nothing."

She regarded me for a minute, then stepped back from the door and nodded in the direction of the barn. "You can find him in the barn. If you see him, why don't you tell him to stay out there?"

I left her standing in the doorway, the light spilling out behind her. On my way to the barn, I stopped at the Cadillac where I'd stashed Jubal's gun. I had the feeling Jubal would be joining us before the night was over, and I wanted to be prepared for any course that might take. I slipped the gun into my jacket pocket.

The barn seemed larger at night, its shadows odd and angular. As I passed between the main row of stalls, I heard an occasional snort and the thump of a hoof, but for the most part everyone had bedded down for the night. I figured if Brig was spending time in the barn, he'd either be in his office or with Kessler. Dworski had told me that Kessler's stall was in the back, away from the others. I imagined that it was probably more spacious as well. I came to the end of the row. To the left was the darkened office and tack room, to the right a short corridor that appeared to open into a larger area, from which a dim glow emanated. I turned that way, proceeding at a normal pace. I wasn't trying to sneak up on Brig, but I didn't think it was necessary to announce myself.

When I rounded the corner of the rear stalls, I came to an abrupt stop. Brig was sitting on the dirt floor propped up against a support beam. His mouth was taped shut and his wrists were bound behind him, linking him to the beam. His white shirt was ripped open and pulled down, exposing his chest. Several small splotches of red blossomed beneath the matted gray chest hair. Kneeling in front of him, smiling down at him like he was a work in progress, was Claude Tanner. She held one of those knives the butchers use for cutting through bone. Its blade was at least eight inches long. She turned to me, knife raised.

Her hair was loose and wild, stark against the black mackinaw she wore. Freed from braids, it streamed to her waist in crimps, parting just enough for a glimpse of her eyes, nose, and the thin line of her mouth. There was a savage quality to her eyes, and when I tried to read them, all reason seemed to have vacated.

"You shouldn't have come," she said, and I was surprised by the steady, even sound to the words.

"What are you doing, Claude?"

She looked up at me, disappointed, as though I were a promising student who'd asked a stupid question. "I'm giving Brig roses."

I approached slowly until I was about ten feet away, and Claude lowered the point of the blade to Brig's chest. She pressed the tip into his flesh and drew it away with a flick of her wrist. Brig winced, his eyes squeezed shut. Placing the bloodied tip at the same spot on his chest, she carved another petal. This time she watched him with a dreamy

smile as she cut again. He kept his eyes shut. She drew the
blade away and cocked her head as though appraising the
work, then, using the blade as a palette knife, with small
circular movements, spread the blood out from the wounds.

"Get away from him, Claude."

I had drawn the gun, but when she looked up at me, she
just gave me a pleasant smile. "We aren't finished yet. But
it will only be a minute." Turning back to Brig, she said,
"We're giving him one rose for every person he has hurt."
Using the tip of the knife, she pointed to one of the "roses."
"This one's for Jubal, and so is this one. I thought my Jubal
deserved two." Moving the blade to another blossom above
his left breast, she continued. "And this one is for me and
then this one . . ." She paused and waited until Brig opened
his eyes to see her. "This one is for that poor girl. Gayle. Who
would still be alive if Brig hadn't sent her out to die in his
place." She shook her head, mildly admonishing him. "You
can't expect other people to die for you. It's not right. And
we have to set things right, don't we Brig?" She placed the
edge of her knife at his throat. "The last rose is going to be
for all of us." Brig's eyes were wide, and sweat was streaming
like rain off his forehead.

I took two steps toward her and she pressed the flat edge
of the blade against Brig's throat. "Please, Quint, no closer.
You may witness our ceremony, but you can't participate."

"Put the knife down, Claude." I held the gun in front of
me with both hands, arms extended. I could feel my own
sweat working its way down my neck.

I moved nearer, but she shifted the knife so that the
business end of the blade touched Brig's throat, and I
stopped. She smiled again. This time there was nothing
pleasant about it. "You can't," she said.

"Neither can you." I swallowed, not believing the words
myself.

"Watch me if you like." Keeping the blade at his throat,
she crept behind him. Brig was making whimpering sounds
through the adhesive tape.

"You can't cut his throat, Claude. That's all wrong." I was grasping at straws of logic, but I knew that threatening her with the consequences of murder was pointless.

She frowned. "What do you mean?"

"That knife's not going to make a rose. Just a line. An ugly line. You'll ruin everything."

She arched an eyebrow at me, as though she were trying to determine my level of sincerity.

"What you've done up to now is good. And it's enough. Don't mess up everything you've done here."

She didn't move, just crouched behind Brig and watched me. I didn't dare get any closer. Behind them, I could hear the rustle of straw as Kessler moved around in his stall. After a minute, Claude drew the blade away from his throat and stood, then slowly moved around him, coming to a stop where she could look down on her work. Then she began to nod. "You're right. It would be wrong." She let go of the knife, and it made a dull thud as it dropped to the floor. Sighing, she thrust her hands into the pockets of her mack.

Brig, situated between Claude and me, began to squirm and make urgent sounds through the tape. Angry with the man's impatience, I shot him a glance. His eyes were practically popping out of their sockets.

Out of the corner of my eye, I saw the glint of steel. By the time I looked, she had brought the pistol to bear on Brig's chest. "Claude!" I cried. A muscle in her jaw twitched, and I fired a split second before she did.

She took the bullet directly in the chest and didn't fall right away, just stood there, mouth agape as though stunned into silence. Then the gun dropped from her hand, and she crumpled to the floor. As her mackinaw swelled around her, she looked like she was melting.

I glanced down at Brig. His eyes were squeezed shut, but he was breathing and apparently hadn't been hit.

I stepped over him and knelt down next to Claude. She watched me, gray eyes confused and hurt, but some of the wildness was gone from them. I brushed a few strands of

hair away from her face and took her hand. "Why?" It was
all I could think of to say.

Her eyes moved so she was looking up at Brig. "He
knows." She groped at the side of her mackinaw. "Take this,"
she said, adding, "I was next." Then she closed her eyes and
stopped breathing. I felt the pulse in her wrist as it faltered
and died. After a minute, I placed her hand on her chest.
"Take this." What was that supposed to mean? I ran my
hand down the mack until I found one of its deep pockets.
In it was an envelope, which I folded and shoved in my
pocket. My hands were shaking so badly I could barely
perform the function. Brig was moaning behind the tape,
but it was like the sound was coming from another dimension. I stared at the gun next to my knee and took several
deep breaths.

After an indeterminate amount of time—maybe seconds,
maybe minutes—I became aware of muffled sounds behind
me. Brig was twisting his neck, trying to work the tape loose.
I loosened one corner, then with a quick yank, ripped it off.
Brig took deep gulps of air. As soon as he could speak, he
said, "Goddamn crazy. She's nuts."

I pulled his shirt up over his shoulders and straightened
the collar. Pulling at the ropes that still bound his hands, he
gave me a guarded look. "Untie me." I didn't move.

He wet his lips. "That gun. Tried to tell you." I just stared
at him. "God, what could have . . . I mean why would
she . . ."

I slowly collected Brig's collar in my fists and pulled him up
an inch or two. I was still shaking, and Brig might have sensed
it as he glanced around, maybe looking for reinforcements.

When I'd collected myself enough to trust my voice, I said,
"I think you know what made her hate you so much she
tried to kill you. And I think you're going to tell me. Now."
I could feel his breath on my face. It smelled sour, like milk
that's been left out too long.

He swallowed. "I don't know what you're talking about.
She was crazy. And I'm starting to wonder about you."

I tightened my grip on his collar, and Brig tilted his head back against the beam. A thin line of blood marked the spot on his throat where Claude's knife had been.

In the stall, Kessler sounded like he was bouncing off walls. He kept making sounds like he was clearing his throat.

"It's all starting to come together."

"What're you talking about?" Brig squirmed at his bindings.

"I know what happened to JoEllen."

He stopped squirming and his eyes narrowed. "Jubal's got a big mouth. That's family business."

"Yeah, well, why don't you think of me as part of the family? I'm in deep enough, dammit." Brig's face was starting to redden, but I kept my grip on his shirt, figuring he'd let me know before he asphyxiated. "You know, it doesn't take a big leap of the imagination to figure it out. Jubal needed twenty-five grand to have enough for the horse. He thought he got that money from Claude's friend, Margaret. But it was from Claude. Only Claude couldn't tell him how she got it, so Margaret agreed to say it was hers." Brig looked up into the rafters, maybe hoping for a distraction. I tightened my grip slightly and continued. "Claude had probably tried everywhere else before she asked you for it. I bet she even knew what you were gonna want from her. But that's how desperate she was to help her husband realize his dream. And sure enough, you said, 'No problem, anything to help my favorite sister-in-law.' But then there were the strings attached. Whatever Jubal or Cody had, you wanted. Just to say you could have it. Whether you needed it or not. And you'd made good on that with just about everything— everything except Claude. She wasn't impressed with your money or your power. And that bugged the shit out of you, didn't it? Where were her priorities? So when she came to you for help, you saw the perfect opportunity to improve your score. And maybe that would've been the end of it, except you went and bought the horse anyway."

"It's not that simple."

"Why not?"

"I wasn't going to buy him. I mean, I was at first. But then I, uh, gave Claude the money and I told Hines I'd changed my mind. But then that damned Jubal goes and rubs my nose in it. Him and all his big plans. Breeder, my ass. I had to buy him. You can see that, can't you?"

"No, I can't." I paused, regarding Brig carefully. Actually, I did know what he was talking about. I didn't understand and hoped that I never would, but I could see Brig goaded by Jubal into making another offer for the horse.

"Besides . . ." His voice trailed off and I jerked at the collar.

"Besides what?"

"Well, Claude and I had this . . . attraction for each other. She wanted it as much as I did."

"If it took twenty-five grand to lure her to your bed, doesn't sound to me like she was real eager."

"Don't you see? She needed an excuse. That was it."

I was beginning to think that Brig had really sold himself on all this. "Then why did she try to kill you?"

Brig opened his mouth to answer, but no sound came out. He was gaping at something behind me, and judging from the look on his face, I'd have guessed that he never heard my question.

"Answer the man."

I didn't have to turn around to know that Jubal had arrived. His voice was low and even and made me real nervous. The pistol hung at his side, its barrel pointing toward the floor.

Speechless, Brig just shook his head.

Without a further glance at Brig, he stepped around us to the body of his wife.

I once spent several excruciating hours at a small airport with a friend waiting to learn the fate of her father's airplane. The Cessna was late, and the tower had lost contact with it in a storm. We feared the worst and prayed for the best. When word came that it had gone down with no survivors, the strings of hope that had been holding her together gave way and she crumbled. That was Jubal. He'd come here understanding Claude's part in the tragedy but never believing it would end like this. He dropped to his knees beside her and bowed his head. His features, gray and haggard, seemed sculpted in granite. For several moments, he didn't move, just knelt there with the gun resting on his thigh. Finally, he reached out to touch her cheek with the back of his hand, hesitated, then began to stroke her face. I had to look away.

Maybe it was a good time to untie Brig's ropes. That was my plan anyway. But the knot was a tight one, and I cursed myself for not carrying my pocket knife. I'd just managed to loosen it when Jubal said, "Don't do that." He looked down at the two of us, the gun pointed at Brig.

I ignored him and yanked the ropes free. Brig immediately began to rub the circulation back into his wrists, then slowly stood to face his brother. Jubal had several inches and a lot more mileage on him.

"Why?" Jubal said. "Everything I ever had you wanted. You had to have it. Why? Compared to you, I didn't have shit."

Brig took a deep breath. "Maybe I just got tired of seeing everything you touched turn to crap. You take something good, like your land or a woman, and you foul it."

Jubal took the gun and placed the barrel right on the bridge of his brother's nose.

"Jubal," I said.

He shook his head. "Nothing to talk about. He killed my Claude. I'm going to kill him. Simple as that. If you try to stop me, I'll kill you too. I don't want to—you're not a bad guy—but nobody's gonna stop me from putting a bullet in this son of a bitch's brain. Shoulda done it thirty years ago."

I stepped between the two of them, shoving them each back a couple feet. Then I turned on Jubal. "Brig didn't kill Claude. I did. His hands were tied. How could he have done it? I killed her." He started to shake his head in denial. As I took a step closer to him, I could feel my control slipping, consumed by rage. Physically, I wasn't much of a match against Jubal or his brother, but that didn't matter. "But I wouldn't have had to kill her if it weren't for you two sons of bitches." I pulled the gun from my pocket and thrust it at Brig, who reacted by grabbing it. "Gayle would be alive too."

"Hey, what the hell are you doing?" It was Jubal who spoke, but Brig looked equally as confused.

"This is what you should have done thirty years ago. Pistols at twenty paces." The two brothers were watching me as though I'd gone mad. Maybe they were right. "Well, how else are you two going to settle this? Talk? That's not the way the Tanners do things."

Brig was examining the gun as though he wasn't real familiar with one.

"Let's face it," I continued, "you can't keep taking pot-shots at each other. You keep missing. You keep hitting innocent people. Who's going to be next? Melissa? Cindy? Will?" I looked from Jubal to Brig and back again. "Anyone got any better ideas?"

Jubal frowned, as though he were seriously considering it, and judging from the look of apprehension on Brig's face, Jubal probably had the advantage.

I stepped away from the two of them. "I'm going to call the police. That ought to give you two long enough to do what you have to do. The way I see it you have three choices." I clicked them off on my fingers. "One, you can kill each other. Two, you can walk out of here without changing much of anything. Or three, you can actually talk to each other." I turned to leave, then stopped. "And you know what I hope? If you're not going to talk, I really hope you use this opportunity to kill each other."

As I walked away from the barn, I felt wired—like I'd just downed five cups of strong, black coffee. Consciously, I was wondering if Cal had gotten hold of Ed Carver, but somewhere in the back of my mind I was bracing for the sound of gunfire. This time I'd know it wasn't the door.

$\triangledown$

25

I GREW UP watching westerns. Back then I even imagined it would be great if there were no such thing as cars, and horses were our major means of transportation. And although I've outgrown that notion, I never got over that sense of satisfaction when the good guys won. It was always easy to tell who they were; not because of their white hats or the way they respected the saloon girls, but because they always left a person or a place in better shape than when they'd first ridden up. Looking back on the havoc that had been wreaked in the past week, my presence had had the opposite effect. Everything I touched had rotted and crumbled.

If I'd noticed that Claude's grip on sanity had been slipping, I might have seen her as a suspect rather than a wife distraught over her husband's predicament. She swore she had waited in the car while Jubal shopped, clinching her husband's alibi for the time of Gayle's death. Jubal saw it as one of his harmless lies. Hell, he *had* been at the store, and just in case no one noticed him, why not say Claude was out in the car? He never imagined that she was using him as her alibi. And if her actions that day weren't enough, there was the note she'd asked me to take, in which she'd confessed to killing Gayle and, albeit a bit prematurely, Brig. Apparently she'd planned to use one bullet from that gun on herself. I'd made that unnecessary.

I tapped a key on my new computer and the screen went black. I replay the scene in the barn over and over again, each time telling myself that she was about to put a bullet in Brig's chest, and I was out of options. If I'd fired a second later, Brig would be dead. I tell myself if I had to do it again, I'd have done the same thing. Maybe someday I'll believe it. Maybe there was a certain inevitability about the way everything turned out, and once things spun into motion, there was no alternate ending.

I'd gone to the cemetery that morning to see Claude's grave. Her middle name was Adele and she was fifty-seven when she died. Crouching beside the fresh sod, I placed the rose at the base of the small white cross. The bud had fully blossomed, its crimson petals smooth and unblemished. A perfect rose, and the last one I would ever buy.

Peanuts groaned in his sleep, and I gave him a little nudge. He liked napping under the computer table. It seemed like I was taking him with me everywhere these days. At first I thought it was out of guilt or worry that he'd be snatched away again, but the other day I caught him looking at me (in my direction at any rate) and it struck me that he was so trusting and nonjudgmental that it was a comfort to have him around. I was still kicking myself for his abduction and the night he spent in a dark basement, but as far as he was concerned, I'd just made a bad choice in boarding kennels. Forgiveness came that easy for him.

I regarded the brand-new computer sitting in front of me on my desk. This, I'd been assured, would make me a more efficient detective. I hit another key and SYNTAX ERROR sprang across the screen. I punched the off switch. Elaine was stopping by in the afternoon to give me a lesson. I'd wait for her.

I had to admit the computer lessons were less painful than the riding lessons. I knew I'd eventually accept this new machine into my life. I'm pretty resilient. Besides, Elaine was a good teacher. So far, it was easy and pleasant to be with her and have her as a friend. I spend a lot of time wondering why it's so hard to tell when love is over. Romantic love, anyway. I wasn't sure, but I thought she'd been out with Carver once or twice. Even that bothered me less than I thought it would.

And Carver. The last few weeks had changed things between us. I wasn't sure how, but they had. Maybe it was because we were actually fighting the same battle this time, and we learned if we had to work together, we could. And then I'm sure Elaine has a civilizing effect on both of us.

Moore had admitted to planting the gun and my dog in Dworski's house. Apparently he'd done all this to ingratiate himself to Brig and become Foxport's police-chief-for-life once Brig became mayor. He figured if he put a nice frame around Jubal Tanner, he'd have Brig's complicity as well as his backing. It almost worked. Almost, but not quite. Carver had been offered his job back, with apologies. He's not sure if he's going to take it. I admire his convictions but hope he doesn't end up going into private practice.

I looked up as I heard a noise in the outer office. Next thing I knew, Jubal Tanner filled the doorway. He wore a brown corduroy jacket over jeans. "You got a minute?"

"Yeah, sure." I pushed my chair back from the computer table and waved him toward a chair.

I hadn't seen him since that night at Windemere almost a week ago. The Tanner house had been empty when I'd come out of the barn, and I wondered where Cindy was, hoping she'd gone after her brother. I used the car phone to call Cal Maitlin, who said he'd just managed to get hold of Carver and that he was on his way. I chain-smoked cigarettes as I waited. Almost twenty minutes later, just as Carver and Rush showed up, the two brothers came out of the barn. Jubal was carrying Claude, and Brig walked a few steps behind him. I don't know what was said between them, but they weren't bloodied or snarling at each other. Maybe being handed the means and the opportunity nudged them out of the pattern. The bottom line was the same any way you write it. They could have used the guns but didn't. It must be nice to have a choice.

After greeting Peanuts with a pat, Jubal removed his hat and sat down, keeping his jacket on. "You need a place to hang your hat."

I nodded. "Sure, Jubal."

He waved his hat, taking in my office. "You get reinstated okay?"

"Yeah, once Artie Fotchke figured out how Erdman had screwed things up for him and his horse business, he told the cops that Erdman had doped my drink and stashed the LSD in my car. He was so ticked off at the guy, I think he would've told them he kidnapped the Lindbergh baby if he thought they'd believe it."

Jubal nodded without much enthusiasm. "That's good," then added, "Oh, you oughta tell that friend of yours—Elaine What's-her-name—that the little Arab is waiting for her. B.J. needs someone to ride her."

Elaine hadn't mentioned the horse and neither had I. Somehow I didn't feel like I'd exactly earned my pay on this one.

As if he could see into my thoughts, he said, "You did what I asked. None of the rest is your fault. Besides, there's no one to ride B.J. anymore. Too small for me. Missy doesn't ride much."

"I'll tell Elaine."

In a familiar gesture, he crossed his leg over the other knee and hung his hat on his boot. It slipped to the floor. Staring at the hat, he shook his head. "I never saw it. Never saw it. She was slipping away from me little by little, and I never saw it." He looked up at me as though he were asking for absolution, but I didn't have any to give.

"No one did" was all I could say. Like everyone involved, he'd have to learn to live with his guilt.

"How's Brig?" I asked.

He frowned and shrugged. "Okay, I guess." He paused for a minute as though chewing over a thought. "Cindy tells me he wants to give me Kessler."

I chuckled. "That would be real generous of him. Giving you a sterile stud horse."

"He doesn't know."

"You never told him?"

Jubal shook his head, a smile tugging at his mouth.

"Why?"

"I guess the humor left the joke a long time ago."

"Won't he find out anyway?"

"Who's gonna tell him?"

He had a point. It wouldn't serve the Hineses or Erdman to talk about it. Erdman had enough problems, and Hines wasn't about to bring it up.

I smiled. I've always been a big fan of irony. "So, if he gives you Kessler . . . that's sort of like extending the proverbial olive branch, isn't it?"

"Maybe. Or maybe just having Kessler around is a bad reminder." He shrugged like it didn't matter either way.

"So what are you going to do if you wind up with this good-looking, but essentially worthless, animal?"

"He's a fine riding horse. Good size for me." He bent down to retrieve his hat, then stood and settled it on his head, giving it a slight twist. "I don't know. I suppose some day the two of us'll go off a cliff together."

As I watched Jubal bid Peanuts a good day and walk out of my office, I made a mental note to steer clear of the high country.